Ruth McEnery Stuart

A Golden Wedding, and Other Tales

Ruth McEnery Stuart

A Golden Wedding, and Other Tales

ISBN/EAN: 9783337023461

Printed in Europe, USA, Canada, Australia, Japan

Cover: Foto ©Andreas Hilbeck / pixelio.de

More available books at **www.hansebooks.com**

A GOLDEN WEDDING

AND

OTHER TALES

By RUTH McENERY STUART

ILLUSTRATED

NEW YORK AND LONDON
HARPER & BROTHERS PUBLISHERS
1900

TO

MY FRIEND

MR. HENRY MILLS ALDEN

CONTENTS

ILLUSTRATIONS

A GOLDEN WEDDING

A GOLDEN WEDDING

A GOLDEN WEDDING

IT was Christmas Eve in New Orleans, and the air was fragrant with the mingled perfume of sweet olive, violets, and roses, while lace curtains, floating in and out of second-story windows, caught and wafted into sunny chambers a hint of orange blossoms lured into untimely bloom by the treacherous wooing of a Southern December.

So Christmas was coming to two old people who sat to-day on the front porch of a little hovel back of town. Each sat in front of a door, and they were separated by a board partition which divided the house into tenements. A man sat on one side, a woman on the other. Both were old, both black, both silent and contemplative.

Though he sat back near his door, in the mingled shadow of the low roof and an orange-tree, we perceive at a glance that the old man was characterized, as to personal appearance, by conspicuous baldness, exaggerated in effect by a luxuriant growth of bushy white hair, which clung about his temples, extending in a low line around the back of his head. A scant, grizzly beard covered his face and chin, and he was apparently entirely toothless.

He had been engaged for several hours in splitting pine kindling, which he tied into little parcels of uniform size.

After he had finished his task to-day, the old man sat for some time quite still, with an air of alert listening.

Presently, however, he rose suddenly (though his motions were nervous and labored), and taking his stool with him, reseated himself near the edge of the gallery, exactly opposite a narrow opening made by a broken plank in the partition.

Knocking here as at a door, while he peered curiously through the aperture, he called out, "Oh, Sister Garrett ! is you home, Sis' Garrett ?"

As " Sister Garrett " rises to respond to the call, we perceive that she too is very old and bent, while a certain fashion of contracting her brows and looking intently before her shows that her dim-looking eyes are failing in vision.

She also takes her chair with her as she approaches the partition wall, and placing it quite near the opening, seats herself with laborious deliberation.

The old man inclined his head in a way almost courtly, as he said, by way of greeting : " I sholy is proud ter see you home, Sis' Garrett. I 'lowed dat I ketched de soun' o' yo' footfalls dis mawnin' on yo' side, an' I listened, an' I 'ain't heerd 'em no mo', an' I kep' a-listenin', 'caze I craved ter heah you a-meanderin' 'round ; but I 'ain't heerd no mo' tell jes now I heerd yer sneeze."

The woman laughed. "Is dat so, Br'er Thormson? I know I is a loud sneezer. De idee o' you takin' note o' me a-sneezin'! Well, well, well! Business mus' be sort o' slow, sho' 'nough, ef you 'ain't got nuttn' better ter do 'n ter set up a-list'nin' ter me a-sneezin'. De Lord save us! You is a case, sho!" And Sister Garrett laughed again— a peal of high-noted laughter worthy of a light-hearted and a younger woman. The inborn spirit of coquetry never dies in some women, and if it seems to be sleeping, it takes only the inspiration of a masculine presence to rouse it into interesting play. Sister Garrett was a woman of this type. If it had been hers to die of old age, the coquette in her would still have died young.

It was the optimistic temper, of which this was an indication, which made her lonely neighbor welcome the sound of her footsteps.

The stolid old man was entirely guiltless of anything in the least degree personal when he referred to her sneezing, and yet the implication of courtesy rather pleased him. He looked through the hole in the wall at the old woman, and laughed.

"Dey's a sociable soun' ter yo' sneeze, Sis' Garrett, an' a man livin' like I does by he's lone se'f, he fin's a heap o' comp'ny in a good, frien'ly sneeze a-comin' f'om 'crost de partitiom. Hit tecks orf a heap o' de lonesomeness o' Chris'mus. Look like bit calls my min' f'om 'way back yonder, an' brings me ter myse'f, like. Time a pusson gits ole, look like Chris'mus is a lonesome day, any way yer tecks it. I trus' you's come home ter stay over Chris'mus, Sister Garrett?"

"Yas, sir; I 'lowed ter come an' set out heah on de po'ch an' sneeze ter keep you comp'ny, Br'er Thormson."

"How you does run on!" said Thompson, foolishly; but the woman continued, more seriously:

"Yas; I come home fur good. I'm done beat out an' burned out a-stan'in' over cook-pots, an' I ain't a-gwine ter do it stiddy no mo'."

"How you gwine do, Sis' Garrett? I knows you ain't a-gwine ter stay home an' set down, dry so!"

"Huccome you so cuyus 'bout me, Br'er Thormson? You is de cuyuses' man! Huccome you know I 'ain't struck de lottery?"

"I jes teckin' a neighborly intruss, Sis' Garrett; I ain't mean no harm."

"Ef you so neighborly, Br'er Thormson, huccome you 'ain't axed me is I run out o' terbacker?"

The old man shuffled to his feet, and soon brought from his room a paper of the weed, his pipe, and a match.

The old woman took her own pipe from her pocket, and presently two columns of smoke, rising from opposite sides, blew into a mingled cloud above the partition, and moved before them toward the south, crossing the old woman's yard.

"Smoke got sociable ways, 'ain't it?" said she, as she watched the misty cloud. "I puffs an' you

"SMOKE GOT SOCIABLE WAYS, AIN'T IT?"

puffs, an' time de partitiom gives 'em a chance, de two smokes look like dee des nachelly goes to-gedder."

"I see dee moves todes de souf," replied the old man, "an' I looks fur a snap o' fros' ter-night, an' I'll be 'j'iced ter see it, ter week up de kin-dlin' trade. Look like a pusson mought starve at dis business ef dis warm winter ain't play out soon."

"I hates a hot Chris'mus," said the old woman.

"I hates it an' I loves it," he replied, with a touch of feeling—"yas, I hates it, 'caze seem like hit's onnachel an' 'ceitful, like pusson a pusson kyant trus', what 'd put up a warm check fur yer ter kiss, an' maybe nex' minute turn de col' shoul-der on yer. I hates it dat-a-way; but ag'in, I loves it on de 'count o' de ricollectioms hit brings me. De happies' day o' my life was a hot Chris'-mus—de day I got ma'yed, when I was yong an' full o' sperit."

The old woman looked at him quickly. "De Thormsons come f'om Georgy, ain't dee?" she asked.

"Yas, 'm, dee comes f'om Georgy," he replied, absently.

Both smoked on in silence for a while. Finally the woman spoke: "Whar you gwine ter eat to-morrer, Br'er Thormson?"

"Who, me? I—I—I don't know, Sis' Garrett. Mos'ly ev'y Chris'mus I goes roun' an' holps some o' my lady frien's cookin' in de big houses, fetch

in wood fur 'em, or maybe pick de tukkey, an' dee
allus persis'es on me a-stayin' ter dinner—but to-
morrer—look like to-morrer—I was jes a-studyin'
'bout dat—ef I could—'f I could—I ain't no cook,
Sis' Garrett; but dar's my big rade rooster step-
pin' roun' so high, an' lookin' so lonesome sence
ole Muffly strayed orf—I was jes lookin' at 'im
an' a-studyin' dat ef I could—'f I could—ef you
could—is you ever fricasseed a chicken, Sis' Garrett?"

"Lord save my soul, Br'er Thormson! I'm a
cook, me! I c'd fricassee a chicken in my sleep,
an' dream 'bout some'h'n else at de same time—jes
put de ingrejums onder my han's."

"What is de ingrejums, Sister Garrett?"

"De ingrejums ter fricassee a chicken? Nemmine 'bout dat. You des gimme de chicken, an'
I won't pester you fur de ingrejums. I allus keeps
a little seasonin' by me. I couldn't 'spect myse'f
fur a cook ef I run out o' my trade-marks."

The old man was pleased. "You talks like a
cook, sho', Sis' Garrett. When you converses dat-
a-way, look like I c'n smell de steam."

"You'll smell it, sho 'nough, ef I passes my
han' over de pot."

"Well, ef you say de word, de ole rade rooster 'll
say he's pra'rs ter-night, an' we'll 'vide up on de
fricassee fur Chris'mus dinner. I been studyin'
'bout de way you was a-talkin' 'bout de smoke
jes now. Maybe de smoke o' our pipes runs togedder fur a sign ter me an' you dat *we* mought

mix in an' out a little mo' neighborly an' sociable
like.   What you say, Sis' Garrett?"

"You kill de rade rooster, an' don't fret 'bout
de smoke."

"An' how we gwine 'vide 'im up? Is you gwine
ter pass my part back froo de hole?"

"I 'lowed you was teckin' a lesson f'om de smoke
des now. Nex' time you studies a lesson, you
study ter de een o' de book. 'Ain't you seed how
de smoke blowed over ter my side? Huccome
you kyan't come over an' eat dinner wid me? *You*
ain't pizen an' *I* ain't pizen, an' Gord knows de
shtewed chick'n, hit ain't a-gwine ter be pizen."

The old man rubbed his hands together, smiled,
and bowed his acknowledgments in a manner gen-
uinely elegant.

"I recedes ter yo' invertatiom wid a full heart,
Sister Garrett, an' ef de Lord spares my life, I'll
shorely be on han'. You done spoke de fatal
word. Time Mr. Highstepper was beginnin' ter
pray now!" he added, laughing immoderately at
his own wit, as he glanced at the rooster, who, all
unconscious, was disporting himself in the sun.
"What time you gwine have dinner, Sister Garrett?"

"'Twouldn't be no Christmus dinner ter me,
less 'n 'twas late," she replied. "Le's have it at
de white folks's time, six o'clock—dat is, ef hit
suit yo' circumstancial convenience."

"All right, Sis' Garrett, all right. Six o'clock
—six o'clock on a Chris'mus! Dat's de time o' day

I got ma'yed—six o'clock on a warm Chris'mus.
I d' know huccome dat comes back ter me ter-
day. I b'lieve hit's de smell o' dem o'ange-
flowers. We had 'em dat day ; dee bloomed out
o' season, jes like dee is now, an' de bride, she had
a whole wreaf ob 'em on 'er haid."

The woman gave him a quick look, as she had
done before. "You say de Thormsons come f'om
Georgy, ain't yer ?" she asked, eagerly.

"Yas, 'm, dat what I say ; dee is come f'om
Georgy."

The old man had risen. "Well, so long, Sis'
Garrett," he said, moving away. "I gwine git a
han'ful o' corn an' bait up Mr. Highstepper, an'
teach 'im 'ligion, 'caze he's boun' fur a hot place.
So long !"

And so they parted. The old woman sat silently ruminating a long time that night before going
to bed.

How strange it was that the old man Thompson had been married on Christmas, and his wife
had worn fresh orange-flowers! How very strange!
All this had happened to her when she was young.
She had been a Christmas bride, and had worn
an orange wreath ; but of course this was in Louisiana, and her husband was tall and straight and
handsome—everything that Thompson was not.
Still, it was strange, and the coincidence filled her
heart with an old yearning. If she could but meet
him once again, this husband of her youth, she
would die happy ; but this was more than she

THE WEDDING, LONG AGO.

could hope for, for it had all happened—she had no idea how many years ago.

It had been an imprudent marriage, ill-advised and unfortunate. She and he had been the property of different families. The evil prophesied had come true. Her husband's owner had moved into another state, and carried all his goods with him, and that had been the end.

After a brief season of happiness, the marriage had brought her only separation and sorrow, and yet she would not part with the memory of this short period for all else that life had brought her.

It was late when she rose from her meditations, knelt for an audible prayer of unusual length, and finally climbed into her high, soft bed, where, surrounded by friends of her youth, and with the sensation of an orange-wreath lying upon her old head, in dreams she fell asleep.

The red rooster was killed that night, picked clean to a feather, and early next morning passed through the partition.

There had been a change in the weather about midnight, and by noon next day a drizzling rain had given way to a light fall of sleet—a transition not uncommon in this Southern city. At five o'clock the sleet was still falling, and at six the storm had grown more violent.

Thompson, rigged *cap-a-pie* in his foxy broadcloth suit, stood looking out upon the weather.

It was time to go, so said the silver watch in his waistcoat pocket, and so said the savory odor that came through the key-hole and under the barred door which separated the two rooms.

Thompson did not know what to do. Even ignoring the question of rain and rheumatism, *how would it look* for a man to go out in such a storm—*just for dinner?*

"Hit 'd look like a pusson was clean starved out, ter go 'way out ter dat front gate an' back ag'in, an' come in wet as a drownded rat, jes— *jes fur grub!*" he soliloquized.

While he stood at the open door, growing momentarily more irresolute as the storm rose in violence, and more eager as the appetizing steam grew in flavor, there came a rap at the partition. He was there in a moment.

"Br'er Thormson," said the expectant 'nostess, "ef you'll len' me a axe I'll prize open de do' 'twix' yo' side an' mine, so's you c'n come froo, ef you'll have de manners an' de perliteness ter nail it up ag'in quick's we gits done dinner. 'Tain't no use fur you ter git drownded out goin' roun', an' de chicken schew, hit's des done up ter de right notch now."

Thompson was most happy to promise to repair any injury resulting from the unbarring of the door, and it was soon open, and the Christmas feast a present reality.

"I hates ter ax yer ter fetch yer knife 'n' fork, Br'er Thormson, but I boun' ter do it, 'less'n we'd borrer back 'n' fo'th—er else I'd 'sult yer by eatin' wid my fingers—"

"Scuse me, scuse me, I pray," said Thompson, bowing and smiling; "I oughter had de sense an' de manners ter fetch—ter fetch de conveniences o' de 'casiom; but I 'ain't been movin' roun' in s'ciety fur—fur so long, I 'ain't got no mo' perliteness 'n one o' dese heah Hottenpotots—er some'h'n' riz in de woods."

With this profuse apology he disappeared, hobbling into his own room, whence he soon returned with the desired implements, adding also a tumbler and a chair, as he had taken note of these further needs during his apology.

A second tour through his apartment resulted in the production of a handsome orange branch, which having stuck in a bottle, he placed now as floral ornament in the centre of the table.

"Look like we ought ter have some sort o' *bouquet* fur ter glorify our eyes an' witness fur de 'casiom," said Thompson, as he stood off in admiration, "an' ter my eyes dat's purty, an' hit's sweet-smellin' too."

"Hit's sweet tell yer git a sniff o' de fricassee, an' dat ain't leave no room fur no fainty flower smell," said the hostess, as she placed the steaming dish opposite Thompson's plate. "Teck a cheer an' set down an' meck yerse'f at home, fur's yer able, Br'er Thormson. What yer see befo' yer ain't sofistercated an' fine, but I gua'ntee hit's clean an' seasonable."

The dinner was fit for a king. The steaming stew, filling the room with its essence, both rich

and delicate, a bowl of snowy, whole-grained rice,
a tin plate of roasted sweet-potatoes, gray with a
hint of ashes upon their coats, a pone of golden
egg-bread, and a pot of coffee, obtrusively aro-
matic, composed the simple *menu.*

It is but fair to observe to his credit that the
eager expression of physical hunger gradually
faded from his old face as the guest, at the invitation of the hostess, raised his right hand solemnly, and, closing his eyes, addressed the throne
of grace with a fervent though brief thanksgiving.

The occasion was in every sense a success,
and the conversation of the guest thickly interspersed with parentheses complimenting the various dishes:

"Umh! Dishere gravy tecks me *'way back!*

"Dey ain't none o' dese heah cooks a-circulatin'
roun' dese days dat knows de true in'ardness o'
cookin'.

"You got dese dumplin's in dis gravy kivered
wid velvet, 'ain't yer? Dee slips down like a soljer gwine home on a furlough.

"Dis heah co'n-brade 'd meck poun'-cake blush
an' clair out.

"Dese heah pertaters is as sugary and mealy-
moufed as a ligislatur candidate!"

Such as these were the overflowing sentiments
of the happy guest, while his hostess, with hospitable insistence, kept his plate filled.

At length, however, Thompson warded off further supply by repeated protest that every crack

was filled up "clair down ter his boots." He moved back a little, still resting his elbow on the table, while the woman drew her chair round to the fire, and the two fell into comfortable after-dinner conversation. As was but natural, these two, both near the end of their lives, soon drifted into retrospection.

"Hit's funny," said the old man, after a pause, as he plucked an orange-flower and held it, man fashion, in the hollow of his palm to his nostril— "hit's funny how de refumeries ob a blorsom kin wuck on a pusson's min', an' raise up ricollectioms o' times an' faces."

He handed the woman a stemless flower. Taking it daintily between her thumb and first finger, she smelt it meditatively.

"An' voices," she added, presently.

"H-how 'd you say dat?"

"An' voices, I say. De flagrams o' dis flower brings back a voice ter me—a voice ob—ob a frien' o' mine."

"Yas, hit do bring back voices too. Look like I c'n shet my eyes an' see a whole passel o' darkies a-standin' roun' a ole-time kyabin, an' a one-arm preacher standin' 'ginst de hyearth a-restin' 'is book orn de mantel-shelf; an' I kin feel myse'f a-walkin' in wid de purties', high-haidedes', bright-eyedes' black gal in de Nunited States. She was all dressed up in some sort o' white fliffy-fluffy dress, wid a whole wreaf o' dese heah blorsoms on 'er haid, an', laws-a-mussy, ef she warn't purty! She a-stan'in'

up, so black an' shinin', in de mids' o' so much
white grandeur, looked jes like one o' dese little
slick blackbirds in a snow-bank! Oh, ef I c'd jes
see 'er once-t ag'in! Ef she's in de lan' o' de livin',
I'd know 'er, sho! In co'se I know she's boun'
ter be changed by de blightin' o' time; but eyes
is eyes, she couldn't nuver lose dem flashy-dashy,
come-ef-yer-dare black eyes, 'less'n blin'ness strick-
en 'er; an' sperit is sperit, an' I know long as she
live she's boun' ter hol' a high haid. We had
jes one little baby—a peart little boy—time de
partin' come. I hope Gord spared 'im ter 'er."

The old woman had been listening alertly all
along, but now she peered into the speaker's face.
"Ain't you say de Thormsons come f'om Georgy?"
she asked, eagerly.

"Y-yas, 'm, dee is. Huccome you keep a-axin'
me is de Thormsons come f'om Georgy? Is yer
knowed any ob 'em?"

Her face was troubled. "No, no, Br'er Thormson, I 'ain't knowed 'em. I des axin' yer *so.*"

The old man continued: "Ef hit was Gord's
will dat I c'd jes see 'er ag'in once mo' 'fo' I die,
an' set down an' talk wid 'er, an' know all 'er ups
an' downs sence I lef' 'er when I went ter Georgy—"

"'Ain't you said you *come* f'om Georgy, Br'er
Thormson?"

"Yas, 'm, dat so. I is come f'om Georgy, but
dis heah what I'm talkin' 'bout now, hit's *away
back yonder*—long 'fo' de 'clarin' o' wah—'fo' my

marster move ter Georgy—when I was a yong buck. I lived in Lou'siana dem days, an' I married, 'ginst de 'visemint o' my marster, a purty little black gal named Cicely, what b'long ter de Morgans on de coas', on de plantation 'j'inin' we's place. In co'se I done passed de mos' o' my life in Georgy, but quick's de wah was over an' Freedom loosen me, I come clair back ter de coas'—I wucked my way down—a-huntin' fur Cicely ; but 'twarn't no use. Her marster done had been kilt in de army, an' look like ev'ything was gone ter rack 'n' ruin, an' I couldn't heah nuttn', an' nobody seem like dee 'membered me, so I come on down heah ter Noo 'Leans—an' let 'lone prayin' fur de sight an' keepin' my eyes open, I done guv up de hunt, 'caze I mought be trablin' cas' while she gwine wes', an' ef hit's de Lord's will, He c'n lan' 'er right heah—an' ef 'tain't, well—maybe hit's fur de bes', 'caze, in co'se, in all dese yeahs she mought o' ceasted ter love me—but I ain't look fur dat, 'caze de way my heart hol' ter her, I b'lieve she done helt ter me too. Ef I c'd jes see 'er ! Dey ain't no gals like her dese days. She was de ole-time sort. Yer 'ain't nuver is met up wid no Morgan people f'om de coas', is yer ?"

The old man had become so much absorbed in his own past that he did not perceive that the woman was silently weeping. The room, lit only by the faint glow of a low fire and the fitful flicker of an expiring candle, was nearly dark.

The old woman steadied her voice by an effort,

2

and made a feeble attempt to straighten her stooped figure.

"You say she got a high haid an' a bright eye —Br'er Thormson—but you ain't 'low dat maybe grievin' an' sayin' nuttn' all dese yeahs mought bring down a proud haid; an' yer know "—her voice trembled—"y-yer know cookin' over a cook-stove, hit nachelly blurs a pusson's eyes."

"I knows all dat," he replied, shaking his head emphatically—"I knows all dat; but—but you 'ain't knowed little Cicely. She warn't none o' de lettin' down sort. In co'se I's perpared ter see 'er gray, maybe, an' maybe show age, but ef she's a-livin', I'm plumb sho she got a quick eye an' a high haid yit."

The old woman's face was twitching nervously. Her dim eyes, doubly dimmed with tears, rested upon the face of the man whom she knew to be the husband of her youth, but there was something in the inborn pride of the woman—call it coquetry if you will—which resented the contrast between his memory's picture and herself.

Finally she said, with wonderful control, though the corners of her mouth were quivering:

"Br'er Thormson, dey's a man what I'd like ter meet up wid ag'in 'fo' I die, please Gord, an' sence you come f'om de coas', maybe you mought o' knowed 'im. He good by de name o' Smiff, Aleck Smiff—"

"Wh-wh-wh-wh-wha'?" the old man stammered, in a bewildered effort to speak; but she paid no attention to him.

"He was a man taller'n you is, but maybe dat
was de way he hol' 'isse'f—he hol' 'isse'f des like
a Presiden'—an' he comb 'is ha'r high up on top
'is haid, des like a rooster wid a proud comb, an'
when he'd open 'is mouf ter talk, 'is voice 'd come
out brave an' strong, des like de deep notes on a
melojum. I'd know dat voice in a chorus o' angels! Ef—ef I c'd meet up wid dat man, Br'er
Thormson, look like my heart 'd turn ter joy,
'caze—'caze he—he was my husban'."

It was all she could do to say these last words,
and she caught her breath nervously as she proceeded:

"I'd sholy know 'im ef I c'd ketch de soun' o'
dat noble voice. Yer 'ain't nuver is met up wid
no man like dat, is yer?"

The old man was peering into her face as one
dazed.

"L—look like I ain't onderstan' yer good," he
said. He was trembling, and his voice, suffering
from agitation, exceeded even its usual quality of
piping thinness.

"I say, yer 'ain't nuver knowed no man like dat,
is yer, f'om de coas', name Aleck Smiff, wid a fine
haid o' black ha'r, an' shinin' white toofs, same as
de milk-white grains on a roas'n' ear, an' a voice
joyous an' persuadin', like a he-bird's song, an'—"

The old man had been weeping silently, but
now he interrupted her by a tremulous wave of
his hand, and with a pathetic effort to steady his
voice, began to answer her:

"L—look like—look like dat when you's a-talk-in' 'bout—hit was a long time ago, Cice—Sis' Garrett, an' yer know a pusson's voice—hit's—hit's boun' ter teck on a high note when age stricken 'im an' 'e begin a-frailin'—"

"In co'se I knows all dat," said she; "I knows all dat. I 'lows fur de wuckin's 'o time on 'im. I ain't spec' ter see 'im skip roun' lively like he done when I knowed 'im; but de voice, an' de way he comb 'is haid, an' dem shinin' white toofs—all dat boun' ter tell on a bordy."

His head sank heavily on his hand, and he was silent for a time. Finally he said: "Ain't yer know, S-Sis'—Sis' Garrett, dat when age an' sorrer stricken a man, ev'ything boun' ter come back on 'im? Dat's huccome dee proves de Book what fo'tell de secon' chil'hood. De toofs, dee all draps out, same as a onteethin' baby; de ha'r on a pusson's haid, hit clair de track too; an' den— look like 'tain' no use fur 'im ter try ter stan' up 'g'ins' dese losses like a man, 'caze time dat high note strack 'im he kyan't play no bluff game; he's jes nachelly bleege ter give up, an' 'low dat de times an' de seasons done beat 'im out."

He hesitated, searching the old woman's face, but she made no sign, and he went on :

"Dat high note look ter me like hit match wid de gorslin's, an' same as a yong buck git de gors-lin's, an' talk high fur a noterfercatiom ter stan' up an' be a man, hit come on 'im ag'in time he gits ole fur a noterfercatiom dat de battle done fit, an' he 'bleege ter give up de fight and let down !"

"L—LOOK LIKE I AIN'T ONDERSTAN' YER GOOD."

He studied his hearer's face for a second pause, but she still seemed looking into space, and was silent. Her pride required that his humiliation should be complete.

"Look like," he resumed—"look like dat high note teck a man twice-t, some'h'n' like de way a ingine blow de trumpit twice-t. Hit blow fus, when de train start orf, ter say dee gwine turn on de steam; an' bimeby hit blow agin, ter ease up, 'caze de statiom's in sight."

Another silence. The old man was greatly tried.

"Ef—ef dis man Smiff been a-pinin' fur you in 'is heart—grief, hit 'll tell on a voice too—an' maybe he mought talk high jes f'om time an' sorrer wuckin' on 'im—an'—an' lonesomeness—an'—an' all dat."

There were tears in his voice now.

"Ef—ef I c'd meet—could meet up wid Cicely, I'd crave ter fine 'er changed, 'caze I knows ef she warn't, she wouldn't have no use fur a ole man like me."

He buried his face in his hands and fell to sobbing.

"Ef—ef she was high-haided—an' peart-eyed —she—she mought turn 'er back on me—an' maybe not know me.—Oh, my Gord !—an' maybe not know me !—But—ef 'er haid was low wid de weight o' time—like mine is—an' 'er eyes was ondimmed wid sorrer—like mine is—an' 'er heart weak wid yearnin'—like mine is—"

His voice, which had failed him piteously at each repetition of the words "like mine is," broke entirely here.

The woman was now also weeping aloud. Rising from her chair, she fell upon her knees at his side. "Hush, Aleck!" she screamed. "Hush, I say! I can't stan' no mo'! Oh, my Gord!" Her head fell upon his knees, and her arms were about his body.

"Glory! glory be ter Gord!" shouted the old man, burying his face upon her neck, while his arms fell over her shoulders.

It was many moments before any word was spoken, save a muffled "Glory!" or "Praise Gord!"

At last, however, the old man wiped his face, and after several futile attempts to speak, said, "Ci-Cicely, wh-whar little Joe?"

But she could not answer. Moving her head from side to side, however, she indicated that she did not know.

The night was far spent when, after having with mingled tears and laughter reviewed their lives, the old couple composed themselves for a quiet talk. Both had been resold soon after their separation, and bore the names of their last owners.

"You know some'h'n', Cicely," said the old man, smiling, when after an interchange of experiences they returned to the question of mutual recognition—"yer know some'h'n', Cicely, I mistrusted de seasonin' o' dat fricasseed chicken f'om de fus'."

"'Twas de o'ange blorsoms what sot me ter studyin', Aleck," said she ; "an' when I'd look acrost de table at yer, an' you 'd talk 'bout marryin' on a Chris'mus, an' havin' de o'ange blooms, seemed like I'd *commence* ter git warm, an' I'd be close-t up ter reconnizin' yer, an' den you'd say some'h'n' 'bout Georgy, an' I'd be col' as ice agin, des like de chillen a-gropin' roun' arter a switch when somebody holler out, ' Now yer hot !' an' 'fo' dee c'n tu'n roun', 'ner one sing out, 'Now yer col' !' An' den when you teched on de baby, I d' know huccome I kep' still— look like we was des 'bleege ter be us, an' den right on top o' dat you 'spon' dat you is come f'om Georgy, an' I was on de rack — wid Chris'- mus an' de o'ange smell, an' seem like you so p'intedly match an' so p'intedly ain't match wid Aleck. Yer voice *is* failed yer some, Aleck ; but when I listens ter it good, seem like de ole ring, hit comes back. Ef you'd o' let 'lone talkin' 'bout Georgy, I'd o' knowed it f'om de fus, but I 'mem- bered dat you went ter Atalanta, an' in co'se Georgy, hit put me orf de track."

"'Tlanta an' Georgy, dee jes de same, Cicely."

"Is dee ? Well, well ! 'Trav'lin' roun' like you's been, a pusson do git educatiom. You mus' scuse my grammar, but I 'lowed dee was two far countries, maybe 'crost de ocean f'om one-'n'er."

"No, no.   'Tlanta, dat's jes, yer mought say, de quality name, an' de people in de cidy what put on style — yer know how dee is — dee jes nachelly 'bleege ter teck on some'h'n' ter look like hit stan' fur grandjer, an' dee claims de name o' 'Tlanta dat-a-way ; an' dem what live roun' in de highways an' byways, dee jes teck on de plain name o' Georgy, dry so."

"Of cose," said she.

The night was far spent, and the old couple still sat talking—living over together in one night of dim retrospection their long lives spent apart.

They wept and laughed many times over the sorrows and surprises of the reminiscence, and these emotions were pathetically mingled as the mother reviewed the life of their child from his infancy, at the time when the father was taken away, to his maturity, and then to the time of the war, when, to use her own words, "look like time he ketched de name o' freedom, he 'ain't had no sense lef', an' run orf an' j'ined de inemy an' turned Yankee, an' nuver was heerd of no mo'."

The old man alternated between laughter and tears over her description of the lad, weeping as she emphasized the points of resemblance to his father in matters of comfort to herself, and laughing as she pursued the subject of heredity further, somewhat in this wise :

"Yas, he was des de spi't 'n' image o' you, Aleck. He walk like you, proud an' bigotified ;

but des strack a bow 'crost de fiddle, an' ev'y
j'int in 'is bordy look like hit 'd loosen up an'
'spon' ter de chune.   An' you know de way you
use ter wrop an' tie up de middle o' yo' ha'r all
de week, an' grease it wid a taller candle ter
open it up of a Sunday—well, little Joe he favored
you dat-a-way.   Look like you is los' yo' ha'r
purty consider'ble, Aleck," she continued, glancing at his bald pate, "but in co'se you 'ain't
been half reg'lated.   Time I gits some goose-
grease an' buggomot an' yarbs, an' bile 'em down
good, an' rub 'em in on de full o' de moon, hit
'll come out ag'in; an' ef it don't, hit 'll nour'sh
an' cher'sh de roots good, an' polish de skin.   Is
yer ever tuck ingon syrup fur yer col', Aleck?"

"I 'ain't got no col', Cicely.   Huccome you ax
me dat?"

"Look ter me like you's a little hoa'se, ain't
yer?"

"Is I?   I d' know ef I is er not.   I 'ain't had
nobody ter catechise me 'bout my cornstitutiom,
an' take no *intruss* in me fur so long, I jes tecks
myse'f as a fines myse'f, an' ax no questioms.   In
co'se, my so'e foot, I knowed dat warn't nachel,
an' I been a-tamperin' wid it good as I could, but
look like hit ain't mendin' none."

"Maybe hit crave a new han', Aleck.   Lif' it
up heah on my knee an' lemme see it."

He raised his foot laboriously, and rested it in
his old wife's lap.   With a tender hand she slipped off the heavy shoe, pulled off an almost

footless sock, and gently unwound the bound ankle.

"You sholy is you," she said, laughing, as she stroked his old foot. "I'd know dat foot in a crowd, de way de big toe treshpash on de nex' one."

"Co'se me me," he responded, with a chuckle. "Ef—ef I 'lowed I was somebordy else a-putt'n' he's foot up in yo' lap so sporntanyus, I'd—I'd shoot 'im sho, perfessor as I is!"

The suffering ankle was tenderly manipulated, and pronounced already better for the sympathetic tending.

"Dey ain't no 'casiom ter nail up de do' no mo', is dey?" said the old man, finally, with a smiling glance at the fallen bar.

"I been a settin' heah ponderin', Aleck," said she, "an' seem ter me, bein' as you an' me stan's high in de chu'ch, an' dey is so much upro'rious doin's an' goin's on dese days, an' so much scandalizin'. we ought ter be calt out ag'in f'om de pulpit fur man an' wife; an' while I ain't say nail de do', I say we better des keep it shet, an' set out on de two sides o' de partitiom (ef a warm spell come ag'in) tell over Sunday, an' den we c'n stan' up in chu'ch ag'in, 'caze you know dee 'ain't got nuttn' but 'cep' des my word an' yo' word ter stan' 'twix' us an' scandalizemint, ef dee choose ter p'int a finger at us."

"What yer mean, Cicely? Is yer mean fur me ter go home?"

" Yas, Aleck. I b'lieve dat's de bes', tell you talks to Br'er Brown an' git 'im ter call us out in chu'ch."

" Dat look like foolishness ter me, Cicely."

" In co'se hit's foolishness 'twix' you an' me, Aleck ; but hit's good hard sense de way we stan's 'fo' de worl'. Ef somebordy 'd come in heah an' fin' dat do' open, an' you maybe on de wrong side, all de splainin' we c'd do arterwards hit 'd on'y aggervate de scandal 'fo' de worl'. You go on home now. Hit's 'mos' day, an' you needs a nap o' sleep 'fo' sunup."

The old man laughed, and waiving further protest, betook himself through the open door to his own apartment. A dim light coming through the window seemed to color the candle-flame a deeper orange. It was the first ray of a rising sun.

" Oh, Cicely," he called, as he stood, candle in hand, at the door—" oh, Cicely, han' me a ole josey er some'h'n' o' yo's, honey, ter hang up over heah, won't yer ? Dis room look like hit's got a sudden spell o' emptiness, an' seem like hit's lonesome as de grave. I 'feerd I mought go ter sleep an' weck up an' mistrus' all dis fur a dream, 'less'n I had a ole ap'on er josey er some'h'n' ter ketch my eyes quick's I opens 'em. Hit 'd he'p me ter pass de time tell Sunday."

" G'way f'om heah, Aleck ! I ain't a-gwine do no sech of a thing ! I ain't gwine have no josey o' mine witnessin' 'ginst me 'fo' de Cornf'ence ;

an' ef some o' dem busybordy br'ers an' sisters
come a-prowlin' roun' heah terreckly ter see de
shape o' de scraps you got lef' f'om Chris'mus
dinner, dee'd spy it out an' set it up 'ginst my
c'a'cter mighty quick. You go on ter baid, Aleck,
an' ef yer git lonesome you des call out, 'Cicely,'
an' I'll 'spon' ter yer, 'caze I's berwildered an'
'plexted in my min' much as you is, an' I ain't
gwine sleep heavy. Good-night, an' Gord bless
yer!"

"Amen," said the old man as he blew out the
candle, and before many minutes a sound of meas-
ured breathing, coming from both rooms, proclaimed the aged pair at rest in that happy land
of youth renewed, of losses restored, of hopes fulfilled—the land of dreams.

Parson Brown was duly interviewed, and con-
curred fully in Sister Garrett's idea of the propri-
ety of a formal announcement, in the presence of
the congregation and of the parties concerned, of
the renewed relations of the old people. Indeed,
he was quite enthusiastic in his delight in prospect of the novel occasion, as well as in congratulations to the soon to be reunited. The old couple
expressed some solicitude as to the manner of proceeding, to which he reassuringly replied in this
wise:

"Hab no reprehensions, my deah br'er an' sister; jes leave ev'ything ter me. Ain't I'm a
preacher? Ain't I'm de shepherd o' de flock? I

is er I *ain't*, one. Ef I *ain't*, I better han' in my designatiom an' clair out, an' go a-fishin'; an' ef I *is*, I sholy is fittn ter conduc' air cer'mony whatsomever what mought arise outn de needs an' de desires o' my flock. Ain't dat so?"

It was so. So said Sister Garrett, and so reiterated Br'er Thormson's nodding head.

"An' as fur yo' part," the minister continued—"as fur yo' part, embellish yo'se'ves accordin' ter de dictates o' yo' desires an' de succumstances o' de 'casiom, an' lookin' neither ter de right ner ter de lef', walk up de middle island o' de chu'ch at the 'p'inted hour, an' teck yo' stan', widout feah an' widout approach, in de presence of a waitin' corngergatiom, an' I'll gua'ntee dat ev'ything shill pass orf ter de comfort o' yo' hearts, ter de 'newin' o' yo' sperits, ter de satersfactiom o' de worl', an' ter de glory o' Gord."

"Amen!" said Sister Garrett.

"Amen!" fervently echoed Br'er Thormson.

On Sabbath morning following this, Br'er Brown announced from the pulpit that at five o'clock on that same afternoon, immediately after the closing exercises of Conference, then in session, there would take place in the church a *golden wedding,* to which all were cordially invited. This was all. He refused further explanation, but laughingly bade the curious "come and see."

Needless to say, the church was crowded to overflowing, for curiosity ran high, both as to the individuals concerned and the exact nature of the promised ceremony. The expectant interest of the waiting congregation proved infectious, and after closing of Conference the dozen or more of ministers present remained, to a man, curious to witness an occasion so rare as a golden wedding.

After a short interval of some disorder, during which ministers and people engaged in social conversation, laughingly surmising as to whom the bridal party should be, a stir at the door announced their approach.

Had not their dress labelled them as the heroes of the hour, it would have been impossible, so great was the crowd, for them to have made their way up the aisle. The throng, pressing to right and left, gave way, however, and arm in arm the old couple, obeying orders, passed up the middle aisle and took their stand before the pulpit.

The groom wore his old broadcloth suit—the very one, by the way, in which he had been married to this same woman a nameless number of years ago.

The bride, modestly attired in an old white muslin, might have escaped special notice in a crowd, excepting for a small spray of natural orange flowers which she wore upon her forehead.

It is a pity to have to write it, but there was a titter of mirth, ill suppressed, unworthy the dignity of the occasion and the place, as the old pair tottered up the aisle.

Brother Brown had stepped down before the

pulpit, and was ready to receive them. Perceiving instinctively that his congregation were not in touch with the spirit of the occasion, he won their attention and deference by a short and earnest prayer; then lowering his voice, addressed them solemnly as follows :

"My deah bredren and sistren in de Lord, you see befo' you a aged couple, bofe o' whom an' each one o' which is no stranger ter you all—Br'er Alexander Thormson, a man in good an' reg'lar standin' in de chu'ch, an' Sister Cicely Garrett, lakwisely respected and respectable 'mongst de sisterhood fur stiddy-goin' piety. It is a fac' well known ter dis corngergatiom dat dese two pussons is been livin' nex' do' ter one-'n'er fur de space o' six mont's er sech a matter, save an' exceptin' sech times as Sister Garrett is been livin' out at service; an' when I 'form you o' de fac' dat dee claims dat dee was married ter one-'n'er long 'fo' de wah, an' 'ain't reconnize one-'n'er tell now, 'tain't fur you ter 'spute dey words, 'caze when you cas'es yo' eyes upon 'em now, as dee stan' heah to-day, you can easy conceive o' de fac' dat de lan'marks *by* which dee *could* o' been reconnized is well-nigh washed away by de surgin' o' de river o' time. Dee claims dat dee was j'ined in de holy instate o' matrermony in de ole days, time dee was yong, an' arter meanderin' roun' de worl', eas' an' wes,' norf an' souf, norfeas' an' norfwes,' so ter speak, ter all de p'ints o' de cumpositiom, dee suddently reconnize one-'n'er, an' now, while dee ain't a-ca'-

culatin' ter ketch up wid all de yeahs what's gone, dee 'low dat dee crave ter come back ter de startin'-p'int, an' start fresh, han' in han'. By de bless'in' o' Gord, when dee skivered one-'n'er, dee was bofe free-handed an' free-hearted ; an' now, wid a free han', dee craves ter jine han's ag'in, an' wid a free heart dee craves ter jine hearts once mo' ; an' ef dey hearts is bofe turned dat-a-way, who gwine say de word ter hender 'em ? Ef anybordy got a word agin it, let 'im *speak now*, er else, as de Bible say, *fo'ever hol' 'is peace.*"

He hesitated, casting his eye over the crowd, upon which the silence of attentive listening had fallen.

"Hit's true," he resumed," dis aged couple is well on in de yeahs, an' look lak dey journey is 'mos' done ; but ef dee got de cour'ge ter teck han's fur de las' mile o' de road, 'tain't fur de laks o' us ter *dis*cour'ge 'em ! An' when I looks at dis o-ole man, ripe in yeahs, as de Book say, an' 'cripit an' failin' in steps, an' I know dey's a woman what's willin' ter stan' up an' teck de spornserbility o' follerin' dat man clean tell 'e gits ter de gate o' de kingdom, I bless de Lord, an' say *dat woman got cour'ge, sho!* She is *born inter de light*, 'caze hit would be a *dark journey fur de onconverted!* An' when my eyes pass ter de bride—'tain't no use fur me ter specify—but when my eye pass ter de bride what stan's befo' me now, a-leanin' fon'ly on de arm o' de groom — dat same groom what done picked an' choosed 'er out, away back yonder time o' de fallin' o' de stars—'tain't no use fur me ter specify, but I raises my eyes ter Heaven an' I say, Bless Gord fur cour'ge ! De bride ain't show no mo' cour'ge 'n de groom is. Bless Gord fur a brave heart an' a kin' heart an' a true heart !

"*Wharfore*," he continued, "in de face o' de fac's, an' in de presence o' you all, I pernounce 'em once mo' *man and wife!*"

Turning to the groom, he added, lowering his voice, "I ain't say s'lute yo' bride, 'caze I know she done been s'luted on de former 'casiom ; howsomever, ef you desires ter 'new yo' salutatiom 'fo' de worl', you is free ter do so."

The old man bent his head and kissed the lips of his old wife. This was taken as the usual signal for congratulations, and the congregation began to move forward.

With a wave of his arm, however, the minister indicated that the golden wedding was not yet over.

Placing bride and groom in chairs within the chancel, he turned again to the congregation. A change of tone denoted that he was now approaching a new branch of the subject.

"I guv out dis mawnin'," he began, "dat dis was gwine ter be a *golden weddin'*, an' what is I mean, my bredren ? Is I mean dat de *preacher* was rich ? No, you know I ain't. Is I mean dat de *groom* was rich ? No, you know he ain't. Is I mean dat de *bride* was rich ? No, you know she ain't. Den what *is* I mean ? What is de signifi-

3

catiom of a golden weddin' ? Hit's de cilebratiom
o' de ma'yage o' two pussons what have de cour'ge
ter stan' up 'fo' Gord an' de worl', arter fifty yeahs,
an' say, 'Amen ! Dee lived through it, an' dee
gwine stan' up ter it !' An' ef dee sorry dee done it,
dee nuver lets on.   Dat's de weddin' part ; an' de
gol' part, dat mean dat ev'ybordy 'bleege ter fetch
a gol' weddin' present. Now fur de gol' part. In
co'se I knows you ain't able ter come up wid pure
gol', but look ter me lak dis is a proud occasiom
ter do double juty wid sech as you is got, an' you
knows yo'se'f dat small change is de squivalent o'
gol' ; an' now I tell yer what I gwine perpose ter
do : I 'ain't c'lected no sal'ry fur two mont's, an'
ef you'll all come up hearty, yong an' ole, wid de
widder's mite, an' swell de collectiom, I tell yer
what I gwine do : I gwine 'vide up even wid
de bride an' groom, an' we'll give 'em a golden
weddin' ter de best o' our stability, 'caze when a
pair o' ole pussons show de cour'ge what dee done
showed ter-day, hit's on'y right ter he'p 'em 'long
an' give 'em a start.   What you say ?"

"Amen !" exclaimed an old man in the front
pew.

"Turn up de hat !" The voice came from the
body of the church this time.

" Ole age boun' ter ketch us all 'f we live," said
another—a white-haired sister.

It was pretty, the generous spirit of this most
ingenuous and sympathetic people.

The collection was the largest ever known.

AFTER THE GOLDEN WEDDING.

When it was over, and the congregation, every individual of which had contributed something, had again come to order, the minister, after offering a short thanksgiving in the name of the beneficiaries, announced that before pronouncing **the** benediction he desired to give a short notice.

"De bride an' de groom," said he, " wants me ter noterfy dis corngergatiom dat on de former 'casiom when dee got ma'yed, dee was j'ined onder de name o' Smiff, bein' as Br'er Thormson at dat time b'long ter de Smiffs, an' seem lak, ef dee goes back ag'in fo' man an' wife, dee boun' by law, ef dee boun' at all, ter teck up dey contrac' onder de same entitlemint dee went by time dee 'sumed de fus spornserbility, an' so now dee gwine leave de name o' Thormson an' teck de name o' Smiff. Dat's de fus p'int ; an' de secon' an' las' p'int is dis: Sis Garrett, jest turned Thormson, and hencefor'ard Smiff, she got a grief on 'er heart on de 'count o' a yong son o' hern an' Br'er Smiff's what strayed orf time o' de wah and 'ain't been heerd of no mo', an' she baigged me ter be sho an' read out from de pul*pit* ter-day a inscriptiom o' de yong man, an' ter spressify de fac' dat 'is pa an' ma crave ter meet up wid 'im ag'in. She say he was name Little Joe, Joe Smiff (she don' know ef he helt ter de Smiff, but she sho he cling ter de Joe) ; an' fur de inscriptiom, de way she got 'im on 'er min', she say he was a lakly yong man, black-complected an' tall an' slim, an' at de time o' de strayin' orf he had orn a blue check home-

spun suit, an' fur face an' shape, she say he look
jes perzac'ly lak 'is pa, an' she furthermo' intreats
dis corngergatiom dat ef dee knows any yong man
name Joe (or even *ain't* name Joe, ef he fulfil
de yether inscriptioms) what 'ain't kep up wid
'is fambly, ter sen' 'im roun' tell dee zamine 'is
p'ints an' see ef he ain't b'longs ter dem. Dats
de way Sister Smiff done calt it out ter me, but ef
dis yong man was b'long ter *me*, I wouldn't cramp
de search by no sech changeable inscriptioms.
Look ter me lak any black-complected yong man,
what is los' 'isse'f f'om 'is ma an' pa, deserve a
hearin', 'caze, when a pusson stops ter consider,
hit's been a long time sence de 'clarin' o' peace,
an' you know a pusson got time ter fatten an' fall
orf in all dis time, an' de homespun suit — yer
kyant fasten dat on 'im no mo', 'caze he's boun'
ter been changed 'is cloze in all dese yeahs—ef
he's fitt'n' *to* ketch up wid—an' when yer come
ter lookin' lak 'is pa "—the speaker shook his
head and smiled—" you know dat's boun' ter be
in 'is mammy's ricollectiom : you an' me 'd nuver
see it, 'caze no yong man gwine look lak Br'er
Smiff look now, not speakin' onrespectful o' de
groom, 'caze we all on de same track ; but now,
on de consideratiom o' dese p'ints, seem ter me de
name o' Smiff 'll do mo' ter ketch up wid dis way-
ward son dan dese changeable inscriptioms ; *wharfore*, I charge you, in de name o' de love o' yo'
chillen, ter open yo' eyes ter see an' yo' ears ter
heah, an' try ter fin' dis prodigums son fur 'em !

His ma an' pa, dee say dee know he's safe, livin'
er daid, 'caze dee's helt 'im up, day an' night, in
de arms o' faith, close-t ter de mercy-seat; but yit,
ef he's in de lan' o' de livin,' dee craves ter lay
dey mortal eyes on 'im ag'in. He was borned
on de Morgan plantation, on de coas', an' was
sol', 'long wid 'is mammy, 'fo' de wah, ter de
Garretts, o' Bayou Gros Tête, f'om w'ich place
he crost over ter Placque*meen*, an' dat's fur as dee
knows."

Turning here toward the ministers, who sat in
a row behind the pulpit, he would have invited
one of them to pronounce the benediction; but
the tallest of their number, known as Brother
Lincoln, had risen, and unbidden was stepping
forward. He was a black man of fifty or thereabouts, conspicuously handsome and of commanding presence, a delegate from one of the upper
parishes. He stepped to the front, as if to address the congregation, hesitated, cleared his
throat, swallowed, essayed to speak, but failed
to command his voice, and finally, turning suddenly, approached the old woman Cicely, and with
a voice broken with a sob, said, "Mammy, heah
little Joe."

The old woman, for the first time during all
the trying ceremony, lost her self-control. With
a shriek, she threw herself into the arms of her
son, whose first word assured her of his identity.

The old father sobbed aloud, trembling piteously, but soon the son drew his mother's with-

ered little form into a chair beside him, next the old man, and, putting his strong arm around him, drew him to himself.

There was not a dry eye in the church, and not a few of the more emotional fell to shouting. In the midst of the wildest excitement, Brother Brown, himself weeping, pronounced a faltering benediction, but the congregation were too much wrought up for dismissal. It was quite dark when at last, after innumerable hand-shakings and many embracings—father and mother leaning each on an arm of the son—they passed out of the church.

The story is told, and yet, before we leave them, let us peep in upon the three as they sit at the home fireside on this first evening. They are in the mother's room, and the son occupies the centre chair, while the old parents on either side gaze fondly upon him.

" Joe," says the old man at length, " wh-whar'd you git de name o' Lincolm, anyhow?"

" Well, yer know, daddy, I 'ain't meant no onrispec' ter you, but I 'ain't nuver spect ter see yer no mo', an' you 'ain't had no name what yer mought say was borned ter yer nohow, an' de name o' Smiff look like hit had so much spornserbility on it a'ready—look like hit's done stood fur so much tell hit don't stan' fur nuttn' no mo' —an' I was a-castin' 'bout fur a name what stood fur freedom—an' dat's huccome I tuck de name o' Lincolm ; but in co'se, ef you sesso — you de

one ter seh de word—an' ef you sesso dat I's
boun' ter teck de name o' Smiff, in co'se I'll—
I'll—"

"No, no! I 'ain't sesso! What you say,
Cicely?"

"Don't pester me 'bout no 'title*mints* to-night,
honey. I des wants ter set down heah an' feas'
my eyes on my baby! Ain't yer see how he
favor you, Aleck? Look at 'is haid. How yer
keep it so purty, Joe?"

"I jes kyards it out wid a kyardin'-comb, same
as I use ter; but I ain't 'ten' ter it much myse'f.
De-Dely, she mos'ly combs an' trains it."

"Who Dely?" asked both the old people at
once, eagerly.

He laughed with some embarrassment. "Wh-
why, Dely—she—she's my wife."

"Umh!" grunted the mother.

"I sesso too!" echoed the father.

"Y-yas—yas, 'm, I ma'yed; yas, sir, I ma'yed.
Why, mammy, I's gittn' ole, me! I got—I got—"

"What you got?" asked both together, again.

"I got—I got—why, mammy, I got a gal big
as you is—yas, 'm, I is."

"'Ain't I tol' yer he was des de perzac' image
o' you, Aleck? I knowed quick as my back was
turned, he ma'y. What else you got, Joe?"

"Who, me? I got a whole passel o' chillen—
boys an' gals, an' an'—boys an' gals, an' boys
an'—"

"Don't say it over no mo', Joe, 'less'n yer mean

dey ain't no een ter 'em. Go orn an' tell us what dey names. Umh! Lord have mussy, Aleck! You an' me's 'bout a dozen gran'mammies and gran'daddies, de way Joe's a-talkin' now. What's de matter wid you, Joe? Why'n't yer talk, an' tell me dey names?"

"I's tellin' yer fas' as I kin, mammy. De oles' one, she name arter you."

The old woman smiled. "Is she? Well, well! —name Cicely, eh?"

Joe scratched his head. The examination was trying.

"No, 'm, not ezzac'ly. Yer see, my wife, she name Delia, an' you name Cicely, an' so I put de two names togedder, Cicely an' Delia, an' dat comes out Celia. She name Celia."

"Mh—hm! Yas, I see. Yer named 'er arter me, an.' calls 'er Celia. I's glad yer splained it out ter me 'fo' yer tol' me de name, 'caze ef I'd a-started backwards on dat, I nuver would o' ketched up wid it. An' de boys, what dee names?"

"Well, de oles' one, he name Aberham, to match in wid de Lincolm; an' den startin' dat-a-way, I was 'bleege ter finish de set, so arter Aberham come Isaac an' Jacob; den come Phil Sheridam an' Gineral Grant, an'—"

"Yer 'ain't thought 'bout namin' none ob 'em Alexander de Great, is yer?" asked the old man, timidly. "Dat's my name, and hit's tooken outn de book; I heerd ole marster sesso."

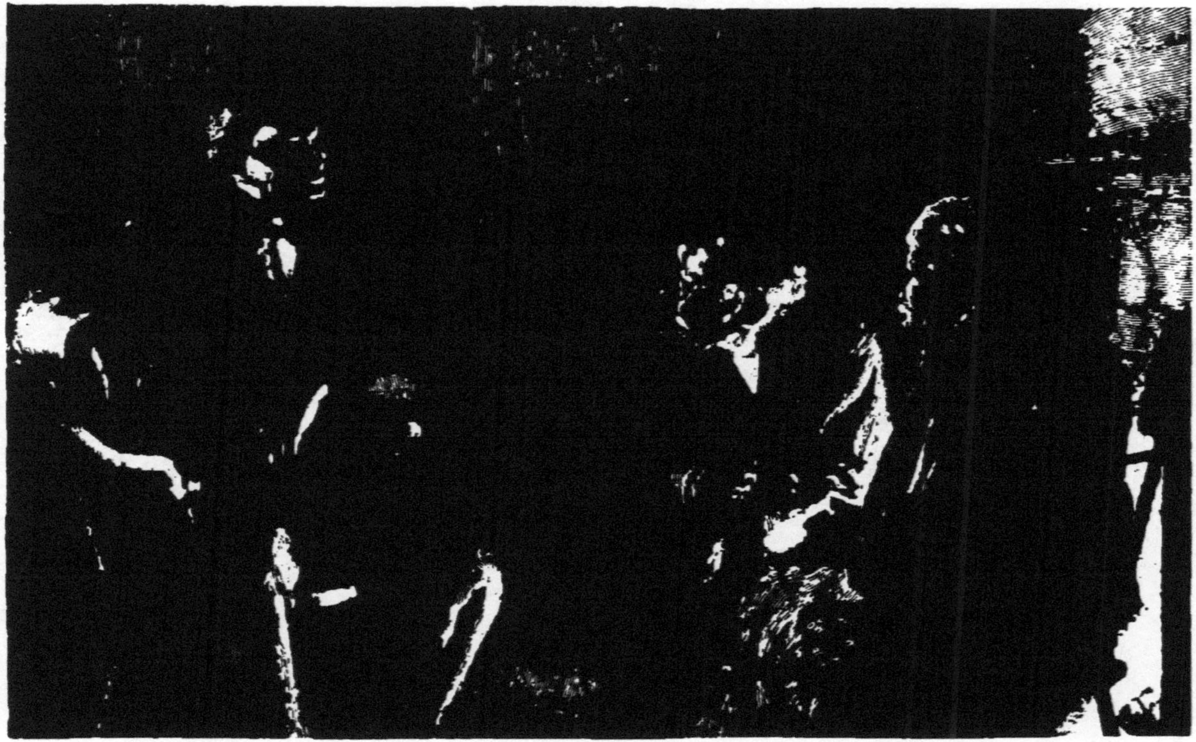

"WHO DELY?"

"I gwine name de nex' one dat, sho, daddy. Hit 'll glorify de whole crowd wid granjer."

But why try to follow them in their artless, original, and most ingenuous talk ?

It was late, and all had gradually subsided into silence, when the old man spoke again. He had been for some time looking at the orange branch which still stood in the bottle on the table. "Cicely," said he, "look ter me like maybe dishere o'ange in de bouquet stood fur little Joe."

"I had dat in my min' all de time, Aleck ; an' dat's huccome I 'ain't bruck it orf; but look ter me now like de branch 'ain't did full juty, 'less'n hit's got 'bout a million o' little o'anges on it, ter stan' fur all o' little Joe's boys an' gals."

"An' I bet yer, ef yer look close-t, you'll fine 'em, too," said the old man.

And it was true.

LAMENTATIONS OF JEREMIAII JOHNSON

LAMENTATIONS OF JEREMIAH JOHNSON

IT was a hot day in August. Groups of cattle stood about in shady spots chewing their cuds, gazing out with mild resignation upon the gleaming field. Horses here and there rolled in the grass to cool themselves; restless hogs moved from one mud puddle to another, grunting a protest against the rising mercury; noisy hens, settling themselves about in gossipy squads under the barnhouse floor, chattered as they scratched down into the substratum of moist sand for cooler spots for their feathered breasts. Such was the picture in Judge Williams's barnyard on this particular August day.

At the extreme end of the enclosure, where a little branch wound its way beneath the shade of a sweet-gum tree, a flock of puddle ducks floated about in the shadow; and here, on the grassy bank, a fat black woman stood before a row of tubs, washing. Across the creek, and it was only a step, and beyond a wild-rose hedge, quite out of sight, perched upon the top crossing of a rail-fence, on guard over the judge's family washing, which lay bleaching in the sun, was the subject

of this sketch—Lamentations of Jeremiah Johnson.

Out in the full glare of the August sun he sat,
with head sunburned and bare. He was black,
tall, lank, and—unpretty, to put it mildly; and
he wore to-day a single garment which partly
covered, but did not ornament, his homely person.
A yellow calico dress, buttoned (or rather un-
buttoned) behind, and caught by a rusty pin mid-
way between neck and waist, boasted a long skirt
which fell nearly to his feet when he stood, but
now, lifted by his projecting knees, it fell in
foliated curves, from which the slender black legs
dangled as dark stamens project from the yellow
calyx of the marsh-lily.

Lamentations was now twelve years old, and yet,
although he was the only child of his mother, he
had never possessed a masculine garment of any
description. He was the last and only survivor
of a family of ten children, and as the others
had all been daughters, who had died at various ages from infancy up to fifteen years,
there were feminine garments of assorted sizes
awaiting him at his birth, from the guinea-blue
baby-frocks to the large dresses of homespun
which lay folded away in his mother's press, an
inheritance into which he was slowly and surely growing, and from which he would fain
have held back, if there had been any relief
at the other end; but Lamentations saw that
the only way out of this dilemma was through

it, and so, if he prayed at all, he prayed *to grow.*

"Ef I could jes grow past dem gal frocks, I'd be willin' ter die de nex' minute, 'caze den I could die like what I *is*, an' *'spect* myself as I on'y *kin* 'spect myself in breeches !   I ain't nuver gwine ter git no ambitioms nor no mannishness s'long's I got ter roam roun' in dese heah yaller-buff gal cloe's !"

In this fashion Lamentations was wont to give vent to his feelings on the subject of his attire ; but he protested secretly, as he found himself the worse always for any open rebellion, his mother often beating him, and declaring that he was "dat proud dat he was a reg'lar ole maid," and that "what was good enough for the angels in Heab'n was good enough for him."   This allusion to his departed sisters generally worked her up to the whipping point, and so Lamentations kept a discreet silence, though he rebelled in secret.

Lamentations' parents, Antony and Priscilla, had been a worldly pair in their youth, and Antony regarded the birth and death of nine daughters consecutively as a visitation of Providence for their early sins.

· "It shorely is a visitatiom, an' a double visita-tiom," he had lamented.   "Fust an' fo'most, de bare fac' o' havin' nine gals han'-runnin' is a visi-tatiom ; an' secon' and hin'most, de losin' ob 'em arter you *is* got 'em is a double correctiom wid de scourgin' rod."

One evening Antony and Priscilla sat inside their cabin door. It was Sunday, and they had been to meeting. On the Sunday before, they had buried their last child, the ninth.

The sun was setting behind the hill, and casting a last ray over the little cemetery at its foot, brought into clear view the row of graves that held the records of their many losses.

Antony gazed intently at them for some time. Finally he said : " P'cilla, I b'lieve dat the visitatiom's done finished! I don't b'lieve Gord's gwine ter give an' teek no mo' gals!"

"Huccome you ca'culatin' so free, I like ter know?" said his wife.

" Well, I's been obserbin', an' a-speculatin'; an' a-settin' heah a-studyin', I's come ter dis conclusiom—"

" What conclusiom is you come ter, Antony?"

" I come ter *dis* conclusiom—dat nine am de fatal figgur. Now you jes lis'n ter me! Look at de signs o' de nines!"

"I knows de signs o' de nines," interrupted Priscilla.

" What signs you know?"

" G'way f'om heah, Antony! You reckin 'caze I ain't learned in the books dat I 'ain't got *no* educatiom! Even a yo'ng kitten, what *is* got de leastest sense in all creatiom, is got sense enough not ter try ter open hits eyes on dis sinful worl' befo' de nine days o' darkness is out."

" ' De nine days o' darkness !' Yer jes struck

it right dar, P'cilla. Now we's all jes de same as new-borned kittens befo' Gord. In fac' *we* ain't 'spornserble fur not *bein'* kittens, an' new-born, an' bline at dat. Now, jes fur de sake o' de argimentatiom o' de subjec', let's us supposin' dat all de worl' *is* new-borned kittens, den it follers, *in* co'se, dat all de worl' is borned bline, which is de case, bein' borned in a state o' sin an mizry. Ain't dat so?"

"You goes so fas' I kyan't keep up wid yer, Antony. Say all dat ag'in. I ain't a-gwine ter give in ter nut'n' what mecks *me* out no varmint, 'less'n I sees de proof, ef you *is* willin' ter argify yo'se'f inter a torm-cat."

"Hush, P'cilla. You's a-runnin' away wid dis subjec' jes de same's a cat runs away wid a mouse. Now you lis'n ter me, 'spornserble, not fur de callin' o' no names, which I ain't a-doin', but fur de sake o' de substantiatiom o' de proof."

"Substantiation of the proof" was too much for Priscilla. The words were well chosen, and gained her respectful attention, while Antony slowly repeated his argument, and in a moment she had agreed that all men were "jes de same as new-borned kittens befo' Gord."

"Well," said Antony, "dat's a fixed fac'. Now, ef we's de same as new-borned kittens, don't you see dat we's got ter go froo our nine days o' darkness befo' we comes out in de light?"

Priscilla saw it.

"Well, now, ain't de losin' of a baby, even

4

ef 'tis a gal baby—ain't dat a day o' darkness ?"

" Dat's so," said Priscilla.

" An' ain't a-losin' *nine* ob 'em goin' froo *nine days o' darkness ?*"

Priscilla raised up her face and assented respectfully. She was convinced.

"Now, look a - heah !" Antony continued. " We's done passed froo de darkness, an' my b'lief is dat Gord's gwine ter raise de visitatiom an' show us de light—dat is, *ef we ac's 'spornserble.*"

" Antony !"

" What yer want, P'cilla ?"

Priscilla eyed him askance as she said, " You talks like you's gitt'n' 'ligion !"

" I ain't a-sayin' I's gitt'n' 'ligion, P'cilla, but I's a-speakin' f'om de innermos'nesses ob my heart."

" Antony !"

" What yer want, P'cilla !"

His wife smiled faintly as she replied, " De time I'll b'lieve you's got 'ligion 'll be de time yer gits de spring-chicken honger an' stays in de baid all night an' nuver bodders 'long o' no hain-rooses !"

Antony did not join in the laugh that followed this, but said, seriously : "You is a awful game-maker, P'cilla, an' I ain't a-denyin' dat I's gi'n yer plenty o' 'casion ter meck game o' me. But look heah !"

He rose slowly from his chair, and, pointing to

the little row of graves, now barely visible in the approaching twilight, he said : " Look a-heah ! A-standin' heah to-night, a-p'intin' ter dat row o' gal graves on de hill-side yonder, each one ob 'em which holds a sign an' a symbol ob a double visi- tatiom, in de givin' an' de teckin' ob a gal chile, I stan' up an' say befo' Gord, dat ef He holps me, I's a-gwine ter ac' 'spornserble an' opright, befo' anudder nine graves gits a start on us, becaze Gord don't do nut'n' by halves, an' ef He's started a-chastisin' us by de fatal nines, He ain't a-gwine ter back down on it !"

Priscilla glanced toward the row of graves and heaved a deep sigh. Then, slowly turning from her husband, she opened the door of a safe at her side, and taking from it a tin plate of cold bacon and greens, and reseating herself with it on her lap, she began to eat them, raising the dark green shreds with her fingers into the air above her head, and slowly lowering them into her capacious mouth. Priscilla was of the earth, earthy. She had mourned heartily and boister- ously over each of her nine bereavements, but her bosom was not the home of sorrow, and when a grief fell into it, it was as an acid falling into an alkali. The effect was effervescent, evanescent, and when once the bubbling ceased, the same acid could not stir it again.

She grew serious at mention of her dead chil- dren, and ate the flabby garlands of greens in grim silence, chewing meditatively, and ruminating almost sadly over each mouthful before elevating another for inspection and consumption.

It was in the spring following this that to the house of Antony and Priscilla came a little son. Antony was in the field "chopping cotton" when the news came to him. He behaved with strange excitement on this occasion, dropping his hoe as he exclaimed: "De visitatiom's done h'isted! Glory be to Gord!" and on the Sunday following he did what, notwithstanding his reformed life, he had never done before. He made a public profession of religion, and, in the language of Brother Williamson, the officiating minister, "Cornsecrated hissef and all o' hisn to de service o' de Lord!"

Antony expressed great concern as to the selection of a name for his son. It must be a Bible name—a name that should be an inspiration to the lad as well as a certificate of his father's piety.

Brother Williamson suggested the names of the gospels, but Antony objected. Matthews and Johns were disgracing the saints all over the country now, "and," he contended, "John Johnson wouldn't do nohow, 'caze hit soun's like a pusson's a-stammerin', an' jes as sho as I'd call John Johnson, I'd git ter Johnin' an' couldn't stop. No, don't gimme none o' dem stutterin' names!"

"How 'bout Mark!" ventured Williamson.

"Mark—Mark," he repeated, reflectively; "a

black Mark?   Don't you know, Brer Williamson, dat a black mark nuver stan's for no good?"

"Dat's so—lookin' at it dat-a-way.   Dat's so. Well, what yer say ter Luke?"

"No, sir!" he quickly replied.   "'Ain't you jes preached las' Sunday ag'in Lukewarm Christians? Dat won't do."

Williamson hesitated; then, counting on his fingers, he slowly said, "Matthew, Mark, Luke, John, Acts — Acts is a good name, Brer Johnson; s'posin' yer names his name Acts?"

Antony hesitated.   There was a suggestion of energy in the name—even a hint of good works; still, he did not seem quite to like it.   Finally he said: "I did know a man once-t what named his boy Ac's, but he come ter it reg'lar.   He had all o' Ac's's. pardners hand-runnin'—Maffew, Mark, Luke, and John; an' hit seems ter me like goin' backward, somehow—like turnin' de 'postles cat-awarmosed, an' treatin' 'em onrespecful, ter name de fust boy Ac's.   De fac' is, Brer Williamson, hit looks ter me kind o' deceitful ter do dat— hit's like sneaking up berhindt 'em like, an' Maffew an' Mark an' Luke an' John would somehow be *slighted!*—an' besides, it don't seem as I's ezzacly got a *right* ter fetch Ac's in heah, ber-hindt a whole passel o' Callines an' M'rias an' seech.   No; I wants ter fine a name what stan's ter hitse'f like—what I could sort o' teck liberties wid movin' outn its place, one dat don't b'longs ter no crowd."

The preacher ventured several other suggestions, but none seemed to suit.

Priscilla, with wifely devotion, wished to call
the boy Antony, but to this he would not listen.

"No, no," he protested; "my name ain't clean
enough. Hit's been mixed up wid too much devil*mint* ter fit dat little angel o' light. Ef I kin
wuck off all de stains what's on it by de time he's
obleeged ter ca'y de Johnson part o' it out inter
de worl', I'll praise Gord."

The babe was nameless for a month.

Finally, one Sunday, Antony came home from
church jubilant. He had found the name to suit
his fancy. The preacher had read it out of the
Bible, and it had a sound of dignity that pleased
him. It seemed to be filled with exhortation and
warning and spirituality. It was "Lamentations
of Jeremiah."

The little babe winced visibly when, on the
next Sabbath, the water of baptism was sprinkled
on his unconscious head, and he became, whether
he willed it or no, "Lamentations of Jeremiah
Johnson."

No one ever had occasion to doubt the sincerity of Antony's conversion. It was a quiet facing
about, an unemotional turning from sinful ways
to a pure life. At first, the good people in the
church were hardly satisfied with the "speritual
evidences" in his case. They were disappointed.
The man who had been the best dancer of the

"double twis'," and could beat every man in the
county "cutting the pigeon wing," would certainly throw some of this muscular vigor into the new
life, and they had looked for great gymnastic
spiritual manifestations, so to speak, in his conversion.

Perhaps religion in his case would even hallow
the "pigeon wing," and sanctify the "double twis'"
—who knew? If Antony had worn a dazed visage and danced down the middle aisle in an ex-
travagant "fling," his would have been considered
a more pronounced conversion. One of the brothers even whispered his disappointment in church
to a neighbor. "I shorely is disapp'inted," he
said. "I 'lowed dat *maybe* Brer Johnson would
sort o' *skipulate* inter grace." But Brer Johnson
did not "skipulate." There was nothing sensational about his case.

For eleven years Antony was a quiet, consistent
Christian member of Chinquepin Chapel, and it is
safe to say that the light of his quiet life did
more to reform the morals of the congregation
and to raise the standard of personal piety among
them than did all the shouting and exhorting done
in the chapel during that time, and his death, occurring when Lamentations was eleven years old,
produced a profound sensation. It was as the
last years of his life had been—full of peace and
a holy trust. The only time he was ever known
to shout was with his passing breath, when, having invoked God's blessing on his little son, his

spirit passed out through a smile on his lips, and he met the grim messenger with a clear though faint "Praise Gord!"

After Antony's death, Priscilla gave up "crap-raisin'" and moved to town. She was a typical negro—improvident, emotional, gossipy, kind-hearted, high-tempered, vain, dishonest, idle, working two or three days in each week and "res'n' up" the remainder, with always a healthy appetite and a "mizry in de bre's'."

She had professed conversion several times, and as often become a backslider. The tips of her fingers led her easily into sin by fastening themselves to her neighbors' goods, but this never brought her into open shame, as did the tips of her *toes*, for Priscilla was an inveterate dancer, and if a revival or camp-meeting drew her into the church, it took only a string band or a fiddle to work her ruin. Indeed, it became a byword that "Sister Johnson shouted all winter and danced out o' grace at every May-day picnic."

Such was Lamentations' mother. During the year of her widowhood, as a visible means of support, she had done the family washing for Judge Williams and his wife; and though the pay for so small an amount of work was proportionally small, there were perquisites in the shape of a cabin rent free, "cold victuals," and sundry opportunities for exercising the weakness of her finger-tips, which made the situation a desirable one. Her cabin—assigned to her on account of its proximity to the creek from which she washed — stood also conveniently near the hen-house on one side and the vegetable garden on the other, while its one window opened over that dazzling, cooling, glowing, seductive temptation to the flesh—the watermelon patch; and so, when Priscilla said that "Gord had been good to her, and she had no 'casion to complain," she meant it.

Lamentations, as we have said, was twelve years old when this story begins. Tall, black, unkempt, arrayed in ill-fitting frocks, with a falsetto voice and a stammering tongue, he was not a thing of beauty; neither was he counted a joy, but rather a sorrow, in the village of Washington, Arkansas, in which he lived. If suspicion of any sort fell upon him, his appearance went far toward its confirmation, not only on account of his ugliness of person, but his peculiar dress gave him a sort of nondescript character, and seemed to brand him as an evil spirit.

Priscilla's one maternal act had been sending him to school. The four months of tuition each year had been enough to make him a fair scholar, as scholarship went in the negro free school of Washington. His education was the one thing about him that his mother respected.

It was vacation now.

As he sat on guard to-day in the crotch of the fence, he seemed to fall into deep meditation. Ever and anon he cast an anxious glance in the direction of the sweet-gum tree, where, though out of sight, he knew his mother stood; then he would gaze wistfully at a pair of trousers which lay bleaching on the grass. He was contemplating doing something which he feared to attempt.

"Ef mammy was on'y a-washin' on de wash-boa'd, 'stid o' renchin' an' a-starchin', I could lis'en an' keep up wid her," he said. Finally, however, the temptation became too great. He slid quickly down from the fence, dropped the yellow dress on the ground, and proceeded hastily to array himself in the judge's pantaloons, suspending them from the shoulders by means of the twine which he took from his whip.

As the old judge was a short and over-fat man, the trousers were not much in the way of a fit. He now selected a vest from the ground, slipped his long black arms through the capacious arm-holes, buttoned it down the front, and, with his thumbs stuck into the pockets, began to strut up and down, surveying himself with evident pride. O, for a mirror! He longed to behold himself in masculine attire. Glancing at the sun, he shifted his position, trying to see his own shadow, but the midday hour denied him even this unsubstantial gratification; and so, satisfying himself with such a survey as he could get of his outline, he resumed his promenade, and began a half-audible soliloquy: "Dey ain't no use o' talkin'! mannishness comes wid breeches! Dey sort o' kin. I feels like I mought be de jedge dis minute. I shorely could 'spect myself in dese heah breeches, even ef dey warn't no tighter'n dese, jes so dey had laigs, an' was s'pendered up wid galluses! I could ac' like a genterman; an' as I *is*, I ain't nothin' an' nobody. Ef I jes had sech as dese, I wouldn't be obleeged ter be a-spittin' terbacker an' a-sayin' cuss-words jes ter show what I is, like I does. I mought have some dignificatioms an' mannerficatioms an'—"

His soliloquy was brought to a sudden close by a loud scream from the direction of the sweet-gum tree. It was his mother's voice. Lamentations had become so absorbed in self-contemplation that a drove of hogs had passed behind him unobserved, leaving their footprints on the bleaching clothes.

Their only exit lay at the end of the Cherokee hedge, a point near Priscilla, and she had taken the alarm. She knew that their familiar porcine hieroglyphs decorated her precious week's washing.

At the sound of her voice, Lamentations turned and saw it all. He was terror-stricken. His first impulse was to get out of the judge's clothing, but haste embarrassed his motions. The twine "galluses" were knotted.

Finally, just as his mother emerged from behind the hedge, the judge's apparel fell to the ground, and he stood before her trembling — a pitiful nude statue of terror. His yellow dress lay just behind him. To take a backward step would expose the judge's trousers. Nearer and nearer came his mother; still Lamentations moved not, neither did he speak. Finally Priscilla came to a halt, and looking at him in mingled anger and alarm, she began:

"Fur Gord's sake, what *is* you a-doin', a-standin' up heah in yo' skin, Lamentations o' Jeremiah Johnson?"

Lamentations began to cry. This indication of natural emotion fanned the flame of her ire, and she continued:

"You *is* de onsettledes', *no*-'countes', beatenes', rapscalliones' nigger dat ever holped a po' sinner ter backslide! You 'ain't got no mo' sperit 'n a suck-aig dorg! What in kingdom come *is* you been doin'!" She approached a step nearer. "*Is* you gwine ter speak, you black buzzard?"

Lamentations was too much frightened to speak. He made a desperate leap in the direction of the yellow dress. Priscilla, thinking he was trying to escape, started and caught him. One of his feet had caught in the twine, and the judge's nether garments trailed after him, becoming more and more entangled about his legs as he danced around his mother, while she laid on blows thick and fast. Oh, the lamentations of Lamentations! As the pantaloons, flying around, brought their own explanation, she became more and more excited, and beat him without mercy. It made no difference which way he turned. Every position presented a bare suggestion for another blow, and it came every time.

Whether this beating provoked him to wrath, or his brief experience in male apparel wrought an inspiration, we cannot say ; but a change came over Lamentations from this time. He became desperate, and various depredations on hen-roosts and melon-patches, even beyond the judge's domain, were laid at his door. The wearer of the yellow dress became a familiar figure in court, but somehow he always managed to escape conviction. Finally, however, justice sought and found him *at home.*

A pair of young Plymouth Rock hens disappeared one night from the roost, and suspicion, confirmed by fresh footprints between the cabin and hen-house, and feathers corresponding with those of the missing chickens hidden in Priscilla's room, fell on the occupants of the cabin.

The footprints were Lamentations', but his mother had hidden the feathers.

On inquiry, it transpired that, the night before, Priscilla had entertained a crowd of her church people on what she had been pleased to call "tucky-hain." Now there were no turkey-hens on the premises, and two fine Plymouth Rocks, nearly as large, were missing. Circumstantial evidence against them was strong.

The judge had mother and son arrested and brought into court—his own court.

Priscilla was called up first. She unblushingly

denied the accusation *in toto,* even weeping over the contemplation of such ingratitude as so base a theft would show. She dwelt at length upon the kindnesses they daily received from the judge's family, and wept afresh over the sad lot of "a po' widderless 'oman an' a orphanless boy, wid nobody ter pertect 'em 'less'n it *was* de jedge, what knowed her po' daid husband," etc. Finally she swore to the truth of all this, and Lamentations was called.

A murmur of suppressed mirth ran through the court as the tall, gaunt wearer of a white swiss dress stalked gawkily upon the stand. Priscilla meant that her son should look his best on this important occasion, and had arrayed him in the Sunday frock of one of his departed sisters. It had belonged to one somewhat younger than Lamentations, and so the fluted ruffles came just to the knees, which, with his legs and feet, were bare. His sunburned hair, usually fluffing out like a mop, was now braided, and stood up in stiff spikes all over his head. He was nervous and embarrassed. Quickly repeating as nearly as he could the substance of his mother's testimony, he offered to swear to the truth of it.

Before presenting the Bible, the judge took occasion to say a word on the sanctity of an oath, and even spoke kindly to the boy as he made a brief allusion to his old father, Antony. Now the one thing sacred to Lamentations was the memory of his father. The judge bade him

think well before laying his hand on the Holy
Book, and handed him the Bible. In taking it,
Lamentations' hand shook, and it fell upon the
floor. It fell open. As the boy stooped to pick
it up, he started—took hold of it—dropped it—
and finally, trembling violently from head to
foot, he approached the judge, and made a full
confession of the theft, humbly begging that he
would not spare him, but punish him as he de-
served. But the judge did spare him, sending
both boy and mother home with only a wholesome admonition.

This was the turning - point in Lamentations'
life.

The old judge, believing that his influence had
brought the confession, took a new interest in the
lad, and the boy in dresses was called from the
cabin in the rear lot to serve in the judge's family, and arrayed, at the age of thirteen years, in
his first pair of " pants."

Notwithstanding many faults of character, such
as idleness and mischief, Lamentations never betrayed the trust of his benefactor. He was his
father's son, and his reformation was honest and
complete.

But this was fifteen years ago. Priscilla died
in grace on the last day of April last year, and
the May-day picnic was postponed that all the
Chinquepin Chapel folk might do her honor.

Lamentations still holds in the judge's family
a position of trust. He is now also the pastor of

Chinquepin Chapel—loved by his people and respected by all.

Just after his appointment to this post I happened to be in the neighborhood, and knowing
something of the young man's history, I went to
hear his inaugural sermon. I was struck by his
changed appearance. No longer a butt of ridicule in skirts did I behold, but a serious youth,
reading from God's word, and exhorting the people to holier living. Briefly reviewing his life
from his youth up, he finally approached the time
of his conversion.

As nearly as I can remember, his words were
these: "I was buried an' steeped in sin, my bredren, an' every time I tried ter rise an' be a man in
my father's image, somethin' holt me back, an' I
'lowed 'twas them frocks, which somehow seemed
to keep me in my mother's image—not meanin'
no disrespec's ter her, my bredren, but it ain't in
nature fur a man ter 'spire when 'pearances is sot
squarely ag'in 'im; but I say now, ef dem gal
clo'es stunted me in de sperit, it was beeaze I was
willin' 'ter *be* holt back, an' wasn't a-strivin' ter
rise. But, my dear bredren, de day I was holten
down de strongest, Gord callt me, an' I tell yer,
my sistren *an'* bredren, ef ever a mannish sperit
was holten down by raiments an' adornments, my
sperit was cramped dat day in dat white swist
frock! I jes felt like I warn't no mo'n one o' dese
heah sky-rockets—a heap o' show-offishness roun'
a little black stick—an' I 'lowed to myse'f dat I

belonged ter de debble, an' I was ready ter say any false words what he put inter my mouf, when dat Bible fell on de flo'. An' when I stooped down ter pick it up, what yer reckin I see? Bless Gord! I see my *own name a-stan'in' on top o' de page!* Yes, my dear bredren, *on de top, an' in dese heah big letters!* Seemed at fust like I was struck bline, an' I heerd Gord a-callin' my name, 'Lamentations o' Jeremiah!' an' de cotehouse an' de jedge an' all de people faded outn my sight, an' I nuver felt dat swist frock no mo'n ef it had o' been breeches, an' I seen my old daddy a-layin' on de baid, with his white haid on de piller, an' seemed like I heerd him a-prayin' ter Gord ter teck an' raise up dis heah po' little black chile ter wuck fur Him, an' ter be His faithful soljer an' servant; an' oh, my bredren, I know den dat Gord done callt me—done callt me, an' showed me my name in de book; an' dar I stood, a ugly black varmint, all furbelowed up in gal finery, an' *chuck-full dat minute o' de jedge's dominicker!* Seemed like I could see myse'f, an' I say ter myse'f, 'I ain't fitten ter 'spond ter sech a call as dis.' An' a big lump riz up in my froat, big as a whole tucky-hain, but I knowed hit warn't de shubshance o' dat dominicker dat was a-chokin' me; hit was the shubshance o' sin! Hit was a-chokin' me, an' I spewed it outn my mouf, an' confessed de trufe, an' de lump went outn my naik, an' peace riz up in my soul!"

The "Amens!" and "Glorys!" came in thick
5

and fast from the responsive congregation as Lamentations continued :

"Yes, Gord call-t me, my bredren, an' showed me my name in de book ; but whar'bouts in de book ? At de bottom o' de page ? No ; He 'ain't lef' me on de mo'ners' bench. In de middle o' de page ? No ; He 'ain't sot me in de mids' o' de corngergatiom. Den whar was it, my bredren ? Hit was on *top o' de page !* Gord done call-t me to de top—done stood me heah in de pulpit ; an' by His grace heah I is ! I tell yer, my bredren, some o' dese heah preachers is gradgerated f'om dishere college an' some f'om dat one, but *I's gradgerated f'om on high !"*

The excitement and enthusiasm were intense when I rose and quietly withdrew from the chapel, and as I walked homeward the words of the familiar hymn came to me :

> "God moves in a mysterious way
> His wonders to perform."

The good old man Antony—densely ignorant, but honest in his conviction—in the one act of faith that seemed most to betray the darkness of his mind, selected this extraordinary name for his son, and this act became the direct means of his reward, in calling his boy from death unto life.

I say this confidently, for, after the test of fifteen years, the man most loved among the people, the one held most dear by the suffering, the sick, and the aged among his race, but the one especially known as the champion of all small boys, is Lamentations of Jeremiah Johnson.

UNCLE MINGO'S "SPECULATIOMS"

"**L**-LORD-A-MUSSY, boss! You d' know nothin'! De idee o' you a-stannin' up dar an' axin' me whar I goes to markit! Hyah! Hyah!

"Well, you see, boss, my markit moves roun'! Some days hit's right heah in front o' my risi*dence*, an' den I goes ter markit wid a drap-line an' a hook; an' some days hit's back heah in de Jedge's giarbage bar'l, an' den I goes wid a hook ag'in—a hook on a stick.

"Don't you go to heavin' an' a-hawkin' an' a-spittin' over my markitin', boss! I'se clean ef I is black, an' I'se pretickilar ef I does go to markit pomiskyus!

"I ain't nuver seed a fresh giarbage bar'l outside o' no quality kitchen do', whar de cook had good changeable habits, whar I couldn't meck a good day's markitin', but I has ter know de habits o' de cook befo' I patternizes a new bar'l, an' dat bar'l's got ter be changed an' scalted out reg'-lar, ef hit gits my trade, caze I nuver eats stale pervisioms.

"In cose, boss, I uses 'scretion long *wid* my hook, 'caze some o' de *contentions* o' de bar'l ain't fittin' fur no genterman ter eat, but sech as dishwater an' coffee-groun's, dee don't tantalize me, caze dee don't hook up, an' I nuver markits wid no dipper, case hit markits *too* pomiskyus!

"Why, boss, ef you was good-hongry, *you'd* eat de kyabbage an' little bacon eens arter I's done washed an' biled 'em!

"De bacon eens wid de little pieces o' twine in 'em looks like dee was jes' lef' *to* be hooked! I tell yer, boss, de wuckins o' Providince is behelt in de leavin' o' dem twine strings.

"You see, yer has ter onderstan' how ter 'scriminate in markitin'. Dey's diff'ent kinds o' scraps. Dey's kitchen scraps an' dish scraps an' plate scraps. De kitchen scraps I uses mos'ly fur seasonin'—de green tops o' de ingons, pa'sley stems, cilery leaves an' sech. De dish scraps is de ch'ice scraps. Dee's fowl kyarcases an' ham bones an' roas' beef bones an' de likes. De plate scraps I ain't nuver fooled wid. I ain't come ter dat yit! I nuver likes ter see de pattern o' nobody's mouf on my victuals! Yer see, I was raised high, boss, an' I ain't nuver got over it.

"Talk about gwine ter markit! I don't want no better markit 'n a fus'-class giarbage bar'l an' 'scriminatiom. Ef I wants ter know who's who, jes' lemme peep in de giarbage bar'l, an' I'll tell yer ef dee's de reel ole-timers er new-sprouters er jes' out-an'-out po' white trash! My old mammy use ter say, 'Show me de cloze-line, an' I'll tell yer who folks is!' an' she could do it, too! but I say, show me de giarbage, an' I'll tell yer ef dee'll parse muster!"

The speaker, an aged, white-haired black man, sat, as he talked, on a log of driftwood on the bank of the Mississippi River at Carrollton, just above New Orleans. I often strolled out for a breeze and quiet smoke on the levee during the warm summer evenings, and it was here that I first met Uncle Mingo. He was a garrulous old negro, who lived alone in a shanty outside the new levee, and was evidently pleased in discovering in me an interested listener.

In reply to his last remark I said, "But you forget, old man, that many of us ' old-timers,' as you call us, are poor now !"

He raised his face in surprise.

"Lord, boss, does you s'pose I's a-talkin' 'bout riches? I's one o' deze befo'-de-war-yers, *an' I knows!* I tell yer, boss, hit ain't on'y de money what mecks de diff'ence, hit's de—hit's de—boss, I wisht I had de book words ter splain it de way I knows it in heah!" He tapped his breast. "Hit's de—de diff'ence in de—in de cornsciousness. Dat's de oniest way I kin splain it. Hit seems ter me de ole-time folks had de inside cornsciousness, an' all dese heah new people ain't got nothin' but de outside cornsciousness ! De outside cornsciousness, hit bristles an' swishes an' wags ter-menjus ; but de inside cornsciousness, hit jis lay low an' keep still, an' hit's gentle in de high places, an' when de waters o' tribulatiom runs ag'in it, hit keeps a stiff upper lip an' don't meck no sign.

"Dar's my ole madam, Miss Annie, now, dat

nse ter smile on ev'y nigger 'long de coas', so 'feerd she mought be a-slightin' some o' she's own people, 'caze she own so many she don't know half on 'em —dar she is now, a-livin' back o' town meckin' yeast cakes fur de Christian Woman's *Exchange*, an', boss, I wish-t you could see her!

"You reckin she talk po' mouf? No, sir! She's mouf warn't cut out by de po' mouf' patterm! She nuver lets on, no more'n ef de ole times was back ag'in.

"I goes ter see her de days my rheumatiz lets up on me right smart—I goes ter see her, an' she sets in dat little front room wid de two little yaller steps a-settin out at de front do', an' she axes me how I come on, an' talks 'long peaceful like, but she nuver specifies!

"No, sir, she nuver specifies! Fur all you could see, she mought have her ca'ge out at de front do' an' be out dar ter see po' white folks on business. Dat house don't fit her, and Marse Robert's po'trit a-hangin' over dat little chimbly look like hit's los', hit look so onnachel.

"I axed Miss Annie one day how long she 'spec's ter live dat-a-way, an' ef Gord forgives me, I ain't a-gwine ter quizzify her no mo'!"

The old man hesitated and looked at me, evidently expecting to be questioned.

"Why, Uncle, didn't she answer you?" I said.

"Oh, yas sir! She answered me; she say, 'Well, Unc' Mingo, I hardly know. I finds it ve'y pleasant an' quiet out heah!'

"'Pleasant an' quiet!' Lord have mussy! An' 'bout a million o' po' chillen a-rippin' an' a-tarrin' up and down de banquette, an' de organ-grinder drowndin' out de soun' o' 'Ole Sweet Beans an' Ba'ley Grow' on her little box steps dat minute!

"I ain't nuver answered her, on'y jes' tunned my haid an' looked at de crowd, an' she say, 'Oh, de chillen, dee are a little noisy, but I meant in a'—some kind o' way—is dey got sich a word as soshual, boss?"

"Social? Yes."

"Dat's hit—in a *soshual* way she say she fine hit's quiet, 'caze, she say, she ain't made no new 'quaintances out dar; an' den she ain't said no mo', on'y axed me ef de ribber's risin', an' I see she done had shet de do' on my quizzifyin'. An' I say ter mysef, 'New 'quaintances'—I reckin not! New 'quaintances in dat mixtry o' Gascons an' Dagos an' Lord knows what! I reckin not. Why, boss, I kin smell de gyarlic jes' a-talkin' 'bout 'em! De Lord!"

"Does she live alone, old man?" I asked.

"Oh, no, sir, she got 'er ma wid 'er!"

"Her ma! I thought you called her 'old madam.'"

"So I is, boss, Miss Annie's we's ole madam, she's jes' lackin' a month o' bein' as ole as me, but *Ole Miss*, she's Miss Annie's ma, she's *ole, ole*. She's one o' dese heah ole Rivolutioners, an' she's gittin' mighty 'cripit an' chil'ish.

"She's got 'er pa's commissiom in de army

sign-t by Gineral Washington.   All we ole fambly servants knows all dat, 'caze we's seen 'em teck it out an' show de han'write *too* many times!

"Yas, sir, she's a ole Rivolutioner, an' in place o' dat, heah she is to-day a-livin' back o' town gratin' cocoanut an' pickin' out *puck*ons."

"Picking pecans!   What do you mean?"

"Ter meck *pralines* ter sell, boss!"

"And how does she sell them, pray?"

"*She* don't sell 'em, bless yo' heart, no!   My daughter, *she* sells 'em!"

"Your daughter!"

"Yas, sir, my younges' gal, Calline.   She's de onies' one o' my chillen what's lef'.   She's de baby.   She mus' be 'long 'bout fifty."

"And you have a daughter right here in New Orleans, and live here by yourself, old man!   Why doesn't she come and take care of you in your old age?"

"An' who gwine to look arter we's white folks? —lif' Ole Miss in an' out o' de baid, an' go of arrants, an' do de pot an' kittle wuck, an' ca'y de yeas' cakes ter de *Ex*change, an' sell *pralines*, an' answer de do'-knocker?   Yer see, boss, de folks at de *Ex*change, dee don't know nothin' 'bout Ole Miss an' Miss Annie.   Yer see Calline, she's dee's pertector!   I ain't a-sufferin', boss, I ain't a-sufferin'!   An' ef I was, hit would be Gord's will; but we ain't made out'n de kine o' stuff ter try ter meck weselves comfable, whilst we's white people's in tribulatiom."

I turned and looked at the old man. A ray from the sun, now setting, across the river, fell into his silver hair and seemed to transform it into a halo around the gentle old face. I had often found entertainment in the quiet stream of retrospective conversation that seemed to flow without an effort from his lips, but this evening I had gotten the first glimpse of his inner life.

"And don't you feel lonely here sometimes, old man?"

"I know hit looks ter you dat-a-way, boss—I know hit looks dat-a-way—but when I sets heah by de water's aidge, you kyant see 'em, but company's all arount me! I'se a-settin' heah an' I ain't settin' heah! I's away back yonder! Sometimes seems like dis levee is de ole plantation, an' out yonder whar de sun's a-shinin' on de water, meckin' a silver road, all de ole-time folks dee comes out dar an' seems like dee talks ter me an' I lives de ole times ag'in!

"Sometimes dee comes one by one down de shinin' road, an' sometimes a whole passel on 'em at once-t, an' seems like dee sets down an' talks ter me.

"Lonesome! If ever I gits lonesome, all I got ter do is ter come heah on de river-bank an' ponder, and when I 'gins ter speculate, heah dee come, a-smilin' jes' like dee was in de ole days, an' sometimes, boss, you mought come ter de top o' de levee dar, an' you mought look out heah an' see me, a ole black dried-up critter, settin' heah in rags, an' maybe at dat minute I mought be a million o' miles f'om heah, a settin' up on top o' Ole Miss's ca'ge, a-drivin' my white folks to chu'ch, an' Marse Robert, de one dat was kilt in de army, a little boy no more'n *so* high, a-settin' up by my side, a-holdin' one rein an' a cluckin' ter de horses!

"I tell yer, boss, when I use ter git up on dat silver-mounted ca'ge, wid my stove-pipe hat on, dey warn't nobody what could o' bought me out. I wouldn't o' sol' out ter de Juke o' Englan'! I was dat puffed out wid stuck-up-ishness!"

He paused, smiling in happy contemplation of his departed glory.

"Uncle," I said, " I am going to ask you something. What was the matter with you last evening?"

"Istiddy? Why, boss?"

"Well, I was sitting out here on the levee with a party of friends, smoking, and while we laughed and told old jokes, I thought I heard some one sobbing—crying out aloud. Peering through the twilight, I saw you just where you sit now. We stopped and listened, and presently I think—yes, I am sure—you were laughing. Would you mind telling me what was the matter?"

"Did you heah me, boss? I reckin you 'lowed dat I was gone 'stracted, didn't you?"

"Well, no, I can't say that, but it did sound queer, out here by yourself."

"An' you'd like ter know de 'casion of it, boss. Well, I'll tell yer, but I'se 'feerd, ef I does tell yer, yer'll 'low dat I'se wus 'stracted 'n yer did befo'. Howsomever, hit was dis-a-way :

"Istiddy mornin' I was a-settin' in my kyabin a-sortin' out my markitin'—a-puttin' a pile o' kyabbage-leaves heah like, and de chicken-haids like heah, an pilin' 'em up accordin' ter dey kinds, when, all on a suddint, a picture o' de ole times come up befo' me, an' in de place o' all dese scraps, I see de inside o' Ole Miss's kitchen, an' seemed like I could heah de chicken a-fryin', an' de hot rolls was piled up befo' me, an' 'fo' I knowed it, seemed like I was a-flyin' roun' de big breckfus-table wid a white ap'on on, an' all de diff'ent kinds o' seasonable steams out'n de dishes come a-puffin' an' a-puffin' up in my face, an' I couldn't get shet ob 'em !

"I tell yer, boss, I nuver is had my day's markitin' look so po' as it did in de presence o' dat visiom o' de ole dinin'-room ! An' when I looked at my chicken-haids, seemed like all dee's eyes was a lookin' at me sort o' gretful, like dee had feelin's fur me, an' like dee 'lowed dat I mought hab feelin's fur dem, seein's we was all havin' hard times togedder.

"Yer can look at me, boss, an' 'cuse me o' high-mindedness, but my stummick turned ag'in' dat victuals, an' I couldn't eat it; an' I upped an' put it back in de baskit, an' I baited a swimp-bag an' a hook, an' I come out heah ter fish fur

my dinner, 'caze I say ter myse'f, ' When giarbage markitin' goes ag'in' yer, yer kyant fo'ce it!'

"Hit warn't 'zacly gwine ag'in' me, but hit was
gwine ag'in' my ricollectioms, an' dey ain't much
diff'ence, 'caze dey ain't much lef' o' me les'n 'tis
ricollectioms.

" Well, boss, ef flingin' dat dinner in de ribber
was chil'ish in me, Gord was mighty good. He
nuver punished me, but humored me, same as we
humors a sp'iled chile, an' gimme good luck wid
de bag an' line, an' I eat off'n fried cat-fish an'
b'iled swimps fur dinner.

" Well, dat was in de mornin'. Dat was my fust
spell o' onsatisfactiom ; an' arter dinner hit sort o'
come on me ag'in, an' I got sort o' lonesome, an'
long todes evenin' I come out heah fur company.

" I d' know how 'tis, but I meets all de ole-time
folks better out heah on de ribber-bank 'n any
place—so I set down an' I commenced ter ponder,
an' treckly heah dee come! An' fus' thing I know,
seemed like I lef' my ole lorg heah, an' slipped
out'n my rheumatiz, an' was out in de silver road
wid de res', a-flyin' an' a-dancin' roun' wid all de
yo'ng boys an' gals what I knowed way back
yonder. Seemed like I *recly was dar*, boss, an'
de wah, an de breckin' up, an' all de tribulatioms
we been pass froo was blotted out, an' I was
yo'ng ag'in !

" An' now, boss, come de strange 'speunce dat
upsot me. Whilst I was a-dancin' in de light an'
ac'in' skittisher 'n a yo'ng colt, I happened ter tu'n

my haid roun' an' look todes de levee, an' I see a
'cripit, lonesome ole man, a-settin' still on a lorg
by hese'f, an' de bones o' 'is laigs a-showin' froo
de holes in 'is breeches.

"Fust, I ain't knowed 'im, tell I looked ag'in,
an' den I seed 'twas me, an' seemed like I was
a-settin' on de outside aidge o' de worl', an' I
kyant tell yer how I felt, boss, but hit sort o'
upsot me. I tried ter laugh an' den I cried. I
knowed I warn't ac'n spornserble, an' hit was
chil'ish in me. Dee does say when a pusson gits
ter a sut'n age dee's obleeged ter ac' chil'ish, an'
I reckin' I mus' be age-in'; but whensomuver I
comes out heah ter ponder, arter dis, I's sholy
gwine ter set heah an' look back, 'caze a-gwine
back an' lookin' dis-a-way don't bring no comfort.

"Ter teck comfort out o' speculatioms, yer has
ter know which een ter start at !"

It seemed to me that the old man was weaker
than usual when he rose to go into his cabin, and
he allowed me to take his arm and assist him.
When we reached his door, I felt reluctant to
leave him alone. "Let me light your candle for
you," I said.

"Candle ! What fur, boss ?"

"Why, so that you may undress and go to bed
comfortably."

"What use is I got fur a candle, boss ? All
dese years I been livin' heah, I ain't nuver is had no
light yit. All I got ter do is ter lay down an'
I's in baid, an' ter git up an' I's up. I ain't prayed

on my knees sence de rheumatiz struck my lef'
j'int."

I slipped a coin into the old man's hand and
left him, but the realization of his lonely and
feeble condition was present with me as I walked
down the levee, across the road, up through the
orange-grove to my comfortable home. I realized
that age and want had met at my own door.
What if the old man should die alone, within
reach of my arm, in an extremity of poverty for
which I should become personally responsible, if
I allowed it to continue?

The question of his relief came again with my
first thoughts next morning, and when Septima's
gentle tap sounded on my door, and she entered,
freshly *tignoned* and aproned—when her black
arm appeared beneath the mosquito-netting with
my morning cup of steaming Mocha, I thought
of the lonely old man in the levee cabin and of
his tremulous handling of his cooking utensils
that moment, perhaps, in the preparation of his
lonely meal.

The picture haunted me, and so the warm
breakfast which Septima carried him was sent as
much for the relief of my own mind as for his
bodily comfort, as was also the dinner which I
myself placed on the tray. The boiled heart of
a cabbage, with a broad strip of bacon, cut far
from the perforation that betrays the string, and
the headless half of a broiled chicken—with no
eye to witness its own humiliation or to glaze in

sympathetic contemplation of the old man's environment of poverty.

In the early afternoon, while the sun was still
high, I yielded to an impulse to go out and see
how my *protégé* was getting along. I found him
sitting with head uncovered in the full glare of
the afternoon sun, outside his cabin door.

"Are you trying to bake yourself, Uncle?" I
said, by way of greeting.

"Oh, no, sir ; no, sir. I's jes' a-settin' out heah
teckin' a little free-nigger-fire ;" and he immediately began thanking me for my slight remem-
brance of him at meal-time.

"You mus' o' been tryin' ter meck my visiom
come true, boss, 'caze when I looked at dat breckfus' dis mornin', hit come back ter me, an' I's
ashamed ter tell yer, but I did ac' chil'ish ag'in,
an' my froat seemed like hit stopped up, an' I
kivered de plate up an' come out heah an' cried
scan'lous. Hit looked like Gord was jes' a-sp'ilin'
me wid humorin' me dat-a-way.

"But treckly dat passed orf, an' I come in an'
sot down, an' seemed like I was mos' starved, I
was dat hongry, but I saved orf a little speck o'
ev'ything you sont me, jes' so dat ef I los' myse'f
in ponderin', an' mistrusted de sho'-nough-ness o'
dat breckfus', I could fetch 'em out fur proof,
'caze hit don't meck no diffe'nce how big visioms
is, dee don't leave no scraps ; an' you know,
boss, jes' livin' like I does, ter myse'f, sort o' on
de aidge bertwix visioms o' de min' an' visioms

6

o' de eye, I does git mixed up some days, an' I
sca'cely knows ef I kin put out my han' an' tech
what I sees or not."

"How long have you been living this way,
Uncle?"

"Well, I d' know ezzactly, boss. I stayed long
wid Ole Miss, down in Frenchtown, s'long's I
could meck a little off'n my buck an' saw, an'
dee quar'ls at me reg'lar now fur leavin' 'em—in-
specially Ole Miss. She so 'feered I mought git
sick an' dee not know. Calline, she comes up
mos'ly ev'y Sunday ter see me, an' fetches me
clean cloze an' a pone o' fresh braid, an' Ole Miss
son's me a little small change, an' I daresn't 'fuse
ter teck it, needer, but I ain't nuver used it.
Lord—no! I couldn't use de money dee mecks
wid dee's white little han's—"

The old man seemed to forget my presence, and
his voice fell almost to a whisper.

"You haven't told me how long you have been
here, Uncle."

"Dat's so, boss—dat's so!" he said, rousing
himself. "I was a-sayin' 'bout leavin' Ole Miss—
I nuver liked it down dar, no how, in Frenchtown,
whar dee lives. Seemed like I couldn't git my
bref good behindt dem close-t rows o' box steps,
an' so when I 'scivered dat I could git reg'lar
wuck a-sawin' drif'-wood up heah, I come up an'
rid down in de kyars ev'y day; but dat was
wearin' on me, an' so— You ricollec' de time o' de
cavin' o' de bank below heah, when two o' my

color, Israel an' Hannah, got drownded? Well, dat sca'd off mos' o' dem what was a-livin' outside o' de new levee, an' dey was a heap o' shanties up an' down de coas' lef' empty, an' I moved inter dis one. Dee's mos'ly caved in now. Ev'y time my daughter heahs now o' de cavin' o' de bank up or down de ribber she comes an' baigs me ter go home—but I ain't afeerd, no, I ain't afeerd. Dis bank's got a stronger holt on de main lan' dan I got on de bank o' Jurdan."

"You talk about Jordan as if it were nothing. Aren't you ever afraid when you think of it, Uncle?"

"Afeerd o' what, boss?"

"Of dying," I answered plainly.

He smiled. "Was you afeerd o' yo' pa when you was little, boss?"

"Why, certainly not."

"Den I ain't afeerd nuther. Ain't Gord we's Father? He done handled me too tender fur me ter be 'feerd o' Him. Yas, He done handled me too tender — an' now, when I's gittin' notionate, He's a-spilin' me wid humorins an' indulgins. Afeerd! No, no!"

The requirements of beauty, as laid down by authorities on the subject, are always resolved into a question of lines and color, of curves and tints—a certain synthesis of corresponding parts into a perfect unit of grace. It may, or may not be, that an analysis would demonstrate that the conditions had been for the moment fulfilled in

the unconscious person of this old negro. I
know not how this may be, but I am sure I never
saw any countenance more spiritual and beautiful
than the gentle brown face he turned upward toward heaven, as in half soliloquy he thus spoke
the childlike trust of his undoubting heart. I
understood now how he might even doubt whether he might not "put out his hand and touch"
the hand of the Giver, who was as real to him as
the gifts with which he felt himself "humored
and indulged."

"Except ye become as little children—" God
give us all such faith as this !

"You are not all recollections after all, Uncle,"
I said.

"Not in de sperit, boss—jes' in de *min'*. Yer
see, de sperit kin go whar de min' kyant foller.
My min' goes back an' picks up ricollectioms
same as you tecks dese heah pressed flowers out'n
a book an' looks at 'em. My min' is de onies'
book I's got, an' de ricollectioms is pressed in
hit same as yo' pressed flowers.

" Gord ain't forbidden us to gyadder de flowers
what He done planted 'long de road, an' de little
flowers we picks up an' ca'ys 'long wid us, dee ain't
a-showin' dat we's forgittin' we's journey's een."

I left the old man with a keener regret than I
had felt the evening before, and I was annoyed
that I could not shake it off. I knew the thing
that I ought to do, but it involved inconvenience
to me which my selfishness resented. I had cul-

tivated the old negro to put him into a book, and now I felt impelled to move him bodily into my *yard*. I could not deal otherwise than gently with this antiquated bunch of aristocratic recollections, nor treat with dishonor the spirit that soared to heights to which I had not attained.

I strolled up the levee and back again several times, always turning before I reached the little cabin; but finally I approached it and seated myself as before on a log on its shady side, facing the old man. "Uncle," I said, plunging headlong into the subject, "I want you to come and live in a cabin in my yard. You can't stay here by yourself any longer!"

"Yer reckin' dee'll min' ef I stays?" he asked apprehensively.

"Reckon who'll mind?"

"De owners o' de kyabin, boss. Yer reckin' dee'll min'?"

"I'm the owner, Uncle, and I don't mind your staying, but I can make you more comfortable in another vacant cabin within my grounds. Won't you come?"

The old man looked troubled. "You's mighty kine an' mighty good; but, boss, ef yer don't min', I'll stay right heah."

"The other cabin is better," I insisted; "the chimney of this is falling now—look at it."

"I know, boss, I know; hit ain't dat—but hit's my white folks. Dee's dat proud dee wouldn't like me ter be berholten ter nobody but

dem. Yer see, I'd be a 'umblin' dem, an' dat
ain't right."

"Well, Uncle," I said, "do you know where
I could get a good, steady old man to come and
stay in my little cabin and look after things? I
am away a good deal, and I want some reliable
man to carry my hen-house key and gather eggs
and vegetables for me. I'd give such a man a
good home, and take care of him."

"H-how did you say dat, boss?"

I repeated it.

"Yer reckin' I'd do, boss?"

"Well, yes, I think you'll do. Suppose you
try it, anyway."

We moved him over that evening, and he
seemed very happy in his new home. He even
wept, as, on entering it, he glanced around at its
homely comforts ; but he was evidently failing,
and it was not long before he often kept his bed
all day.

He had been with us a month, when, one evening,
he sent for me. "Set down heah, boss, please,
sir," he said. "I wants ter talk ter yer. I's wor-
ried in my min' 'bout my people—my white folks.
Dis worry*mint* ain't nuver come ter me fur nothin',
an' I's 'sturbed in de sperit."

"Aren't you sick yourself, Uncle?" I asked,
for he looked very feeble.

"No, sir, I ain't sick. I's jes' a-nearin' home.
Some days hit seems ter me I kin heah de ripple
o' de water, I's dat near de aidge. De bank's

nigh cavin', but Gord's a-lettin' me down mighty tender—mighty tender.

"But dat ain't what meck me son' fur you, boss. I's troubled 'bout my people. I had a warnin' in my dream las' night, de same warnin' I had when Marse Robert was kilt, an' when Ole Boss died, an' when all we's troubles come; an' I 'spicion now dat hit's Ole Miss gone—an' would yer min' 'quirin' 'bout 'em fur me, boss?"

Thrusting his hand nervously under his pillow, he brought out a little soiled package, wrapped and tied in the corner of an old bandana handkerchief.

"An' won't yer, please, sir, ter teck dis little package wid yer, an' ef Ole Miss *is* daid, jes' give dis ter Calline fur me? Don't 'low nothin' ter nobody else—jes' give hit ter Calline, an' say as I sont it. Hit's twenty dollars what I saved f'om my wood-sawin', 'long wid all de change Ole Miss sont me.

"I done saved it by, 'g'inst de comin' o' dis time fur Ole Miss, an' maybe dee mought be sca'ce o' small change. Dee's *add*ress is in dar."

Untying the handkerchief, I found on a scrap of paper the name of a street and number, but no name of a person. Sometimes pride survives *after* a fall.

"Tell Calline," the old man continued, "I say hit's all fur Ole Miss's buryin', an' don't specify ter Miss Annie, caze she's dat proud she moughtn't teck it, but Ole Miss wouldn't kyah—she wouldn't kyah. Ef I 'lowed dat Ole Miss would kyah, I wouldn't fo'ce it on her, 'caze I wouldn't have no right—but she wouldn't kyah.

"She nussed me when I was a baby—Ole Miss did.

"My mammy, she nussed Miss Annie reg'lar, an' yer know she an' me is jes' a month older 'n one-'n'er, an' you know how women folks is, boss, jes' changin' roun' an' a-nussin' one-'n'er's babies, jes' fur fun, like. Ole Miss cay'ed me roun' an' played wid me, same as you'd pet a little black kitten, an' soon's I could stan' up dee'd meek me clap an' dance, an' I couldn't sca'cely talk befo' dee had me a-preachin' an' a-shoutin'.

"Dee had me fur a reg'lar show when dee had company. Dee jes' out an' out sp'iled me. I was jes' riz up wid 'em all, right in de house ; an' den, all indurin o' de war, when all we's men folks was away, I slep' at Ole Miss's do', an' Calline, she slep' on a pallet in dee's room, 'twix dee's two baids.

"Dat's de reason we loves one-'n'er. We's done seen good an' bad times togedder—good an' bad times—togedder."

His voice faltered—I looked at him quickly. He seemed suddenly to have fallen asleep. I felt his pulse gently, so as not to rouse him. It was weak and flickering, but not alarmingly so, I thought. Calling Septima, and bidding her sit with the old man for a while, I left him. About bedtime she summoned me to come into the cabin. Mingo had fainted. He was reviving when I entered, and his eyes moved with uncertain glance about the room.

When he saw me he smiled. "Tell Ole Miss, don't be afeerd," he said ; "I's a-sleepin' at de do'."

His mind was wandering. He lay in a semiconscious state for an hour or more, then he seemed to be sinking again, but reaction came a second time.

"Hit's a-cavin' in !—cavin' in easy an' slow—He's a-lettin' me down—mighty tender."

Suddenly a new light shone in his eyes. "Heah dee come—down de shinin' road—Marster !"

So the end came. At this supreme moment, when his spirit passed away, his face wore again that expression of exquisite beauty, that illumination as with a spiritual light from within, that had glorified it once before when he spoke of the surpassing love of God.

Early next morning, a neat old colored woman came in haste for Uncle Mingo. It was Caroline. The old lady, "Ole Miss," had died during the night, and Caroline had come for her father. Finding the levee cabin empty, she had made inquiries and been directed here. She was in great distress over her new sorrow, and seemed much disturbed lest the old man had missed her.

I insisted that I was his debtor to at least the paltry sum needed for his burial—and was it not so ? We pay directly or indirectly for the priv-

ilege of hearing sermons; we pay for stories of
self-sacrifice and devotion ; we pay for poetry ;
we pay for pictures of saints. I had gotten all
these, and what had I given? One month's rent
of an old cabin and a few crumbs from my table.

And in another sense still, I was old Mingo's
debtor. Had he not made known to me the silent
suffering of two Southern gentlewomen? And
inasmuch as every true Southern man feels himself to be the personal champion and friend of
every needy Southern woman, I might now become, in this small matter, a friend to the lonely
lady who hid her pride, as well as her poverty, in
the little grief-stricken house on a shabby street
"back of town."

I asked this much, but a dainty note in a tremulous feminine hand "thanked Monsieur most
heartily for all his kindness, and for his present
generous offer, but assured him that the privilege
of caring for the body of one of the most beloved
of her old servants was one which his former
mistress could not forego." There was no signa-
ture; but what was the need of one ?

A plain black hearse, followed by a single carriage, in which Caroline sat alone, came in the
afternoon for the remains of Uncle Mingo.
Moving slowly down St. Charles Street to Canal,
they turned down and across, out four, five
squares, then down again, till, finally, hesitating a few moments, they fell into line with another hearse that stood before a pair of box-steps

in a tenement row, and continued to the old St. Louis Cemetery.

The old lady sleeps her last sleep in a marble bed, the stateliest in a stately row. I started as I read the name: "These people here—and in want! Robert—'Marse Robert'— Yes— No, it cannot be! We were friends—in the army together—he was killed at Shiloh. Something must be done—but how? I must inquire—down town —at the Pickwick — or maybe through Caroline—"

As, in the old days, Mingo slept outside his mistress's door, so, in a little grave all his own, in the corner of the family lot, he sleeps now at her feet.

THE WIDDER JOHNSING

> "Monkey, monkey, bottle o' beer,
> How many monkeys have we here?
>   One, two, three—
>   Out goes she!"

"'TAIN' no use ter try ter hol' 'er. She des gwine f'om fits ter convulsions, and f'om convulsions back inter fits!"

Sister Temperance Tias raised her hands and spoke low. She had just come out of the room of sorrow.

Jake Johnson was dead, and Lize Ann Johnson again a widow.

The "other room" in the little cabin was crowded with visitors—the old, the young, the pious, the thoughtless, the frivolous—all teeming with curiosity, and bursting into expressions of sympathy, each anxious to look upon the ever-interesting face of death, every one eager to "he'p hol' Sis' Lize Ann."

But Temperance held sway on this as on all similar occasions on the plantation, and no one would dare to cross the threshold from "the other room" until she should make the formal announcement, "De corpse is perpared ter receive 'is frien's," and even then there would be the tedium of precedence to undergo.

It was tiresome, but it paid in the end, for long before midnight every visitor should have had his turn to pass in and take a look. Then would begin an informal, unrestricted circulation between the two rooms, when the so-disposed might " choose pardners," and sit out on the little porch, or in the yard on benches brought in from the church, and distributed about for that purpose.

Here they would pleasantly gather about in groups with social informality, and freely discuss such newly discovered virtues of the deceased as a fresh retrospect revealed, or employ themselves with their own more pressing romances, as they saw fit.

There were many present, inside and at the doors, who eagerly anticipated this later hour, and were even now casting about for "pardners"; but Sister Temperance was not one of these. Now was the hour of her triumph. It was she alone, excepting the few, selected by herself, who were at this moment making a last toilet for the departed, who had looked upon the face of the dead.

She was even ahead of the doctors, who, as the patient had died between visits, did not yet know the news.

As she was supreme authority upon the case in all its bearings, whenever she appeared at the door between the two rooms the crowd pressed eagerly forward. They were *so* anxious for the very latest bulletin.

"F'om convulsions inter fits! Umh!" repeated the foremost sister, echoing Temperance's words.

"Yas, an' back ag'in!" reiterated the oracle. "She des come thoo a fit, an' de way she gwine orn now, I s'picion de nex' gwine be a reverind convulsion! She taken it hard, I tell yer!" And Sister Temperance quietly, cruelly closed the door, and withdrew into the scene of action.

"Sis' Lize Ann ought ter be helt," ventured a robust sister near the door.

"Or tied, one," added another.

"I knowed she keered mo' fur Brer Jake 'n she let orn," suggested a third. "Lize Ann don't mean no harm by her orf-handed ways. She des kep' 'er love all ter 'erse'f."

So ran the gossip of "the other room," when Temperance reappeared at the door.

"Sis' Calline Taylor, yo' services is requi'ed." She spoke with a suppressed tone of marked distinctness and a dignity that was inimitable, whereupon a portly dame at the farthest corner of the room began to elbow her way through the crowd, who regarded her with new respect as she entered the chamber of death, a shrill scream from the new-made widow adding its glamour to her honors, as, with a loud groan, she closed the door behind her.

A stillness now fell upon the assembly, disturbed only by an occasional moan, until Sister

7

Phyllis, a leader in things spiritual, broke the silence.

"Sis' Calline Taylor is a proud han' ter hol' down fits, but I hope she'll speak a word in season fur sperityal comfort."

"Sis' Tempunce callin' out Scripture ev'y time she see 'er ease up," said old Black Sal. "Lize Ann in good han's, po' soul! Look like she *is* got good 'casion ter grieve. Seem like she's born ter widderhood."

"Po' Jake! Yer reck'n she gwine bury 'im 'longside o' Alick an' Steve?"—her former husbands.

"In co'se. 'Tain' no use dividin' up grief an' sowin' a pusson's sorrer broadcas', 'caze—"

The opening door commanded silence again.

"Brer Jake's face changin' mightily!" said Temperance, as she stood again before them. "De way hit's a-settlin', I b'lieve he done foun' peace ter his soul."

"Is 'is eyes shet?"

"De lef' eye open des a leetle *teenchy tinechy* bit."

"Look fur a chile ter die nex'—a boy chile. Yer say de lef' eye open, ain't yer!"

"Yas—de one todes de chimbly. He layin' catti-cornders o' de baid, wid 'is foots ter de top."

"Catti-cornders! Umh!"

"Yas, an' wid 'is haid down todes de foot."

"Eh, Lord! Haids er foots is all one ter po' Jake now."

"Is yer gwine plat 'is fingers, Sis' Tempunce?"

"His fingers done platted, an' de way I done twissen 'em in an' out, over an' under, dee gwine stay tell Gab'iel call fur 'is han' !"

"Umh !"

"Eh, Lord ! An' is yer done comb 'is haid, Sis' Tempunce ?"

"I des done wropp'n an' twissen it good, an' I 'low' ter let it out fur de fun'al to-morrer. I knowed Jake 'd be mo' satisfider ef he knowed it 'd be in its fus' granjer at the fun'al—an' Sis' Lize Ann too. She say she 'ain't nuver is had no secon'-class buryin's, an' she ain' *gwine* have none. Time Alick died she lay in a trance two days, an' de brass ban' at de fun'al nuver fazed 'er ! An' y' all ricollec' how she taken ter de woods an' had ter be ketched time Steve was kilt, an' now she des a-stavin' it orf brave as she kin on convulsions an' fits ! Look like when a pusson taken sorrer so hard, Gord would sho'ly spare de scourgin' rod."

"Yas, but yer know what de preacher say— 'Gord sen' a tempes' o' win' ter de shorn lamb.'"

"Yas indeedy," said another, a religious celebrity, "an' we daresn't jedge de Jedge !"

"Maybe sometimes Gord sen' a tempes' o' win' ter de shorn lamb ter meek it run an' hide in de Shepherd's fol'. Pray Gord dis searchin' win' o' jedgmint gwine blow po' Sis' Lize Ann inter de green pastures o' de kingdom !"

"Amen !" came solemnly from several directions.

An incisive shriek from within, which startled the speakers into another awe-stricken silence, summoned Temperance back in haste to her post.

Crowds were gathering without the doors now, and the twinkle of lanterns approaching over the fields and through the wood promised a popular attendance at the wake, which, after much tedious waiting, was at last formally opened. Temperance herself swung wide the dividing door, and hesitating a moment as she stood before them, that the announcement should gain in effect by a prelude of silence, she said, with marked solemnity:

"De corpse is now perpared ter receive 'is frien's! Ef," she continued, after another pause —"ef so be any pusson present is nigh kin ter de lately deceasted daid corpse, let 'em please ter step in fust at de haid o' de line."

A half-minute of inquiring silence ensued, and that the first to break it by stepping forward was a former discarded wife of the deceased caused no comment. She led by the hand a small boy, whom all knew to be the dead man's son, and it was with distinct deference that the crowd parted to let them pass in. Just as they were entering, a stir was heard at the outer door.

"Heah comes de corpse's mammy and daddy," one said, in an audible whisper.

It was true. The old parents, who lived some miles distant, had just arrived. The throng had fallen well back now, clearing a free passage across the room. With a loud groan and extended arms, Temperance glided down the opening to meet the aged couple, who sobbed aloud as they tremulously followed her into the presence of the dead.

The former wife and awe-stricken child had already entered, and that they all, with the new-made widow, who rocked to and fro at the head of the corpse, wept together, confessed sharers in a common sorrow, was quite in the natural order of things.

The procession of guests now began to pass through, making a circuit of the table on which the body lay, and as they moved out the door, some one raised a hymn. A group in the yard caught it up, and soon the woods echoed with the weird rhythmic melody. All night long the singing continued, carried along by new recruits as the first voices grew weary and dropped out. If there was some giggling and love-making among the young people, it was discreetly kept in the shadowy corners, and wounded no one's feelings.

The widow took no rest during the night. When exhausted from violent emotion, she fell .into a rhythmic moan, accompanied by corresponding swaying to and fro of her body—a movement at once unyielding and restful.

The church folk were watching her with a keen interest, and indeed so were the worldlings, for this was Lize Ann's third widowhood within the short space of five years, and each of the other funerals had been practically but an inaugural ser-vice to a most remarkable career. As girl first, and twice as widow, she had been a conspicuous and, if truth must be told, rather a notorious fig-ure in colored circles. Three times she had vol-untarily married into quiet life, and welcomed with her chosen partner the seclusion of wedded domesticity ; but during the intervals she had played promiscuous havoc with the matrimonial felicity of her neighbors, to such an extent that it was a confessed relief when she had finally walked up the aisle with Jake Johnson, as, by taking one woman's husband, she had brought peace of mind to a score of anxious wives.

It is true that Jake had been lawfully wedded to the first woman, but the ceremony had occurred in another parish some years before, and was practically obsolete, and so the church, taking its cue from nature, which does not set eyes in the back of one's head, made no indiscreet retrospec-tive investigations, but, in the professed guise of a peace-maker, pronounced its benediction upon the new pair.

The deserted wife had soon likewise repaired her loss, whether with benefit of clergy or not, it is not ours to say, but when she returned to mourn at the funeral, it was not as one who had refused to be comforted. She felt a certain secret triumph in bringing her boy to gaze for the last time upon the face of his father. It was more than the childless woman, who sat, acknowledged chief mourner, at the head of the corpse could do.

There was a look of half-savage defiance upon her face as she lifted the little fellow up and said, in an audible voice :

"Take one las' look at yo' daddy, Jakey. Dat's yo' own Gord-blessed father, an' you ain't nuver gwine see 'im no mo', tell yer meet 'im in de Kingdom come, whar dey ain't no marryin', neither *givin'* in marriage"; and she added, in an undertone, with a significant sniffle, "nur borryin', nuther."

She knew that she whom it could offend would not hear this last remark, as her ears were filled with her own wails, but the words were not lost upon the crowd.

The little child, frightened and excited, began to cry aloud.

"Let 'im cry," said one. "D'ain't nobody got a better right."

"He feel his loss, po' chile !"

"Blood's thicker'n water ev'y time."

"Yas, blood will tell. Look like de po' chile's heart was rendered in two quick's he looked at 'is pa."

Such sympathetic remarks as these, showing the direction of the ultimate sentiment of the people, reached the mother's ears, and encouraged her to raise her head a fraction higher than before, as, pacifying the weeping child, she passed out and went home.

The funeral took place on the afternoon following, and, to the surprise of all, the mourning widow behaved with wonderful self-control during all the harrowing ceremony.

Only when the last clod fell upon the grave did she throw up her hands, and with a shriek fall over in a faint, and have to be "toted" back to the wagon in which she had come.

If some were curious to see what direction her grief would take, they had some time to wait. She had never before taken long to declare herself, and on each former occasion the declaration had been one of war—a worldly, rioting, rollicking war upon the men.

During both her previous widowhoods she had danced longer and higher, laughed oftener and louder, dressed more gaudily and effectively, than all the women on three contiguous plantations put together; and when, in these well - remembered days, she had passed down the road on Sunday evenings, and chosen to peep over her shoulders with dreamy half-closed eyes at some special man whom it pleased her mood to ensnare, he had no more been able to help following her than he had been able to help lying to his wife or sweetheart about it afterward.

The sympathy expressed for her at Jake's funeral had been sincere. No negro ever resists any noisy demonstration of grief, and each of her moans and screams had found responsive echo in more than one sympathetic heart.

But now the funeral was over, Jake was dead and gone, and the state of affairs so exact a restoration to a recent well-remembered condition that it was not strange that the sisters wondered with some concern what she would do.

They had felt touched when she had fainted away at the funeral, and yet there were those, and among them his good wife, who had not failed to observe that she had fallen squarely into Pete Richards's arms.

Now every one knew that she had once led Pete a dance, and that for a time it seemed a question whether he or Jake Johnson should be the coming man.

Of course this opportune fainting might have been accidental, and it may be that Pete's mother was supercensorious when, on her return from the funeral, she had said, as she lit her pipe:

"Dat gal Lize Ann is a she-devil."

But her more discreet daughter-in-law, excepting that she thrashed the children all round, gave no sign that she was troubled.

For the first few months of her recovered widowhood Lize Ann was conspicuous only by her absence from congregations of all sorts, as well as by her mournful and persistent refusal to speak with any one on the subject of her grief, or, indeed, to speak at all.

There was neither pleasure nor profit in sitting down and looking at a person who never opened her lips, and so, after oft-repeated but ineffectual visits of condolence, the sisters finally stopped visiting her cabin.

They saw that she had philosophically taken up the burden of practical life again, in the shape of a family washing, which she carried from the village to her cabin poised on her head, but the old abandon had departed from her gait, and those who chanced to meet her in the road said that her only passing recognition was a groan.

Alone in her isolated cabin, the woman so recently celebrated for her social proclivities ranged her wash-tubs against the wall ; alone she soaked, washed, rinsed, starched, and ironed ; and, when the week's routine of labor was over, alone she sat within her cabin door to rest.

For a long time old Nancy Price or Hester Ann Jennings, the two superannuated old crones on the plantation, moved by curiosity and an irresistible impulse to "talk erligion" to so fitting a subject, had continued occasionally to drop in to see the silent woman, but they always came away shaking their heads and declining to stake their reputations on any formulated prophecy as to just how, when, where, or in what direction Lize Ann would come out of her grief. That she was deliberately poising herself for a spring they felt sure, and yet their only prognostications were always prudently ambiguous.

When, however, the widow had consistently for five long months maintained her position as a broken-hearted recluse not to be approached or consoled, the people began to regard her with a degree of genuine respect; and when one Sunday morning the gathering congregation discovered her sitting in church, a solitary figure in black, on the very last of the Amen pews in the corner, they were moved to sympathy.

She had even avoided a sensational entrance by coming early. Her conduct seemed really genuine, and yet it must be confessed that even in view of the doleful figure she made, there were several women present who were a little less comfortable beside their lovers and husbands after they saw her.

If the wives had but known it, however, they need have had no fear. Jake's deserted wife and child had always weighed painfully upon Lize Ann's consciousness. Even after his death they had come in, diverting and intercepting sympathy that she felt should have been hers. When she married again she would have an unencumbered, free man, all her own.

As she was first at service to-day, she was last to depart, and so pointedly did she wait for the others to go, that not a sister in church had the temerity to approach her with a welcoming hand, or to join her as she walked home. And this was but the beginning. From this time forward the little mourning figure was at every meeting, and when the minister begged such as desired salvation to remain to be prayed for, she knelt and stayed. When, however, the elders or sisters sought her out, and, kneeling beside her, questioned her as to the state of her soul, she only groaned and kept silence.

The brethren were really troubled. They had never encountered sorrow or conviction of sin quite so obstinate, so intangible, so speechless, as this. The minister, Brother Langford, had remembered her sorrowing spirit in an impersonal way, and had colored his sermons with tender appeals to such as mourned and were heavy-laden with grief.

But the truth was, the Reverend Mr. Langford, a tall, handsome bachelor of thirty years or thereabouts, was regarded as the best catch in the parish, and had he been half so magnetic in his personality or half so persuasive of speech, all the dusky maids in the country would have been setting their feathered caps for him.

When he conducted the meetings there were always so many boisterous births into the Kingdom all around him, when the regenerate called aloud as they danced, swayed, or swooned for "Brother Langford," that he had not found time to seek out the silent mourners, and so had not yet found himself face to face with the widow. Finally, however, one Sunday night, just as he passed before her, Lize Ann heaved one of her very best moans.

He was on his knees at her side in a moment. Bending his head very low, he asked, in a voice soft and tender, laying his hand the while gently upon her shoulder, "'Ain't you foun' peace yit, Sis' Johnsing?"

She groaned again.

"What is yo' mos' chiefes' sorrer, Sister Johnsing? Is yo' heart mo' grieveder f'om partin' wid yo' dear belovin' pardner, or is yo' soul weighted down wid a sense o' inhuman guilt? Speak out an' tell me, my sister, how yo' trouble seem ter shape itse'f."

But the widow, though she turned up to him her dry beseeching eyes, only groaned again.

"Can't you speak ter yo' preacher, Sis' Johnsing? He crave in 'is heart ter he'p you."

Again she looked into his face, and now, with quivering lip, began to speak : "I can't talk heah, Brer Langford ; I ain't fittin'; my heart's clean broke. I ain't nothin' but des a miser'ble outcas'. Seem lak even Gord 'isse'f done cas' me orf. I des comes an' goes lak a hongry suck-aig dorg wha' nobody don't claim, a-skulkin' roun' heah in a back seat all by my lone se'f, tryin' ter pick up a little crumb wha' fall f'om de table. But seem lak de feas' is too good fur me. I goes back ter my little dark cabin mo' harder-hearted an' mo' sinfuler 'n I was befo'. Des de ve'y glimsh o' dat empty cabin seem lak hit turn my heart ter stone."

She dropped her eyes, and as she bent forward, a tear fell upon the young man's hand.

His voice was even tenderer than before when he spoke again. "It is a hard lot, my po' sister, but I am positive sho' dat de sisters an' brers o' de chu'ch would come ter you an' try ter comfort yo' soul ef you would give 'em courage fur ter do so."

"You don't know me, Brer Langford, er you wouldn't name sech a word ter me. I's a *sinner*, an' a sinner what *love sin*. Look lak de wus a sin is, de mo' hit tas'es lak sugar in my mouf. I can't trus' myse'f ter set down an' talk wid dese heah brers an' sisters wha' *I* knows is one-half sperityal an' fo'-quarters playin' ketcher wid de devil. I can't *trus*' myse'f wid' em tell Gord set my soul free f'om sin. I'd soon be howlin' happy on de devil's side des lak I was befo', facin' two-forty on de shell road ter perditiom."

"I see, my po' sister—I see whar yo' trouble lay."

"Yas, an' dat's huccome I tooken *tol*' yer, 'caze I knowed you is got de sperityal eye *to* see it. You knows I's right when I say ter you dat I ain't gwine set down in my cabin an' hol' speech wid *nobody* less'n 'tis a thoo-an'-thoo sperityal pusson, lak a preacher o' de gorspil, tell my soul is safe. An' dey ain't no minister o' de sperit wha' got *time* ter come an' set down an' talk wid a po' ongordly widder pusson lak me. I don't *spect* 'em ter do it. De shepherds can't teck de time to run an' haid orf a ole frazzled-out black sheep lak I is, what 'd be a *dis*grace ter de fol', anyway. Dey 'bleege ter spen' dey time a-coaxin' in de purty sleek yo'ng friskin' lambs, an' I don't blame 'em."

"Don't talk dat-a-way, Sis' Johnsing—don't talk dat-a-way. Sence you done specified yo' desire, I'll call an' see you, an' talk an' pray wid you in yo' cabin whensomever you say de word. I knows yo' home is kivered by a cloud o' darkness an' sorrer. When shill I come to you?"

"De mos' lonesomes' time, Brer Langford, an' de time what harden my heart de mos', is in de dark berwilderin' night-times when I fus' goes home. Scem lak ef I c'd des have some reel Gordly man ter come in wid me, an' maybe call out some little passenger o' Scripture to comfort me, tell I c'd des ter say git usen ter de lonesomeness, I c'd maybe feel mo' cancelized ter de Divine will. But, co'se, I don't *expec'* no yo'ng man lak you is ter teck de *trouble* ter turn out'n yo' path fur sech as me."

"I will do it, Sis' Johnsing, an' hit will be a act o' pleasurable Christianity. When de meet'n' is over, ef you will wait, er ef you will walk slow, I will overtaken you on de road quick as I shets up de church-house, an' I pray Gord to give me de seasonable word fur yo' comfort. Amen, an' Gord bless yer!"

Lize Ann had nearly reached her cabin when the reverend brother, stepping forward, gallantly placed his hand beneath her elbow, and aided her to mount the one low step which led to her door.

As they entered the room, he produced and struck a match, while she presented a candle,

which he lit and placed upon the table. Neither
had yet spoken. If he had his word ready, the season for its utterance seemed not to have arrived.

"'Scuse my manners, Brer Langford," she said,
finally, "but my heart is so full, seem lak I can't
fine speech. Take a rock'n'-cheer an' set down tell
I stirs de fire ter meck you welcome in my po' little shanty."

The split pine which she threw upon the coals
brought an immediate illumination, and as the
young man looked about the apartment he could
hardly believe his eyes, so thorough was its trans-
formation since he had seen it on the day of the
funeral.

The hearth, newly reddened, fairly glowed with
warm color, and the gleaming white pine floor
seemed fresh from the carpenter's plane. Dainty
white muslin curtains hung before the little square
windows, and from the shelves a dazzling row of
tins reflected the blazing fire a dozen times from
their polished surfaces.

The widow leaned forward before him, stirring
the fire; and when his eyes fell upon her, his as-
tonishment confirmed his speechlessness. She had
removed her black bonnet, and the heavy shawl,
which had enveloped her figure, had fallen behind
her into her chair. What he saw was a round,
trig, neatly clad, youngish woman, whose face,
illumined by the flickering fire, was positively
charming in its piquant assertion of grief. Across
her shapely bosom lay, neatly folded, a snowy

kerchief, less white only than her pearly teeth, as, smiling through her sadness, she exclaimed, as she turned to her guest:

"Lor' bless my soul, ef I 'ain't raked out a sweet 'tater out'n deze coals! I 'feerd you'll be clair disgusted at sech onmannerly doin's, Brer Langford ; but when dey ain't no company heah, I des kivers up my 'taters wid ashes an' piles on de live coals, an' let 'em cook. I don't reck'n you'd even ter say *look* at a roas' 'tater, would you, Brer Langford ?"

The person addressed was rubbing his hands together and chuckling. "Ef yer tecks *my* jedgmint, Sis' Johnsing, on de pretater question, roas'in' is de onies way *to* cook 'em."

His hostess had already risen, and before he could remonstrate she had drawn up a little table, lifted the potato from its bed, and laid it on a plate before him.

"Ef you will set down an' eat a roas' 'tater in my miser'ble little cabin, Brer Langford, I 'clar' fo' gracious hit 'll raise my sperits mightily. Gord knows I wushes I had some'h'n good *to* offer you, a-comin' in out'n de col'; but ef you'll please, sir, have de mannerliness ter hol' de candle, I'll empty my ole cupboard clean inside outen but I'll fin' you *some'h'n* 'nother to spressify yo' welcome."

Langford rose, and as he held the light to the open safe, his eyes fairly glared. He was hungry, and the snowy shelves were covered with open

8

vessels of tempting food, all more or less broken, but savory as to odor, and most inviting.

"I 'clare, Sis' Johnsing — I 'clare!" were the only words that the man of eloquent speech found to express his appreciation and joy, and his entertainer continued:

"Dis heah cupboard meeks me 'shame', Brer Langford. Dey ain't a thing fittin' fur sech as you *in* it. Heah's a pan o' col' 'tater pone an' some cabbage an' side meat, an' dis heah's a few ords an' eens o' fried chicken an' a little passel o' spare-ribs, piled in wid co'n-brade scraps. Hit don't look much, but hit's all clean. Heah, you gimme de candle, an' you retch 'em all down, please, sir; an' I ain't shore, but ef I don't disremember, dey's de bes' half a loaf o' reeson-cake 'way back in de fur corner. Dat's hit. Now, dat's some'h'n like. An' now pass down de butter; an' ef yer wants a tumbler o' sweet milk wid yo' 'tater, you'll haf ter hop an' go fetch it. Lis'n ter me, fur Gord sake, talkin' ter Brer Langford same as I'd talk ter a reg'lar plantation nigger!"

Langford hesitated. "Less'n you desires de sweet milk, Sis' Johnsing—"

"I does truly lak a swaller o' sweet milk wid my 'tater, Brer Langford, but seem lak 'fo' I'd git it fur myse'f I'd do widout it. Won't you, please, sir, teck de candle an' fetch it fur me? Go right thoo my room. Hit's in a bottle, a-settin' outside de right-han' winder des as you go in."

Langford could not help glancing about the

widow's chamber as he passed through. If the other room was cozy and clean, this one was charming. The white bed, dazzling in its snowy fluted frills, reminded him of its owner, as she sat in all her starched freshness to-night. The polished pine floor here was nearly covered with neatly fringed patches of carpet, suggestive of housewifely taste as well as luxurious comfort.

He had returned with the bottle, and was seating himself, when the disconsolate widow actually burst into a peal of laughter.

"Lord save my soul!" she exclaimed, "ef he 'ain't gone an' fetched a bottle o' beer! You is a caution, Brer Langford! I wouldn't 'a' had you know I had dat beer in my house fur nothin'. When I was feelin' so po'ly in my fus' grief, seem lak I craved sperityal comfort, an' I went an' bought a whole lot o' lager-beer. I 'lowed maybe I c'd drink my sorrer down, but 'twarn't no use. I c'd drink beer all night, an' hit wouldn't nuver bring nobody to set in dat rockin'-cheer by my side an' teck comfort wid me. Does you think fur a perfesser ter teck a little beer ur wine when he feels a nachel faintiness is a fatal sin, Brer Langford?"

"Why, no, Sis' Johnsing. Succumstances alter cases, an' hit's de *succumstances* o' *drinkin'* what mecks de *altercations;* an' de way I looks at it, a Christian man is de onies pusson who oughter dare to *trus'* 'isse'f wid de wine cup, 'caze a sinner don' know when ter *stop.*"

"Dat soun' mighty reason'ble, Brer Langford. An' sence you fetched de beer, now you 'bleege ter drink it. But please, sir, go, lak a good man, an' bring my milk, on de tother side in de winder."

The milk was brought, and the Rev. Mr. Langford was soon smacking his lips over the best supper it had been his ministerial good fortune to enjoy for many a day.

As the widow raked a second potato from the fire, she remarked, in a tone of inimitable pathos:

"Seem lak I can't git usen ter cookin' fur one. I cooks fur two ev'y day, an' somehow I fines a little spec o' comfort in lookin' at de odd po'tion, even ef I has ter eat it myse'f. De secon' 'tater on de hycarth seem lak hit stan's fur company. Seein' as you relishes de beer, Brer Langford, I's proud you made de mistake an' fetched it. Gord knows *some*body better drink it! I got a whole passel o' bottles in my trunk, an' I don't know what ter do wid 'em. A man what wuck an' talk an' preach hard as you does, he *need* a little some-'h'n' 'nother ter keep 'is cour'ge up."

It was an hour past midnight when finally the widow let her guest out the back door, and as she directed him how to reach home by a short-cut through her field, she said, while she held his hand in parting:

"Gord will bless you fur dis night, Brer Langford, fur you is truly sakerficed yo'se'f fur a po' sinner; an' I b'lieve dey's mo' true 'ligion in comfortin' a po' lonely widderless 'oman lak I is, what

'ain't got nobody *to* stan' by 'er, dan in all de sermons a-goin'; an' now I gwine turn my face back
todes my lonely fireside wid a *better hope* an' a
firmer trus', 'caze I knows de love o' Gord done
sont you ter me. My po' little brade an' meat
warn't highfalutin' nur fine, but you is shared it
wid me lak a Christian, an' I gi'n it ter you wid a
free heart."

Langford returned the pressure of her hand,
and even shook it heartily during his parting
speech :

"Good-night, my dear sister, an' Gord bless
you ! I feels mo' courageous an' strenk'n'd myse'f sence I have shared yo' lonely fireside, an',
please Gord, I will make it my juty as well *as* my
pleasure to he'p you in a similar manner whensomever you desires my presence. I rejoices to
see that you is tryin' wid a brave heart to rise
f'om yo' sorrer. Keep good cheer, my sister, an'
remember dat the Gord o' Aberham an' Isaac an'
Jacob—de patriots o' de Lord—is *also* de friend
ter de fatherless *an'* widders, an' to them that are
desolate an' oppressed."

With this beautiful admonition, and a last distinct pressure of the hand, the Rev. Mr. Langford
disappeared in the darkness, carefully fastening
the top button of his coat as he went, as if to
cover securely the upper layer of raisin-cake which
still lay, for want of lower space, just beneath it
within.

He never felt better in his life.

The widow watched his retreating shadow until she dimly saw one dark leg rise over the rail as he scaled the garden fence; then coming in, she hooked the door, and throwing herself on the floor, rolled over and over, laughing until she cried, verily.

"Stan' back, gals, stan' back!" she exclaimed, rising. "Stan' back, I say! A widder done haided yer off wid a cook-pot!" With eyes fairly dancing, she resumed her seat before the fire. She was too much elated for sleep yet. "I 'clare 'fo' gracious, I is a devil!" she chuckled. "Po' Alick—an' po' Steve—an' po' Jake!" she continued, pausing after each name with something that their spiritual presences might have interpreted as a sigh if they were affectionately hovering near her. "But," she added, her own thoughts supplying the connection, "Brer Langford gwine be de stylishes' one o' de lot." And then she really sighed. "I mus' go buy some mo' beer. Better git two bottles. He mought ax fur mo', bein' as I got a trunkful." And here alone in her cabin she roared aloud. "I does wonder huccome I come ter be sech a devil, anyhow? I 'lowed I was safe ter risk de beer. Better git a dozen bottles, I reck'n; give 'im plenty rope, po' boy! Well, Langford honey, good-night fur to-night! But perpare, yo'ng man, perpare!" And chuckling as she went, she passed into her own room and went to bed.

The young minister was as good as his promise,

and during the next two months he never failed
to stop after every evening meeting to look after
the spiritual condition of the " widder Johnsing,"
while she, with the consummate skill of a prac-
tised hand, saw to it that without apparent fore-
thought her little cupboard should always supply
a material entertainment, full, savory, and varied.
If on occasion she lamented a dearth of cold dishes, it was that she might insist on sharing her
breakfast with her guest, when, producing from
her magic safe a ready-dressed spring chicken or
squirrel, she would broil it upon the coals in his
presence, and the young man would depart thoroughly saturated with the odor of her delightful
hospitality.

Langford had heard things about this woman
in days gone by, but now he was pleased to realize that they had all been malicious inventions
prompted by jealousy. Had he commanded the
adjectives, he would have described her as the
most generous, hospitable, spontaneous, sympathetic, vivacious, and witty, as well as the most
artless of women. As it was, he thought of her
a good deal between visits ; and whether the
thought moved backward or forward, whether it
took shape as a memory or an anticipation, he
somehow unconsciously smacked his lips and swallowed. And yet, when one of the elders questioned him as to the spiritual state of the still
silent mourner, he knit his brow and answered,
with a sigh :

"It is hard ter say, my brothers—it is hard ter say. De ole lady do nourish an' cherish 'er grief mightily; but yit, ef we hol' off an' don't crowd 'er, I trus' she'll come thoo on de Lord's side yit."

If there had been the ghost of a twinkle in his interlocutor's eye, it died out, abashed at itself at this pious and carefully framed reply. The widow was indeed fully ten years Langford's senior —a discrepancy as much exaggerated by outward circumstances as it was minimized in their fireside relations.

So matters drifted on for a month longer. The dozen bottles of beer had been followed by a second, and these again by a half-dozen. This last reduced purchase of course had its meaning. Langford was reaching the end of his tether. At last there were but two bottles left. It was Sunday night again.

The little cupboard had been furnished with unusual elaboration, and the savory odors which emanated from its shelves would have filled the room but for the all-pervading essence of bergamot with which the widow had recklessly deluged her hair. Indeed, her entire toilet betrayed exceptional care to-night.

She had not gone to church, and as it was near the hour for dismissal, she was a trifle nervous, feeling confident that the minister would stop in, ostensibly to inquire the cause of her absence. She had tried this before, and he had not disappointed her.

Finally she detected his familiar announcement, a clearing of his throat, as he approached
the door.

"Lif' up de latch an' walk in, Brer Wolf," she
laughingly called to him; and as he entered she
added, "Look lak you come in answer to my
thoughts, Brer Langford."

"Is dat so, Sis' Johnsing?" he replied, chuckling with delight. "I knowed *some'h'n'* 'nother
drawed me clean over f'om de chu'ch in de po'in'-
down rain."

"Is it a-rainin'? I 'clare, I see yer brung
yo' umber*el;* but sett'n' heah by de fire, I nuver
studies 'bout de ele*mints.* I been studyin' 'bout
some'h'n' mo'n rain or shine, *I* tell yer."

"Is yer, Sis' Johnsing? What you been studyin' 'bout?"

"What I been studyin' 'bout? Nemmine what
I been studyin' 'bout! I studyin' 'bout *Brer
Langford* now. De po' man look so tired an' fraz-
zled out, 'is eyes looks des lak dorg-wood blorsoms. You is des nachelly preached down, Brer
Langford, an' you needs a morsel o' some'h'n'
'nother ter stiddy yo' cornstitutiom." She rose
forthwith, and set about arranging the young
man's supper.

"But you 'ain't tol' me yit huccome you 'ain't
come ter chu'ch ter-night, Sis' Johnsing?"

"Nemmine 'bout dat now. I ain't studyin'
'bout gwine ter chu'ch now. I des studyin' 'bout
how ter induce de size o' yo' eyes down ter dey

nachel porportiom. Heah, teck de shovel, an' rake
out a han'ful o' coals, please, sir, an' I'll set dis
pan o' rolls ter bake. Dat's hit. Now kiver de
led good wid live coals an' ashes. Dat's a man!
Now time you wrastle wid de j'ints o' dis roas'
guinea-hen, an' teck de corkscrew an' perscribe
fur dis beer bottle, and go fetch de fresh butter
out'n de winder, de rolls 'll be a-singin' 'Now is
de accepted time!'"

It was no wonder the young man thought her
charming.

Needless to say, the feast, seasoned by a steady
flow of humor, was perfect. But all things earthly
have an end, and so, by-and-by, it was all over.
A pattering rain without served to enhance the
genial in-door charm, but it was time to go.

"Well, Sis' Johnsing, hit's a-gittin' on time fur
me ter be a-movin'," said the poor fellow at length,
for he hated to leave.

"Yas, I knows it is, Brer Langford," the hostess
answered, with a tinge of sadness, "an' dat ain't
de wust of it."

"How does you mean, Sis' Johnsing?"

"'Ain't I tol' yer, Brer Langford, ter-night dat
my thoughts was wid you? Don't look at me so
quizzical, please, sir, 'caze I got a heavy sorrer in
my heart."

"A sorrer 'bout me, Sis' Johnsing? How so?"

"Brer Langford—I—I been thinkin' 'bout you
all day, an'—an'—ter come right down ter de
p'int, I—I—" She bit her lip and hesitated. "I

'feerd I done put off what I ought ter said ter you tell look lak hit 'll 'mos' bre'k my heart *to* say it."

"Speak out, fur Gord sake, Sis' Johnsing, an' ease yo' min'! What is yo' trouble?"

She seemed almost crying. "You—you—you mustn't come heah no mo', Brer Langford."

"Who—me? Wh-wh-what is I done, Sis' Johnsing?"

"My Gord! how *kin* I say it? You 'ain't done nothin', my dear frien'. You has been Gord's blessin' ter me; but—but—I 'clare 'fo' Gord, how *kin* I say de word? But—don't you see yo'se'f how de succumstances stan'? You is a yo'ng man li'ble to fall in love wid any lakly yo'ng gal any day, an' ter git married, an', of co'se, dat's right; but don't you see dat ef a po' lonesome 'oman lak me put *too* much 'pendence orn a yo'ng man lak you is, de time gwine come when he gwine git *tired* a-walkin' all de way f'om chu'ch in de po'in'-down rain des fur charity ter comfort a lonely sinner pusson lak I is; an'—an' settin' heah by myse'f ter-night, I done made up my min' dat I gwine scuse you f'om dis task while I *kin* stand it. Of co'se I don't say but hit 'll be hard. You is tooken me by de han' an' he'ped me thoo a dark cloud, but you an' me mus' say far'well ter-night, an' you—you mustn't come back no mo'."

Her face was buried in her hands now, and so she could not see her guest's storm-swept visage as he essayed to answer her.

"You—you—you—you—talkin' 'bout *you* c'n

stan' it, Sis' Johnsing, an'—an'—seem lak you 's
forgitt'n' all *'bout me.*" His voice was trembling.
"I—I knows I ain't nothin' but a no-'count yo'ng
striplin', so ter speak, an' you is a mannerly lady
o' speunce, but hit do seem lak 'fo' you'd send me
away, des lak ter say a yaller dorg, you'd—you'd
ax me could *I* stan' it; an'—an', tell de trufe, I
can't stan' it, an' I ain't *gwine* stan' it, 'less'n you
des nachelly, p'int-blank, out an' out, shets de do'
in my face."

"Brer Langford—"

"Don't you say Brer Langford ter me no mo,'
ef you please, ma'am; an'—an' I ain't gwine call
you Sis' Johnsing no mo', nuther. You is des, so
fur as you consents, hencefo'th an' fo'ever mo', in
season an' out'n season—des my Lize Ann. You
knows yo'se'f dat we is come ter be each one-'n'ners
heart's delight." He drew his chair nearer, and,
leaning forward, seized her hand, as he continued:
"Leastwise, dat's de way *my* heart language hitse'f. I done tooken you fur my sweetness 'fo' ter-
night, Lize Ann, my honey."

But why follow them any further? Before he
left her, the widow had consented, with becoming
reluctance, that he should come to her on the following Sunday with the marriage license in his
pocket, *on one condition,* and upon this condition
she insisted with unyielding pertinacity. It was
that Langford should feel entirely free to change
his mind, and to love or to marry any other woman within the week ensuing.

Lize Ann arrived late at service on the following Sunday evening. Her name had just been announced as a happy convert who rejoiced in new-found grace; and when she stepped demurely up the aisle, arrayed in a plain white dress, her face beaming with what seemed a spiritual peace, the congregation were deeply touched, and, eager to welcome her into the fold, began to press forward to extend the right hand of fellowship to one who had come in through so much tribulation. It was a happy time all round, and no one was more jubilant than the young pastor, who seemed, indeed, to rejoice more over this recovered lamb than over the ninety-and-nine within the fold who had not gone astray.

The young girl converts of recent date, never slow to respond to any invitation which led to the chancel, were specially demonstrative in their affectionate welcome, some even going so far as to embrace the new "sister," while others were moved to shout and sing as they made the tour of the aisles.

When, however, as soon as congratulations were over, it was formally announced that this identical convert, Mrs. Eliza Ann Johnsing, was then and there to be joined in the holy estate of matrimony to the Reverend Julius Cæsar Langford, the shock was so great that these same blessed damosels looked blankly one upon the other in mute dismay for the space of some minutes, and when presently, as a blushing bride, Lize Ann again turned to them for congratulations, it is a shame to have to write it, but they actually did turn their backs and refuse to speak to her.

The emotions of the company were certainly very much mixed, and the two old crones, Nancy Price and Hester Ann Jennings, sitting side by side in a front pew, were seen to nudge each other as, their old sides shaking with laughter, they exclaimed:

"What I tol' yer, Sis' Hest' Ann?"

"What I tol' yer, Sis' Nancy?"

"Dat's des what we tol' one-'n'ner Lize Ann gwine do!"

Though no guests were bidden to share it, the wedding supper in the little cabin that night was no mean affair, and when Langford, with a chuckling, half-embarrassed, new-proprietary air drew the cork from the beer bottle beside his plate, Lize Ann said,

"Hit do do me good ter see how you relishes dat beer."

But she did not mention that it was the last bottle, and maybe it was just as well.

CHRISTMAS GIFTS

CHRISTMAS GIFTS

CHRISTMAS on Sucrier plantation, and the gardens are on fire with red flames of salvia, roses, geraniums, verbenas, rockets of Indian shot, brilliant blazes of coreopsis, marigold, and nasturtium, glowing coals of vivid portulaca.

Louisiana acknowledges a social obligation to respond to a Christmas freeze ; but when a guest tarries, what is one to do ?

She manufactures her ice, it is true. Why not produce an artificial winter ? Simply because she does not care for it. If she did— ? Such things are easily arranged.

Still, when he comes, *a guest*, she would not forget her manners and say him nay, any sooner than she would shrug her shoulders at a New England cousin or answer his questions in French.

She does the well-bred act to the death, summons her finest, fairest, most brilliant and tender of flower and leaf to await his coming: so to-day all her royal summer family are out in full court dress, ready to prostrate themselves at his feet.

This may be rash, but it is polite.

Her grandfather was both ; and so the " Creole

State," in touch with her antipodal brother in ancestor-worship, is satisfied.

But winter, the howling swell, forgetful of provincial engagements, does not come. Still, the edge of his promise is in the breeze to-day, and the flaring banana leaves of tender green look cold and half afraid along the garden wall.

The Yule log smoulders lazily and comfortably in the big fireplace, but windows and doors are open, and rocking-chairs and hammocks swing on the broad galleries of the great house.

It is a rich Christmas of the olden time.

Breakfast and the interchange of presents are over.

Cautious approaches of wheels through the outer gates during the night, in the wee short hours when youth sleeps most heavily, have resulted in mysterious appearances : a new piano in the parlor ; a carriage, a veritable ante-bellum chariot, and a pair of bays, in the stable ; guns, silver-mounted trappings, saddles, books, pictures, jewels, and dainty confections, within and piled about the stockings that hung around the broad dining-room chimney.

For there were sons and daughters on Sucrier plantation.

An easy-going, healthy, hearty, and happy man, of loose purse - strings and lax business habits, old Colonel Slack had grown wealthy simply because he lived on the shore where the tide always came in — the same shore where since '61 the

waters move ever to the sea, and those who waited where he stood are stranded.

His highest ambitions in life were realized.
His children, the elect by inheritance to luxurious
ease, were growing up about him, tall, straight,
and handsome, and happily free from disorgan-
izing ambitions, loving the fleece-lined home-nest.

The marriage of an eldest daughter, Louise, to
a wealthy next-door planter, five miles away, had
seemed but to add a bit of broidery to the borders
of his garment.

His pretty, dainty wife, in lieu of wrinkles, had
taken on avoirdupois and white hair, and instead
of shrivelling like a four-o'clock had bloomed into
a regal evening-glory.

So distinctly conscious of all these blessings was
the old colonel that his atmosphere seemed always charged with the electric quality which was
happiness ; but on occasions like to-day, when the.
depths of his tendernesses were stirred within him
by the ecstasy of giving and of receiving thanks
and smiles and thanks again from "*my* handsome
wife," "*my* fine children," "*my* loyal slaves"—
ah, this was the electric *flash!* It was joy! It
was delight and exuberance of spirit! It was
youth returned! It was Christmas!

In his heart were peace and good-will all the
year round, and on Christmas—hallelujahs.

He had often been heard to say that if he ever
professed religion it would be on Christmas ;
and, by the way, so it was, but not *this* Christmas.

A tender-souled, good old man was he, yet thoughtless, withal, as a growing boy.

Down in the quarters, this morning, the negroes, gaudily arrayed in their Sunday best, were congregated in squads about the benches in front of their cabins, awaiting the ringing of the plantation bell which should summon them to "the house" to receive their Christmas packages.

In the grove of China-trees around which the cabins were ranged, a crowd of young men and maidens flirted and chaffed one another on the probable gifts awaiting them.

One picked snatches of tunes on a banjo, another drew a bow across an old fiddle, but the greater number were giddily spending themselves in plantation repartee, a clever answer always provoking a loud, unanimous laugh, usually followed by a reckless duet by the two "musicianers."

Sometimes, when the jokes were too utterly delicious, the young "bucks" would ecstatically hug the China-trees or tumble down upon the grass and bellow aloud.

"What yer reck'n ole marster gwine give you, Unc' Torm?" said one, addressing an old man who had just joined the group and sat sunning his shiny bald head.

"'Spec' he gwine give Unc' Torm some hair-ile, ur a co'se comb," suggested a pert youth.

"Look like he better give you a wagon-tongue ur a bell-tongue, one, 'caze yo' tongue ain't long 'nough," replied Uncle Tom quietly, and so the joke was turned.

"I trus' he gwine give Bow-laigged Joe a new pair o' breeches !"

"Ef he do, I hope dey'll be cut out wid a circular saw !" came a quick response, which brought a scream of laughter.

"Wonder what Lucindy an' Dave gwine git ?"

Lucinda and Dave were bride and groom of a month.

In a minute two big fellows were screaming and holding their sides over a whispered suggestion, when the word "cradle" escaped and set girls and all to giggling.

"Pity somebody wouldn't drap some o' you smart boys on a *corn-cradle* an' chop you up," protested the bride, with a toss of her head.

"De whole passel ob 'em wouldn't make nothin' but rotten-stone, ef dee was *grine* up," suggested Uncle Tom, with an intolerant sniffle.

"Den you mought use us fur tooth-powder," responded the wit again, and the bald-headed old man, confessing himself vanquished, good-naturedly bared his toothless gums to join in the laughter at his own expense.

A sudden clang of the bell brought all to their feet presently, and, strutting, laughing, prancing, they proceeded up to the house, the musicians tuning up afresh *en route*, for in the regular order of exercises arranged for the day they were to play an important part.

The recipients were to be ranged in the yard in line, about fifty feet from the steps of the back veranda where the master should stand, and, as their names should be called, to dance forward, receive their gifts, courtesy, and dance back to their places.

At the calling of the names music would begin.

The pair who by vote should be declared the most graceful should receive from the master's hand a gift of five dollars each, with the understanding that it should supply the eggnog for the evening's festivities, where the winners should preside as king and queen.

An interested audience of the master's family, seated on the veranda back of him, was a further stimulant to best effort.

The packages, all marked with names, were piled on two tables, those for men on one and the women's on the other, and the couples resulting from a random selection from each caused no little merriment.

All had agreed to the conditions, and when Lame Phœbe was called out with Jake Daniels, a famous dancer, they were greeted with shouts of applause.

Phœbe, enthused by her reception, and in no wise embarrassed by a short leg, made a virtue of necessity, advancing and retreating in a series of graceful bows, manipulating her sinewy body so dextrously that the inclination towards the left foot was more than concealed, and for the first time in his life Jake Daniels came in second best, as, amid deafening applause, Lame Phœbe bowed and wheeled herself back among the people.

Then came Joe Scott, an ebony swell, with Fat Sarey, a portly dame of something like three hundred avoirdupois — a difficult combination again.

That Sarey had not danced for twenty years was not through reluctance of the flesh more than of the spirit, for she was "a chile o' de kingdom," both by her own profession and universal consent.

Laughing good-naturedly, with shaking sides she stepped forward, bowed first to her master and then to her partner, and, raising her right hand, began, in a wavering, soft voice, keeping time to the vibrating melody by easy undulations of her pliable body, to sing :

"Dey's a star in de eas' on a Chris'mus morn.
  Rise up, shepherd, an' foller !
Hit'll lead ter de place whar de Saviour's born.
  Rise up, shepherd, an' foller !
Ef yer take good heed ter de angels' words,
You'll forgit yo' flocks an' forgit yo' herds,
  An' rise up, shepherd, an' foller !
    Leave yo' sheep an'
    Leave yo' lamb an'
    Leave yo' ewe an'
    Leave yo' ram, an'
Rise up, shepherd, an' foller !"

Joe took his cue from the first note, and, accommodating his movements to hers, elaborating them profusely with graceful gestures, he fell in with a rich, high tenor, making a melody so tender and true that the audience were hushed in reverential silence.

The first verse finished, Sarey turned slowly, and by an uplifted finger invited all hands to join in the chorus.

Rich and loud, in all four parts, came the effective refrain :

    " Foller, foller, foller, foller,
      Rise up, shepherd, rise an' foller,
        Foller de Star o' Bethlehem !"

Still taking the initiative, Sarey now bent easily and deeply forward in a most effusive parlor salutation as she received her gift; while Joe, as ever quick of intuition, also dispensed with the traditional dipping courtesy, while he surrendered himself to a profound bow which involved the entire length of his willowy person.

Turning now, without losing for a moment the rhythmic movement, they proceeded to sing a second verse :

  "Oh, dat star's still shinin' dis Chris'mus day.
    Rise, O sinner, an' foller !
   Wid an eye o' faith you c'n see its ray.
    Rise, O sinner, an' foller !
   Hit'll light yo' way thoo de fiel's o' fros',
   While it leads thoo de stable ter de shinin' cross.
    Rise, O sinner, an' foller !

> Leave yo' father,
> Leave yo' mother,
> Leave yo' sister,
> Leave yo' brother,
> An' rise, O sinner, an' foller !"

A slightly accelerated movement had now brought the performers back to their places, when the welkin rang with a full all-round chorus:

> "Foller, foller, foller, foller,
> Rise, O sinner, rise an' foller,
> Foller de Star o' Bethlehem !"

A few fervid high-noted "Amens !" pathetically suggestive of pious senility, were succeeded now by a silence more eloquent than applause.

Other dancers by youthful antics soon restored hilarity, however, and for quite an hour the festivities kept up with unabated interest.

Finally a last parcel was held up—only one—and when the master called, " Judy Collins !" adding, " Judy, you'll have to dance by yourself, my girl !" the excitement was so great that for several minutes nothing could be done.

Judy Collins, by a strange coincidence, was the only " old maid " on the plantation, and, as she was a dashing, handsome woman, she had given the mitten at one time or another to nearly every man present.

That she should have to dance alone was too much for their self-control.

The women, convulsed with laughter, held on to one another, while the men shrieked aloud.

Judy was the only self-possessed person present.

Before any one realized her intention, she had seized a new broom from the kitchen porch near, and stepped out into the arena with it in her hand.

Judy was grace itself. Tall, willowy, and lithe, stately as a pine, supple as a mountain-trout, she glided forward with her broom.

Holding it now at arm's-length, now balancing it on end and now on its wisps, tilting it at hazardous angles, but always catching it ere it fell, poising it on her finger-tips, her chin, her forehead, the back of her neck, keeping perfect time the while with the music, she advanced to receive her parcel, which, with a quick movement, she deftly attached to the broom-handle, and, throwing it over her shoulder, danced back to her place.

The performance entire had proven a brilliant success, and Judy's dance a fitting climax.

Needless to say, Judy insisted on keeping the broom.

The awarding of the prizes by acclamation to Joe Scott and Fat Sarey was the work of a moment, prettily illustrating the religious susceptibility of the voters.

Then followed a "few remarks" from the speaker of the occasion, and a short and playful response from the master, when the crowd dispersed, opening their bundles *en route* as they returned merrily to their cabins.

The parcels had been affectionately prepared. Besides the dresses, wraps, and shoes given to all,

there were attractive trinkets, bottles of cologne,
ribbons, gilt ear-rings or pins for the young
women, cravats, white collars, shirt-studs, for the
beaux, and for the old such luxuries as tobacco,
walking-canes, spectacles, and the like, with small
coins for pocket-money.

This year, in addition to the extra and expected
"gift," each young woman received, to her delight, a flaring hoop-skirt; and such a lot of balloons as were flying about the plantation that
morning it would be hard to find again.

Happy and care-free as little children were they,
and as easily pleased.

Having retired for the moment necessary for
their inflation and adornment, the younger ele-
ment, balloons and beaux, soon returned to their
popular holiday resort under the China-trees.

Though the branches were bare, the benches
beneath them commanded a perennial fair-weather
patronage; for where a bench and a tree are,
there will young men and maidens be gathered
together.

Lame Mose was there, with his new cushioned
crutch, and Phil Thomas the preacher, looking
ultra-clerical and important in a polished beaver;
while Lucinda and Dave, triumphant in the cumu-
lative dignity of new bride-and-groomship, hoop-
skirt and standing collar, actually strutted about
arm in arm in broad daylight, to the intense
amusement of the young folk, who nudged one
another and giggled as they passed.

Such was the merry spirit of the group when Si, a young mulatto household servant, suddenly appeared upon the scene.

"'Cindy," said he, "marster say come up ter de house—dat is, ef you an' Dave kin part company fur 'bout ten minutes."

"I don' keer nothin' 'bout no black ogly-lookin' some'h'n-'nother like Dave, nohow!" exclaimed Lucinda flirtatiously, as she playfully grasped Si's arm and proceeded with him to the house, leaving Dave laughing with the rest at her antics.

The truth was that, confidently expecting the descent of some further gift upon her brideship, Lucinda was delighted at the summons, and her face beamed with expectancy as she presented herself before her master.

"Lucindy," said he, as she entered, "I want you to mount Lady Gay and ride down to Beechwood this morning, to take some Christmas things to Louise and her chicks."

Lucinda's smile broadened in a delighted grin.

A visit to Beechwood to-day would be sure to elicit a present from her young mistress, "Miss Louise," besides affording an opportunity to compare presents and indulge in a little harmless gossip with the Beechwood negroes.

Lady Gay stood, ready saddled, waiting at the door. After a little delay in adjusting the assertive springs of her hoop-skirt to the pommel of the saddle, Lucinda started off in a gallop.

When she entered the broad hall at Beechwood,

the family, children and all, recognizing her as an ambassador of Santa Claus, gathered eagerly about her, and as boxes and parcels were opened in her presence her eyes fairly shone with pleasure. Nor was she disappointed in her hope of a gift herself.

"I allus did love you de mos' o' all o' ole Miss's chillen, Miss Lou," she exclaimed presently, opening and closing with infantile delight a gay feather-edged fan which Louise gave her.

"I does nachelly love red. Red seem like hit's got mo' color in it 'n any color."

"Dis heah's a reg'lar courtin'-fan," she added to herself, as she followed the children out into the nursery to inspect their new toys, fanning, posing, and flirting as she went. "Umph! ef I'd 'a' des had dis fan las' summer I'd 'a' had Dave all but crazy."

After enjoying it for an hour or more, she finally wrapped it carefully in her handkerchief and put it for safe keeping into her pocket. In doing so, her hand came in contact with a letter which she had forgotten to deliver.

"Law, Miss Lou!" she exclaimed, hurrying back, "I mos' done clair forgittin' ter gi' you yo' letter wha' ole marster tol' me ter han' you de fus' thing."

"I wondered that father and mother had sent no message," replied Louise, opening the note. Her face softened into a smile, however, as she proceeded to read it.

"Why, you wretch, Lucindy!" she exclaimed, laughing, "you've kept me out of my two best Christmas gifts for an hour. I always wanted to own Lady Gay, and father writes that you are a fine, capable girl."

Lucinda cast a quick, frightened look at Louise and caught her breath.

"And I am so glad to know that you are pleased. Why didn't you tell me that you were a Christmas gift when you came?"

There was no longer any doubt. Lucinda could not have answered to save her life. The happy-hearted child of a moment ago was transformed into a desperate, grief-stricken woman.

"Why, Lucindy!" Louise was really grieved to discern the tragic look in the girl's face. "I am disappointed. I thought you loved me. I thought you would be delighted to belong to me—to be my maid—and not to work in the field any more—and to have a nice cabin in my yard—and a sewing-machine—and to learn to embroider—and to dress my hair—and to—"

The growing darkness in Lucinda's face warned Louise that this conciliatory policy was futile, and yet, feeling only kindly towards her, she continued,

"Tell me, Lucindy, why you are distressed. Don't you really wish to belong to me? Why did you say that you loved me the best?"

Words were useless. Louise was almost frightened as she looked again into the girl's face. Her eyes shone like a caged lion's, and her bosom rose and fell tumultuously.

After many fruitless efforts to elicit a response, Louise called her husband, and together they tried by kind assurances to pacify her ; but it was vain. She stood before them a mute impersonation of despair and rage.

"You'd better go out into the kitchen for a while, Lucindy," said Louise finally, "and when I send for you I shall expect you to have composed yourself." Looking neither to right nor left, Lucinda strode out of the hall, across the gallery, down the steps, through the yard to the kitchen, gazed at by the assembled crowd of children both black and white.

"'Cindy ain't but des on'y a little while ago married," said Tildy, a black girl who stood in the group as she passed out.

"Married, is she ?" exclaimed Louise, eagerly grasping at a solution of the difficulty. "That explains. But why didn't she tell me ? There must be some explanation. This is so unlike father. We are to dine at Sucrier this afternoon. Go, Tildy, and tell Lucindy that we will see what can be done."

"Fo' laws-o'-mussy sakes, Miss Lou, please, ma'am, don't sen' me ter 'Cindy now. 'Cindy look like she gwine hurt somebody."

If she could have seen Lucinda at this moment, she might indeed have feared to approach her. When she had entered the kitchen a little negro who had followed at her heels had announced to the cook and her retinue,

"'Cindy mad caze ole marster done sont 'er fur a Chris'mus-gif' ter Miss Lou."   Whereupon there were varied exclamations :

"Umph !"

"You is a sorry-lookin' Chris'mus gif', sho !"

"I don't blame 'er !"

"What you frettin' 'bout, chile? You in heab'n here !"

"De gal's married," whispered some one in stage fashion, finally.

"Married !" shrieked old Silvy Ann from her corner where she sat peeling potatoes. "Married ! Eh, Lord ! Time you ole as I is, you won't fret 'bout no sech. Turn 'im out ter grass, honey, an' start out fur a grass-widder. I got five I done turned out in de pasture now, an' ef dee sell me out ag'in, Ole Abe'll be a-grazin' wid de res' !

"Life is too short ter fret, honey ! But ef yer *boun'* ter fret, fret 'bout *some'h'n'!* Don't fret 'bout one o' deze heah long-laigged, good-fur-nothin' sca'crows name' Mister Man ! Who you married ter, gal ?"

"She married ter cross-eyed Dave," some one answered.

"Cross-eyed ! De Lord ! Let 'im go fur what he'll fetch, honey ! De woods roun' heah is full o' straight-eyed ones, let 'lone game-eyes !" And the vulgar old creature encored her own wit with an outburst of cracked laughter.

"Ain't you 'shame' o' yo'se'f, Aunt Silvy Ann! 'Cindy ain't like you; she *married — wid a preacher.*"

"Yas, an' *unmarried 'dout no preacher!* What's de good o' lockin' de do' on de inside wid a key, ef you c'n open it f'om de outside 'dout no key? I done kep' clair o' locks an' keys all my life, an' nobody's feelin's was hurt."

While old Silvy Ann was running on in this fashion, Texas, the cook, had begun to address Lucinda:

"Don't grieve yo' heart, baby. My ole man stay mo' fur 'n ole marster's f'om heah — 'way down ter de cross-roads t'other side de bayou. How fur do daddy stay, chillen?" she added, as she broke red pepper into her turkey-stuffing.

"Leb'n mile," answered four voices from as many little black pickaninnies who tumbled over one another on the floor.

"You heah dat! *Leb'n mile,* an' ev'y blessed night he come home ter Texas! Yas, ma'am, an' 'is lone star keep a lookout fur 'im too—a candle in de winder an' a tin pan o' 'membrance on de hyearth."

Seeing that her words produced no effect, Texas changed her tactics.

Approaching Lucinda, she regarded her with admiration: "Dat's a quality collar you got on, 'Cindy. An', law bless my soul, ef de gal 'ain't got on hoops! You gwine lead de style on dis planta—"

10

Texas never finished her sentence.

Trembling with fury, Lucinda snatched the collar from her neck and tore it into bits ; then, making a dive at her skirts, she ripped them into shreds in her frantic efforts to destroy the hoop-skirt.

Dragging the gilt pendants from her ears, tearing the flesh as she did so, she threw them upon the floor, and, stamping upon them, ground them to atoms.

Attracted next by her new brogans, she kicked them from her feet and hurled them, one after another, into the open fire. No vestige of a gift from the hand that had betrayed her would she spare.

While all this was occurring in the kitchen, a reverse side of the tragedy was enacting in the house.

A few moments after Lucinda's departure, while Louise and her husband were yet discussing the situation, another messenger came from Sucrier, this time a man, and again a gift, the " note" which he promptly delivered proving to be a deed of conveyance of " two adult negroes, by name Lucinda and David." Then followed descriptions of each, which it was unnecessary to read.

The bearer seemed in fine spirits.

" Ole marster des sont me wid de note, missy," said he, courtesying respectfully, "an' ef yer please, ma'am, I'll go right back ef dey ain't no answer. We havin' a big time up our way ter-day."

"Why, don't you know what this is, Dave?"

"Yas, 'm, co'se I knows. Hit's—hit's a letter. Law, Miss Lou, yer reck'n I don' know a letter when I see it?"

"Yes, but this letter says that you are not to go back. Father has sent you as a Christmas gift to us."

"Wh—wh—h—how you say dat, missy?"

"Please don't look so frightened, Dave. From the way you all are acting to-day, I begin to be afraid of myself. Don't you want to belong to me?"

"Y—y—yas, 'm, but yer see, missy, I—I—I's married."

The hat in his hand was trembling as he spoke.

"And where is your wife?" Could it be possible that he did not know?

"She — sh — she—" The boy was actually crying. "She stay wid me. B—b—but marster des sont 'er on a arrant dis mornin'. Gord knows whar he sont 'er. I 'lowed maybe he sont 'er heah, tell 'e sont me."

The situation, which was plain now, had grown so interesting that Louise could not resist the temptation to bring the unconscious actors in the little drama together, that she might witness the happy catastrophe.

She whispered to Tildy to call Lucinda.

That Lucinda should have been summoned just at the crisis of her passion was most inopportune.

Tildy stood at a distance as she timidly delivered the message.   Indeed, all the occupants of the kitchen had moved off apace and stood aghast and silent.

As soon as Lucinda heard the command, however, without even looking down at herself, with head still high in air and her fury unabated, she followed Tildy into the presence of her mistress.

Louise was frightened when she looked upon her; indeed it was some moments before she could command herself enough to speak.

The girl's appearance was indeed tragic.

In tearing the ribbon from her hair she had loosened the ends of the short braids, which stood in all directions.   Her ears were dripping with blood, and her torn sleeve revealed her black arm, scratched with her nails, also bleeding.

Below her tattered skirt trailed long, detached springs, the dilapidated remains of the glorious structure of the morning.

Her tearless eyes gave no sign of weakening, and the veins about her neck and temples, pulsating with passion, were swollen and knotted like ropes.

She seemed to have grown taller, and the black circles beneath her eyes and about her swelling lips imparted by contrast an ashen hue grimly akin to pallor to the rest of her face.

As her mistress contemplated her, she was moved to pity.

"Lucindy"—she spoke with marked gentleness—"I showed you all our Christmas gifts this morning; but after you went out we received another, and I've sent for you to show you this too."

She hesitated, but not even by a quivering muscle did Lucinda give a sign of hearing.

"Look over there towards the library door, Lucindy, and see the nice carriage-driver father sent me."

Ah! now she looked.

For a moment only young husband and wife regarded each other, and then, oblivious to all eyes, the two Christmas gifts rushed into each other's arms.

The fountains of her wrath were broken up now, and Lucinda's tears came like rain. Crying and sobbing aloud, she threw her long arms around little Dave, and, dragging him out into the floor, began to dance.

Dave, more sensitive than she, abashed after the first surprise, became conscious and ashamed.

"Stop, 'Cindy! I 'clare, gal, stop! Stop, I say!" he cried, trying in vain to wrest himself from her grasp.

"You 'Cindy! You makes me 'shame'! Law, gal! Miss Lou, come here to 'Cindy!"

But the half-savage creature, mad with joy, gave no heed to his resistance as she whirled him round and round up and down the hall.

"Hallelujah! Glory! Amen! Glory be ter

Gord, fur givin' me back dis heah little black, cross-eyed, bandy-legged nigger! Glory, I say!"

The scene was not without pathos. And yet—how small a thing will sometimes turn the tide of emotion! By how trifling a by-play does a tragedy become comedy!

In her first whirl, the trailing steels of Lucinda's broken hoop-skirt flew over the head of the cat, who sat in the door, entrapping her securely.

Round and round went poor puss, terror-stricken and wildly glaring, utterly unable to extricate herself, until finally a reversed movement freeing her, she sprang with a desperate plunge and an ear-splitting "*Miaou!*" by a single bound out of the back door.

This served to bring Lucinda to a consciousness of her surroundings.

Screaming with laughter, she threw herself down and rolled on the floor.

In rising, her eyes fell for the first time, with a sense of perception, upon herself.

Suddenly conscience-stricken, she threw herself again before her mistress.

"Fur Gord sake, whup me, Miss Lou!" she began; "whup me, ur put me in de stocks, one! I ain't no mo' fitt'n fur a Chris'mus gif' 'n one o' deze heah tiger-cats in de show-tent. Des look heah how I done ripped up all my purties, an' bus' my ears open, an' broke up all my hoop-granjer, all on 'count o' dat little black, cross-eyed nigger! I tell yer de trufe, missy, I ain't no bad-hearted nigger! You des try me! I'll hoe fur yer, I'll plough fur yer, I'll split rails fur yer, I'll be yo' hair-dresser, I'll run de sew'-machine fur yer, I'll walk on my head fur yer, ef yer des leave me dat one little black scrooched-up some'h'n'-'nother stan'in' over yonner 'g'inst de do', grinnin' like a chessy-cat. He ain't much, but, sech as 'e is an' what dey is of 'im, fur Gord sake, spare 'im ter me! Somehow, de place whar he done settled in my heart is des nachelly my *wil'-cat spot.*"

Sitting in her rags at her mistress's feet, in this fashion she approached the formal apology which she felt that her conduct demanded.

Somehow the conventional formula, "I ax yo' pardon," seemed inadequate to the present requirement.

She hardly knew how to proceed.

After hesitating a moment in some embarrassment, she began again, in a lower tone :

"Miss Lou, dis heah's Chris'mus, ain't it?"

"Yes ; you know it is."

"An' hit's de day de Lord cas' orf all 'is glory an' come down ter de yearth, des a po' little baby a-layin' in a stable 'longside o' de cows an' calves, ain't it?"

"Yes."

"An' hit's de day de angels come a-singin' 'peace an' good-will,' ain't it?"

"Yes."

"Miss Lou—"

"Well?"

"On de 'count o' all dat, honey, won't yer please, ma'am, pass over my wil'-cat doin's dis time, mistus?"

She waited a moment, and, not understanding how a rising lump in her throat kept her mistress silent, continued to plead:

"Fur Gord sake, mistus, I done said all de scripchur' I knows. What mo' kin I say?"

"What—what—what—what—what's all this?"

It was old Colonel Slack, standing in the front hall door.

At the sound of his voice, the three grandchildren ran to meet him, Louise following.

"You dear old father!" she exclaimed, kissing him. "You've grown impatient and come after us!"

"Certainly I have. What sort of spending the day do you call this? It's two o'clock now. But what's all this?" he repeated, approaching Lucinda, who had risen to her feet.

Dave had gradually backed nearly out of the door.

"Why, Lucindy, my girl! you look as if you'd had a tiff with a panther."

"Tell de trufe, marster, I done been down an' had a han'-ter-han' wrastle wid Satan ter-day, an' he all but whupped me out."

"How did you happen to send these poor children to us separately, father?" said Louise. "They have been almost broken-hearted, each thinking the other was to stay at Sucrier."

"Well, well, well! I am the clumsiest old blunderer! It's from Scylla to Charybdis every time. I didn't want my people to suspect they were going, just because it's Christmas, you know, and saying good-bye will cast a sort of shadow over things. Dave and Lucindy are immensely popular among the darkies. I knew they'd be glad to come; it's promotion, you see. Never thought of a misunderstanding. And so you poor children thought I wanted to divorce you, did you? And you, Lucindy, flew into a tantrum and tore the clothes off your back? I don't blame you. I'd tear mine off too. Rig her up again somehow, daughter, and let her go up to the dance to-night."

Opening his pocket-book, he took out two crisp five-dollar bills.

Handing one of them to Lucinda, he said :

"Here, girl, take this, and—don't you tell 'em I said so, but I thought you beat the whole crowd dancing this morning, anyhow. And Dave, you little cross-eyed rascal you, step up here and get your money. Here's five dollars to pay for spoiling your Christmas. Now, off with you !"

As they passed out, Lucinda seized Dave's arm, and when last seen as they crossed the yard she was dragging the little fellow from side to side, dancing in her rags and flirting high in air the red fan, which by some chance had escaped destruction in her pocket.

Magnificent in a discarded ball-dress of her new

mistress, Lucinda was the centre of attraction at the Sucrier festival that evening, and when questioned in regard to her toilet of the morning, she answered, with a playful toss of the head:

"What y'all talkin' 'bout, niggers? I wushes you ter on'erstan' dat I's a house-gal now! Yer reck'n I gwine wear common ornamints, same as you fiel'-han's?"

"BLINK"

"BLINK"

"BLINK"

I.

IT was nearly midnight of Christmas Eve on Oakland Plantation. In the library of the great house a dim lamp burned, and here, in a big arm-chair before a waning fire, Evelyn Bruce, a fair young girl, sat earnestly talking to a withered old black woman, who sat on the rug at her feet.

"An' yer say de plantatiom done sol', baby, an' we boun' ter move?"

"Yes, mammy, the old place must go."

"An' is de 'Onerble Mr. Citified buyed it, baby? I know he an' ole marster sot up all endurin' las' night a-talkin' and a-figgurin'."

"Yes. Mr. Jacobs has closed the mortgage, and owns the place now."

"Who tol' yer, honey? Is ole marster sesso?"

"No, mammy. Father seemed so depressed that I followed Mr. Jacobs out this morning, and asked him all about it, and he told me."

"He 'ain't talked no way sassy ter yer 'bout it, is he, baby? 'Ain't put on no 'bove-ish ways? Deze heah permissiom-merchams, dee puts on a heap o' biggoty an' super*flu*ousness sometimes when dee steps inter de royal kingdoms, an' 'ray deyselves in robes made fur bigger folks."

"Mr. Jacobs spoke very kindly, mammy. I think he is truly sorry."

"An' when is we gwine, baby?"

"The sooner the better. I wish the going were over."

"An' whar'bouts is we gwine, honey?"

"We will go to the city, mammy—to New Orleans. Something tells me that father will never be able to attend to business again, and I am going to work—to make money."

Mammy fell backward. "W-w-w-work! Y-y-you w-w-work! Wh-wh-why, baby, what sort o' funny, cuyus way is you a-talkin', anyhow?"

"Many refined women are earning their living in the city, mammy."

"Is you a-talkin' sense, baby, ur is yer des a-bluffin'? Is yer axed yo' pa yit?"

"I don't think father is well, mammy. He says that whatever I suggest we will do, and I am *sure* it is best. We will take a cheap little house, father and I—"

"Y-y-you an' yo' pa! An' wh-wh-what 'bout me, baby?" Mammy would stammer when she was excited.

"And you, mammy, of course."

"Umh! umh! umh! An' so we gwine ter trabble! An' de' Onerble Mr. Citified done closed de morgans on us! Ef-ef I'd o' knowed it dis mornin' when he was a-quizzifyin' me so sergacious, I b'lieve I'd o' upped an' sassed 'im, I des couldn't o' helt in. I 'lowed he was teckin' a mighty frien'ly intruss, axin' me do we-all's *puck*on-trees bear big *puck*ons, an'—an' ef de well keep cool all summer, an'—an' he ax me— he ax me—"

"What else did he ask you, mammy ?"

"Scuze me namin' it ter yer, baby, but he ax me who was buried in we's graves—he did fur a fac'. Yer reck'n dee gwine claim de graves in de morgans, baby ?"

Mammy had crouched again at Evelyn's feet, and her eager brown face was now almost against her knee.

"All the land is mortgaged, mammy."

"Don't yer reck'n he mought des nachelly scuze de graves out'n de morgans, baby, ef yer ax 'im mannerly ?"

"I'm afraid not, mammy, but after a while we may have them moved."

The old bronze clock on the mantel struck twelve.

"Des listen. De ole clock a-strikin' Chris'mus gif' now. Come 'long, go ter baid, honey. You needs a res', but I ain' gwine sleep none, 'caze all dis heah news what you been a-tellin' me, hits gwine ter run roun' in my haid all night, same as a buzz-saw."

And so they passed out, mammy to her pallet in Evelyn's room, while Evelyn stepped to her father's chamber.

Entering on tiptoe, she stood and looked upon his face. He slept as peacefully as a babe. The anxious look of care which he had worn for years had passed away, and the flickering fire revealed the ghost of a smile upon his placid face. In this it was that Evelyn read the truth. The crisis of effort for him was past. He might follow, but he would lead no more.

Since the beginning of the war Colonel Bruce's history had been the oft-told tale of loss and disaster, and at the opening of each year since, there had been a flaring up of hope and expenditure, then a long summer of wavering promise, followed by an inevitable winter of disappointment.

The old colonel was, both by inheritance and the habit of many successful years, a man of great affairs, and when the crash came he was too old to change. When he bought, he bought heavily. He planted for large results. There was nothing petty about him, not even his debts. And now the end had come.

As Evelyn stood gazing upon his handsome, placid face her eyes were blinded with tears. Falling upon her knees at his side, she engaged for a moment in silent prayer, consecrating herself in love to the life which lay before her, and as she rose she kissed his forehead gently, and passed to her own room.

Mammy, in spite of her own prediction of sleeplessness, was already snoring before the fire.

Evelyn could not sleep yet. She felt so keenly that her own decision must be the pivot upon which their future lives must turn, that all her faculties of heart and mind were alert. As she sank into a chair, her eyes fell on the portraits upon the walls. Here were the uniformed soldier brothers, young and handsome, now only a misty memory of her childhood—there, in a frame of silver daisies, a baby sister, who had died before Evelyn was born. Only a spirit sister this, and yet to-night her heart went out with a strong yearning to this baby face in a cloud. If this little sister, but a year her senior, had lived, how lovingly the two might plan and work together now! And here, above the mantel, is the face of her mother. The gentle eyes of the picture seem to shed a benediction upon her as she looks into them, and for a moment the other world and this seem almost to touch, so real does Heaven become when it takes our mothers.

At last her eyes fall upon mammy, old, faithful mammy, asleep at her feet, her very presence here an act of devotion, for since Evelyn's mother's death mammy had forsaken her own soft bed, and come here, protesting that she was "gitt'n' clair sp'iled, an' no 'count anyhow, sleepin' in a funniture bed."

On the table at Evelyn's side lay several piles of manuscript, and as these attracted her, she turned her chair, and fell to work sorting them into packages, which she laid carefully away.

11

These papers, representing much of labor and patience, were the visible foundation upon which she hoped ultimately to build an independence.

Evelyn had always loved to scribble, but only within the last few years had the idea of writing for money come to her as a possible escape from threatened poverty. Gleaning those which seemed best of her early writings, she had revised, polished, and corrected them so far as she could, and, if the whole truth must be told, she had even sent several manuscripts to editors of magazines, but somehow, like birds too young to leave the nest, they all found their way back to her. With each failure, however, she had become more determined to succeed, but in the mean time—*now* —she must earn a living. This was impracticable here. In the city all things were possible, and to the city she would go. She would at first accept one of the tempting situations offered in the daily papers, improving her leisure by attending lectures, studying, observing, cultivating herself in every possible way, and after a time she would try her hand again at writing.

It was nearly day when she finally went to bed, but she was up early next morning. There was much to be considered. Many things were to be done.

At first she consulted her father about everything, but his invariable answer, "Just as you say, daughter," transferred all responsibility to her.

A letter to her mother’s old New Orleans friend,
Madame Le Duc, briefly set forth the circumstances, and asked Madame’s aid in securing a
small house. Other letters sent in other directions
arranged various matters, and Evelyn soon found
herself in the vortex of a move. She had a wise,
clear head and a steady, resolute hand, and in old
mammy a most efficient deputy. The old woman
seemed, indeed, positively ubiquitous as she bus-
tled about, forgetting nothing, packing, suggest-
ing, and, spite of herself, frequently protesting ;
for, if the truth must be spoken, this move to the
city was violating all the traditions of mammy’s
life.

“ Wh-wh-wh-why, baby ! Not teck de grimestone !” she exclaimed one day, in reply to Evelyn’s protest against her packing that ponderous
article. “ How is we gwine sharpen de spade an’
de grubbin’-hoe ter work in the gyard’n ?”

“ We sha’n’t have a garden, mammy.”

“ No gyard’n !” Mammy sat down upon the
grindstone in disgust. “ Wh-wh-wh-what sort o’
a fureign no-groun’ place is we gwine ter,
anyhow, baby ? Honey !” she continued, in a
troubled voice, “ co’se you know I ain’t got educatiom, an’ I ain’t claim knowledge ; b-b-b-but
ain’t you better study on it good ’fo’ we goes ter
dis heah new country ? Dee tells me de cidy’s a
owdacious place. I been heern a heap o’ tales,
but I ’ain’t say nothin’. Is yer done prayed over
it good, baby ?”

"Yes, dear. I have prayed that we should do only right. What have you heard, mammy?"

"D-d-d-de way folks talks, look like death an' terror is des a-layin' roun' loose in de cidy. Dee tell *me* dat ef yer des nachelly blows out yer light fur ter go ter baid dat dis heah someh'n' what stan' fur wick, hit 'll des keep a-sizzin' an' a-sizzin' out, des like sperityal steam ; *an' hit's clair pizen!*"

"That is true, mammy. But you see, we won't blow it out. We'll know better."

"Does yer snuff it out wid snuffers, baby, ur des fling it on de flo' an' tromp yer foots on it ?"

"Neither, mammy. The gas comes in through pipes built into the houses, and is turned on and off with a valve, somewhat as we let water out of the refrigerator."

"Um-hm ! Well done ! Of co'se ! On'y, in place o' water what *put out* de light, hit's in'ardly filled wid someh'n' what *favor* a blaze."

"Exactly."

Mammy reflected a moment. "But de grimestone gotter stay berhime, is she ? An' is we gwine leave all de gyard'n tools an' implemers ter de 'Onerble Mr. Citified ?"

"No, mammy ; none of the appurtenances of the homestead are mortgaged. We must sell them. We need money, you know."

"What is de impertinences o' de homestid, baby ? You forgits I ain't on'erstan' book words."

“Those things intended for family use, mammy. There are the carriage-horses, the cows, the chickens—”

“Bless goodness fur dat! An’ who gwine drive ’em inter de cidy fur us, honey?”

“Oh, mammy, we must sell them all.”

Mammy was almost crying. “An’ what sort o’ entry is we gwine meck inter de cidy, honey— empty - handed, same es po’ white trash? D-d-d-don’t yer reck’n we b-b-better teck de chickens, baby? Yo’ ma thunk a heap o’ dem Brahma hains an’ dem Clymoth Rockers—dee looks so courageous.”

It was hard for Evelyn to refuse. Mammy loved everything on the old place.

“Let us give up all these things now, mammy; and after a while, when I grow rich and famous, I’ll buy you all the chickens you want.”

At last preparations were over. They were to start to-morrow. Mammy had just returned from a last tour through out-buildings and gardens, and was evidently disturbed.

“Honey,” she began, throwing herself on the step at Evelyn’s feet, “what yer reck’n? Ole Muffly is a-sett’n’ on fo’teen aigs, down in de cotton seed. W-w-we can’t g’way f’m heah an’ leave Muffly a-sett’n’, hit des nachelly can’t be did. D-d-don’t yer reck’n dee’d hol’ back de morgans a little, tell Muffly git done sett’n’?”

It was the same old story. Mammy would never be ready to go.

"But our tickets are bought, mammy."

"An' like as not de 'Onerble Mr. Citified 'll shoo ole Muffly orf de nes' an' spile de whole sett'n'. Tut! tut! tut!" And groaning in spirit, mammy walked off.

Evelyn had feared, for her father, the actual moment of leaving, and was much relieved when, with his now habitual tranquillity, he smilingly assisted both her and mammy into the sleeper. Instead of entering himself, however, he hesitated.

"Isn't your mother coming, daughter?" he asked, looking backward. "Or—oh, I forgot," he added, quickly. "She has gone on before, hasn't she?"

"Yes, dear, she has gone before," Evelyn answered, hardly knowing what she said, the chill of a new terror upon her.

What did this mean? Was it possible that she had read but half the truth? Was her father's mind not only enfeebled, but going?

Mammy had not heard the question, and so Evelyn bore her anxiety alone, and during the day her anxious eyes were often upon her father's face, but he only smiled and kept silent.

They had been travelling all day, when suddenly, above the rumbling of the train, a weak, bird-like chirp was heard, faint but distinct; and presently it came again, a prolonged "p-e-e-p!"

Heads went up, inquiring faces peered up and down the coach, and fell again to paper or book, when the cry came a third time, and again.

Mammy’s face was a study. “ ’Sh—’sh—’sh ! don’ say nothin’, baby,” she whispered, in Evelyn’s ear ; “ but dis heah chicken in my bosom is a-ticklin’ me so I can’t hardly set still.”

Evelyn was absolutely speechless with surprise, as mammy continued by snatches her whispered explanation :

“ Des ’fo’ we lef’ I went ’n’ lif’ up ole Muffly ter see how de aigs was comin’ orn, an’ dis heah aig was pipped out, an’ de little risidenter look like he eyed me so bersecchin’ I des nachelly couldn’t leave ’im. Look like he knowed he warn’t right-eously in de morgans, an’ ’e crave ter clair out an’ trabble. I did hope speech wouldn’t come ter ’im tell we got off’n deze heah train kyars.”

A halt at a station brought a momentary silence, and right here arose again, clear and shrill, the chicken’s cry.

Mammy was equal to the emergency. After glancing inquiringly up and down the coach, she exclaimed aloud, “ Some’h’n’ in dis heah kyar soun’ des like a vintrilloquer.”

“ That’s just what it is,” said an old gentleman opposite, peering around over his spectacles. “ And whoever you are, sir, you’ve been amusing yourself for an hour.”

Mammy’s ruse had succeeded, and during the rest of the journey, although the chicken developed duly as to vocal powers, the only question asked by the curious was, “ Who can the ventriloquist be ?”

Evelyn could hardly maintain her self-control, the situation was so utterly absurd.

"I does hope hit's a pullet," mammy confided later; "but I doubts it. Hit done struck out wid a mannish movemint a'ready. Muflly's aigs allus hatches out sech invig'rous chickens. I gwine in de dressin'-room, baby, an' wrop 'im up agin. Feel like he done kicked 'isse'f loose."

Though she made several trips to the dressing-room in the interest of her hatchling, mammy's serene face held no betrayal of the disturbing secret of her bosom.

At last the journey was over. The train crept with a tired motion into the noisy depot. Then came a rattling ride over cobble-stones, granite, and unpaved streets; a sudden halt before a low-browed cottage; a smiling old lady stepping out to meet them; a slam of the front door—they were at home in New Orleans.

Madame Le Duc seemed to have forgotten nothing that their comfort required, and in many ways that the Creole gentlewoman understands so well, she was affectionately and unobtrusively kind. And yet, in the life Evelyn was seeking to enter, Madame could give her no aid. About all these new ideas of women—ladies—going out as bread-winners, Madame knew nothing. For twenty years she had gone only to the cathedral, the French Market, the cemetery, and the Chapel of St. Roche. As to all this unconventional American city above Canal Street, it was there

and spreading (like the measles and other evils) ;
everybody said so ; even her paper, *L'Abeille*, referred to it in French—resentfully. She believed
in it historically ; but for herself, she *"never
travelled," excepting*, as she quaintly put it, in her
"acquaintances"—the French streets with which
she was familiar.

The house Madame had selected was a typical
old-fashioned French cottage, venerable in scaling
plaster and fern-tufted tile roof, but cool and
roomy within as uninviting without. A small inland garden surprised the eye as one entered the
battened gate at its side, and a dormer-window in
the roof looked out upon the rigging of ships at
anchor but a stone's-throw away.

Here, in the chamber above, Evelyn installed
her father. Furnishing this spacious upper room
with familiar objects, and pointing out the novelties of the view from its window, she tried to interpret his new environment happily for him, and
he smiled, and seemed content.

It was surprising to see how soon mammy fell
into line with the new order of things. The
French Market, with its "cuyus fureign folks an'
mixed talk," was a panorama of daily unfolding
wonders to her. "But huccome dee calls it
French?" she exclaimed, one day. "I been lis-
tenin' good, an' I hear 'em jabber, jabber, jabber
all dey fanciful lingoes, but I 'ain't heern nair one
say *polly fronsay*, an' yit I know dats de riverend
book French." The Indian squaws in the market,

sitting flat on the ground, surrounded by their wares, she held in special contempt. "I hol's myse'f *clair* 'bove a Injun," she boasted. "Dee ain't look jinnywine ter me. Dee ain't nuther white folks nur niggers, nair one. Sett'n' dee-selves up fur go-betweens, an' sellin' sech grass-greens as we lef' berhindt us growin' in de wil-derness!"

But one unfailing source of pleasure to mammy was the little chicken, "Blink," who, she de-clared, "named 'isse'f Blink de day he blinked at me so skancified out'n de shell. Blink 'ain't said nothin' wid 'is mouf," she continued, eying him proudly, "'caze he know eye-speech set on a chicken a heap better'n human words, mo' in-special on a yo'ng half-hatched chicken like Blink was dat day, cramped wid de aig-shell behime, an' de morgans starin' 'im in de face befo', an' not knowin' how 'e gwine come out'n 'is trouble. He des kep' silence, an' wink all 'is argimints, an' 'e wink to the p'int, too!"

In spite of his unique entrance into the world and his precarious journey, Blink was a vigorous young chicken, with what mammy was pleased to call "a good proud step an' knowin' eyes."

Three months passed. The long, dull summer was approaching, and yet Evelyn had found no employment. Advertised positions had proven unsuitable or inaccessible, and indeed, sometimes the most inviting but delusions and snares. But Evelyn had not been idle. Sewing for the market-folk, decorating palmetto-fans and Easter-eggs, which mammy peddled in the big houses, she had earned small sums of money from time to time. Enforced leisure she recognized as opportunity for study, and her picturesque surroundings an open book.

Impressions of the quaint old French and Spanish city, with its motley population, were carefully jotted down in her note-book. These first descriptions she afterward rewrote, discarding weakening detail, elaborating the occasional triviality which seemed to reflect the true local tint —a nice distinction, involving conscientious hard work. How she longed for criticism and advice !

A year ago her father, now usually dozing in his chair while she worked, would have been a most able and affectionate critic ; but now— She rejoiced when a day passed without his asking for her mother, and wondering why she did not come.

And so it was that in her need of sympathy Evelyn began to read her writings, some of which had grown into stories, to mammy. The very exercise of reading aloud—the sound of it—was helpful. That mammy's criticisms should have proven valuable in themselves was a surprise, but it was even so.

II.

"A pusson would know dat was fanciful de way hit reads orf, des like a pusson 'magine some'h'n' what ain't so."

Such was mammy's first criticism of a story which had just come back, returned from an editor. Evelyn had been trying to discover wherein its weakness lay.

Mammy had caught the truth. The story was unreal. The English seemed good, the construction fair, but—it was "*fanciful.*"

The criticism set Evelyn to thinking. She laid aside this, and read another manuscript aloud.

"I tell yer, honey, a-a-a pusson 'd know you had educatiom, de way you c'n fetch in de dicksh'-nary words."

"Don't you understand them, mammy?" she asked, quickly, catching another idea.

"Who, me? Law, baby, I don't crave ter on'er-stan' all dat granjer. I des ketches de chune, an' hit sho is got a glorified ring."

Here was a valuable hint. She must simplify her style. The tide of popular writing was, she knew, in the other direction, but the *best* writing was *simple.*

The suggestion sent her back to study.

And now for her own improvement she rewrote the "story of big words" in the simplest English she could command, bidding mammy tell her if there was one word she could not understand.

In the transition the spirit of the story was necessarily changed, but the exercise was good. Mammy understood every wood.

"But, baby," she protested, with a troubled face, "look like *hit don't stan' no mo';* all its granjer done gone. You better fix it up des like it was befo', honey. Hit 'mines me o' some o' deze heah fine folks what walks de streets. You know *folks what 'ain't got nothin' else,* dee des nachelly *'bleege* ter put on finery."

How clever mammy was! How wholesome the unconscious satire of her criticism! This story, shorn of its grandeur, could not stand indeed. It was weak and affected.

"You dear old mammy," exclaimed Evelyn, "you don't know how you are helping me."

"Gord knows I wushes I could holp you, honey. I 'ain't nuver is craved educatiom befo', but now, look like I'd like ter be king o' all de smartness, an' know all dey is in de books. I wouldn't hol' back *nuth'n* f'om yer, baby."

And Evelyn knew it was true.

"Look ter me, baby," mammy suggested, another night, after listening to a highly imaginative story—"look ter me like ef—ef—ef you'd des write down some *truly truth* what is ac-*chilly* happened, an' glorify it wid educatiom, hit 'd des nachelly stan' in a book."

"I've been thinking of that," said Evelyn, reflectively, laying aside her manuscript.

"How does this sound, mammy?" she asked, a week later, when, taking up an unfinished story, she began to read.

It was the story of their own lives, dating from the sale of the plantation. The names, of course, were changed, excepting Blink's, and, indeed, until he appeared upon the scene, although mammy listened breathless, she did not recognize the characters. Blink, however, was unmistakable, and when he announced himself from the old woman's bosom his identity flashed upon mammy, and she tumbled over on the floor, laughing and crying alternately. Evelyn had written from her heart, and the story, simply told, held all the wrench of parting with old associations, while the spirit of courage and hope, which animated her, breathed in every line as she described their entrance upon their new life.

"My heart was teched f'om de fus', baby," said mammy, presently, wiping her eyes; "b-b-b-but look heah, honey, I'd—I'd be wuss'n a hycoprite ef I let dat noble ole black 'oman, de way you done specified 'er, stan' fur me. Y-y-yer got ter change all dat, honey. Dey warn't nothin' on top o' dis roun' worl' what fetched me 'long wid y' all but 'cep' 'caze I des *nachelly love yer*, an' all dat book granjer what you done laid on me I *don' know nothin' 't all about it*, an' yer got ter *teck it orf*, an' write me down like I is, des a po' ole nigger wha' done fell in wid de Gord-blessedes' white folks wha' ever lived on dis yearth, an'—an' wha' gwine *foller* 'em an' *stay by 'em*, don' keer whicherway dee go, so long as 'er ole han's is able ter holp 'em. Yer got ter change all dat, honey.

"But Blink! De laws-o'-mussy! Maybe hit's 'caze I been hatched 'im an' raised 'im, but look ter me like he ain't no *dis*grace ter de story, no way. Seem like he sets orf de book. Yer ain't gwine say nothin' 'bout Blink bein' a frizzly, is yer? 'Twouldn't do no good ter tell it on 'im."

"I didn't know it, mammy."

"Yas, indeedy. Po' Blink's feathers done taken on a secon' twis'," she replied, with maternal solicitude. "I d' know huccome he come dat-a-way, 'caze we 'ain't nuver is had no frizzly stock 'mongs' our chickens. Sometimes I b'lieve Blink tumbled 'isse'f up dat-a-way tryin' ter wriggle 'isse'f outn de morgans. I hates it mightily. Look like a frizzly can't put on granjer no way, don' keer how mannerly 'e hol' 'isse'f."

The progress of the new story, which mammy considered under her especial supervision, was now her engrossing thought.

"Yer better walk straight, Blink," she would exclaim—"yer better walk straight an' step high, 'caze yer gwine in a book, honey, 'long wid de a'stokercy!"

One day Blink walked leisurely in from the street, returning, happily for mammy's peace of mind, before he had been missed. He raised his wings a moment as he entered, as if pleased to get home, and mammy exclaimed, as she burst out laughing:

"Don't you come in heah shruggin' yo' shoulders at me, Blink, an' puttin' on no French airs. I believe Blink been out teckin' French lessons," she added, as she shut the gate. And taking her pet into her arms, she continued, addressing him:

"Is you crave ter learn fureign speech, Blinky,· like de res' o' dis mixed-talkin' settle*mint?*   Is you 'shamed o' yo' country voice, honey, an' tryin' ter ketch a French crow?   No, 'e ain't," she added, putting him down at last, but watching him fondly.   "Blink know he's a Bruce.   An' he know he's folks is in tribulatiom, an' hilar'ty ain't bercome 'im — dat's huccome Blink 'ain't crowed none — *ain't it, Blink?*"

And Blink wisely winked his knowing eyes. That he had, indeed, never proclaimed his roosterhood by crowing was a source of some anxiety to mammy.

"Maybe Blink don't know he's a rooster," she confided to Evelyn one day.   "Sho 'nough, honey, he nuver is seed none!   De neares' ter 'isse'f what he knows is dat ole green polly what set in de figtree nex' do', an' talk Gascon.   I seed Blink 'istidd'y stan' an' look at 'im, an' den look down at 'isse'f, same as ter say, 'Is I a polly, ur what?'   An' den 'e open an' shet 'is mouf, like 'e tryin' ter twis' it, polly-fashion, an' hit won't twis', an' den 'e des shaken 'is haid, an' walk orf, like 'e heavy-hearted an' mixed in 'is min'.   Blink don' know what 'spornserbility lay on 'im ter keep our courage up.   You heah me, Blink!   Open yo' mouf, an' crow out, like a man !"

But Blink was biding his time.

During this time, in spite of strictest economy, money was going out faster than it came in.

"I tell yer what I been thinkin', baby," said

mammy, as she and Evelyn discussed the situation. "I think de bes' thing you can do is ter hire me out. I can cook y' alls breckfus' soon, an' go out an' meck day's work, an' come home plenty o' time ter cook de little speck o' dinner you an' ole boss needs."

"Oh, no, no! You mustn't think of it, mammy."

"But what we gwine do, baby? We des *can't* get out'n *money*. Hit *won't do!*"

"Maybe I should have taken that position as lady's companion, mammy."

"An' stay 'way all nights f'om yo' pa, when you de onlies' light ter 'is eyes? No, no, honey!"

"But it has been my only offer, and sometimes I think—"

"Hush talkin' dat-a-way, baby. Don't yer pray? An' don't yer trus' Gord? An' ain't yer done walked de streets tell you mos' drapped down, lookin' fur work? An' can't yer teck de hint dat de Lord done laid orf yo' work *right heah in de house?* You go 'long now, an' cheer up yo' pa, des like you been doin', an' study yo' books, an' write down true joy an' true sorrer in yo' stories, an' glorify Gord wid yo' sense, an' don't pester yo'se'f 'bout ter-day an' ter-morrer, an'—an'—an' ef de gorspil is de trufe, an'—an' ef a po' ole nigger's pra'rs mounts ter Heaven on de wings o' faith, Gord ain't gwine let a hair o' yo' haid perish."

But mammy pondered in her heart much concerning the financial outlook, and it was on the day after this conversation that she dressed herself with unusual care, and, without announcing her errand, started out.

Her return soon brought its own explanation, however, for upon her old head she bore a huge bundle of unlaundered clothing.

"What in the world!" exclaimed Evelyn; but before she could voice a protest, mammy interrupted her.

"Nuver you min', baby! I des waked up," she exclaimed, throwing her bundle at the kitchen door. "I been preachin' ter you 'bout teckin' hints, an' 'ain't been readin' my own lesson. Huccome we got dis heah nice sunny back yard, an' dis bustin' cisternful o' rain-water? Huccome de boa'din'-house folks at de corner keeps a-passin' an' a-passin' by dis gate wid all dey fluted finery orn, ef 'twarn't ter gimme a hint dat dey's wealth a-layin' at de do', an' me, bline as a bat, 'ain't seen it?"

"Oh, but, mammy, you can't take in washing. You are too old; it is too hard. You *mustn't*—"

"Ef-ef-ef-ef you gits obstropulous, I-I-I gwine whup yer, sho. Y-y-yer know how much money's a-comin' out'n dat bundle, baby? *Five dollars!*" This in a stage-whisper. "An' not a speck o' dirt on nothin'; des baby caps an' lace doin's rumpled up."

"How did you manage it, mammy?"

"Well, baby, I des put on my fluted ap'on—an'

you know it's ironed purty—an' my clair-starched
neck-hankcher, an'—-an' *my business face*, an' I helt
up my haid an' walked in, an' axed good prices,
an' de ladies, dee des tooken took one good look
at me, an' gimme all I'd carry. You know washin' an' ironin' is my pleasure, baby."

It was useless to protest, and so, after a moment, Evelyn began rolling up her sleeves.

"I am going to help you, mammy," she said,
quietly but firmly; but before she could protest,
mammy had gathered her into her arms, and carried her into her own room. Setting her down at
her desk, she exclaimed:

"Now, ef *you* goes ter de wash-tub, dey ain't
nothin' lef' fur *me* ter do but 'cep'n ter *set down
an' write de story*, an' you know I can't do it."

"But, mammy, I *must* help you."

"Is you gwine *meck* me whup yer, whe'r ur no,
baby? Now I gwine meck a bargain wid yer.
You set down an' write, an' *I* gwine play de pianner on de washbode, an' ter-night you c'n read orf
what yer done put down, an' ef yer done written
it purty an' sweet, you c'n come an' turn de flut-
in'-machine fur me ter-morrer. Yer gwine meck
de bargain wid me, baby?"

Evelyn was so touched that she had not voice
to answer. Rising from her seat, she put her arms
around mammy's neck and kissed her old face, and
as she turned away a tear rolled down her cheek.
And so the "bargain" was sealed.

Before going to her desk Evelyn went to her

father, to see that he wanted nothing. He sat, as
usual, gazing silently out of the window.

"Daughter," said he, as she entered, "are we
in France?"

"No, dear," she answered, startled at the question.

"But the language I hear in the street is
French ; and see the ship masts—French flags
flying. But there is the German too, and English, and last week there was a Scandinavian.
Where are we truly, daughter ? My surroundings
confuse me."

"We are in New Orleans, father—in the French
Quarter. Ships from almost everywhere come to
this port, you know. Let us walk out to the
levee this morning, and see the men-of-war in
the river. The air will revive you."

"Well, if your mother comes ? She might come
while we were away."

And so it was always. With her heart trembling within her, Evelyn went to her desk. "Surely," she thought, "there is much need that I
shall do my best." Almost reverentially she took
her pen, as she proceeded with the true story she
had begun.

"I done changed my min' 'bout dat ole 'oman
wha' stan' fur me, baby," said mammy that night.
"You leave 'er des like she is. She glorifies de
story a heap better'n my nachel se'f could do it.
I been a-thinkin' 'bout it, an' *de finer that ole*

'oman ac', an' de mo' granjer yer lay on 'er, de better yer gwine meck de book, 'caze de ole gemplum wha' stan' fur ole marster, his times an' seasons is done past, an' he can't do nothin' but set still an' wait, an'—an' de yo'ng missus, she ain't fitten ter wrastle on de outskirts; she ain't nothin' but 'cep' des a lovin' sweet saint, wid 'er face set ter a high, far mark—"

"Hush, mammy!"

"*I'm a-talkin' 'bout de book, baby, an' don't you interrup' me no mo'!* An' *I say ef dis ole 'oman wha' stan' fur me, ef-ef-ef she got a weak spot in 'er, dey won't be no story to it.* She de one wha' got ter *stan' by de battlemints an' hol' de fort.*"

"That's just what you are doing, mammy. There isn't a grain in her that is finer than you."

"'Sh! dis ain't no time fur foolishness, baby. Yer 'ain't said nothin' 'bout yo' ma an' de ole black 'oman's baby bein' borned de same day, is yer? An' how de ole 'oman nussed 'em bofe des like twins? An'—an' how folks 'cused 'er o' starvin' 'er own baby on de 'count o' yo' ma bein' puny? (*But dat warn't true.*) Maybe yer better leave all dat out, 'caze hit mought spile de story."

"How could it spoil it, mammy?"

"Don't yer see, ef folks knowed dat dem white folks an' dat ole black 'oman was *dat close-t*, dey wouldn't be no principle in it! Dey ain't nothin' but *love* in *dat*, an' de ole 'oman *couldn't he'p 'erse'f, no mo'n I could he'p it!* No right-minded pusson is gwine ter deny dey own heart. Yer better leave all dat out, honey. B-b-but deys some'h'n' else wha' been lef' out, wha' b'long in de book. Yer ain't named de way de little mistus sot up all nights an' nussed de ole 'oman time she was sick, an'—an'—an' de way she sew all de ole 'oman's cloze; an'—an'—an' yer done lef' out a heap o' de purtiness an' de sweetness o' de yo'ng missis! Dis is a book, baby, an'—an'— yer boun' ter do jestice!"

In this fashion the story was written.

"And what do you think I am going to do with it, mammy?" said Evelyn, when finally, having done her very best, she was willing to call it finished.

"Yer know some'h'n', baby? Ef-ef-ef I had de money, look like I'd buy dat story myse'f. Seem some way like I loves it. Co'se I couldn't read it; but my min' been on it so long, seem like, ef I'd study de pages good dee'd open up ter me. What yer gwine do wid it, baby?"

"Oh, mammy, I can hardly tell you! My heart seems in my throat when I dare to think of it; but *I'm going to try it.* A New York magazine has offered five hundred dollars for a best story—*five hundred dollars!* Think, mammy, what it would do for us!"

"Dat wouldn't buy de plantatiom back, would it, baby?" Mammy had no conception of large sums.

"We don't want it back, mammy. It would

pay for moving our dear ones to graves of their own ; we should put a nice sum in bank ; you shouldn't do any more washing ; and if we can write one good story, you know we can write more. It will be only a beginning."

"An' I tell yer what I gwine do. I gwine pray over it good, des like I been doin' f'om de start, an' ef hit's Gord's will, dem folks 'll be moved in de sperit ter sen' 'long de money."

And so the story was sent.

After it was gone the atmosphere seemed brighter. The pending decision was now a fixed point to which hope, no longer a vague abstraction, tended.

The very audacity of the effort seemed inspiration to more ambitious work, and during the long summer, while in her busy hands the fluting-machine went round and round, Evelyn's mind was full of plans for the future.

Finally, December, with its promise of the momentous decision, was come, and Evelyn found herself full of anxious misgivings.

What merit entitling it to special consideration had the little story ? Did it bear the impress of self-forgetful, conscientious purpose, or was this a thing only feebly struggling into life within herself—not yet the compelling force that indelibly stamps itself upon the earnest labor of consecrated hands ? How often in the silent hours of night did she ask herself questions like this !

At last it was Christmas Eve again, and Satur-

day night. When the days are dark, what is so
depressing as an anniversary — an anniversary
joyous in its very essence ? How one Christmas
brings in its train memory-pictures of those gone
before !

This had been a hard day for Evelyn. Her
heart felt weak within her, and yet, realizing that
she alone represented youth and hope in the little
household, and feeling need that her own courage should be sustained, she had been more than
usually merry all day. She had clandestinely
prepared little surprises for her father and mammy, and was both amused and touched to discover
the old woman secreting mysterious little parcels
which she knew were to come to her to-morrow.

"Wouldn't it be funny if, after all, I should
turn out to be only a good washer-woman, mammy ?" she said, laughing, as she assisted the old
woman in pinning up a basket of laundered
clothing.

"Hit 'd be funnier yit ef *I'd* turn out inter
one o' deze heah book-writers, wouldn't it ?" And
mammy laughed heartily at her own joke. "Look
like I better study my a-b abs, fus', let 'lone puttin' 'em back on paper wid a pen. I tell you
educatiom's a-spreadin' in dis fam'ly, sho. Time
Blink run over de sheet out a-bleachin' 'is*tidd*y,
he written a Chinese letter all over it. Didn't
you, Blink ? What de matter wid Blink anyhow, to-day ?" she added, taking the last pin
from her head-kerchief. "Blink look like he

nervous some way 's evenin'. He keep a-walk·
in' roun', an' winkin' so slow, an' retchin' 'is
neck out de back do' so cuyus. Stop a-battin'
yo' eyes at me, Blink ! Ef yo' got some'h'n ter
say, *say it !*"

A sudden noisy rattle of the iron door-knocker
—mammy trotting to the door—the postman—a
letter ! It all happened in a minute.

How Evelyn's heart throbbed and her hand
trembled as she opened the envelope ! "Oh,
mammy !" she cried, trembling now like an aspen
leaf. " *Thank God !*"

"Is dee d-d-d-done sont de money, baby ?"
Her old face was twitching too.

But Evelyn could not answer. Nodding her
head, she fell sobbing on mammy's shoulder.

Mammy raised her apron to her eyes, and
there's no telling what "foolishness" she might
have committed had it not been that suddenly,
right at her side, arose a most jubilant screech.

Blink, perched on the handle of the clothes-
basket, was crowing with all his might.

Evelyn, startled, raised her head, and laughed
through her tears, while mammy threw herself at
full length upon the floor, shouting aloud.

"'Tell me chickens ain't got secon'-sight !" she
exclaimed, finally, wiping her eyes. " Blink see'd
—he see'd— Laws-o'-mussy, baby, look yonder
at dat little yaller rooster stan'in' on de fence.
Dat what Blink see. Co'se it is !"

JESSEKIAII BROWN'S COURTSHIP

JESSEKIAH BROWN'S COURTSHIP

JESSEKIAH BROWN, a fat, bow-legged fellow of forty years or thereabouts, enjoyed the double distinction of being the fattest man as well as the oldest bachelor of his color on the plantation.

He had been a general beau in colored circles ever since he had begun to wear shoes to church, about twenty-five years ago. The " young ladies " he had " gone with " and " had feelin's about " were now staid matrons, mothers of grown sons and daughters, and yet Jessekiah had never been known to speak a serious word of love to any woman.

It was a common thing for the old wives on the place to say, as they sat together on the levee and laughed to see him still playing the beau, "Po' Ki! I don't b'lieve pos'tive he know how ter out an' out cote a gal !"

And this was true, or at least it was half the truth. The other half was that Jessekiah had never been able to make up his mind decidedly as to the identical woman he wished to marry.

His was a case of ultra all-round susceptibility resulting in an embarrassment of emotions. It is probable that a certain indecision amounting to a psychological idiosyncrasy had descended to Ki by direct maternal inheritance, as it is related on reliable authority that his good mother had been utterly unable, even while she stood at the baptismal font with her babe, to decide whether his name should be Jesse or Hezekiah, and an embarrassed effort to change it at the last moment resulted in the unique cognomen which distinguished him through life.

There had been times in Jessekiah's life when he had *almost decided* that some special woman was the undisputed possessor of his affections, but they were fleeting moments.

On the old levee just opposite his present cabin he had once been sitting with Diana Forbes, a copper-skinned lass of seventeen years, for whom he had long confessed a soft spot in his soft heart, and the moonlight and a white gown she wore on that occasion had settled the question — for the moment.

He had even gotten as far as " Roses " in his avowal of love, when a silvery laugh, descending all the way from high C to inaudibility, had floated to him from the quarters.

Jessekiah could never propose to another girl while he heard Silv'y Simms laugh, and so, instead of saying " Roses is red an' vi'lets blue," and becoming hopelessly involved on the second line, he had coughed and remarked :

" Roses smells a heap mo' sweeter, ter my min',

'n honeysuckles does. Which you lak de moes', Miss Diana?"

And so the crisis had passed.

The only distinction Ki had attained as a person of superior years among the youth of the plantation was the title of brother.

"Brer Brown" had long ago "professed," and while never attaining any celebrity either as a speaker or worker in the fold, neither had he introduced shame in any shape, which was saying a good deal.

Ki's life, as care-free as that of the humming-bird that flits at will from flower to flower, and apparently as sunny and bright, was yet not without its trials. For years a certain single woman on the place, as huge as himself, hence familiarly known as "Fat Ann," had been his *bête noire.*

It was not enough that every one took special delight in teasing him about her, but the woman herself, in spite of years of avoidance on his part, seemed to have a fancy for him.

The bitterest hours of Ki's life had been on account of Fat Ann.

Any joke that threw their names together, any premeditated pairing off of couples that left him as her escort, was regarded as great fun. And it was one of those jokes that never wear out.

So it happened that on a certain memorable occasion Ki, suddenly finding himself allotted to walk with her at a cake walk, actually disgraced his manhood by genuine tears.

Happily, however, they were not shed in Ann's presence, and when she met him with a smiling salutation, and took his arm with her best effort at a flourish, there was something within him that felt challenged to a best effort—for in his heart poor Jessekiah was something of a gentleman—and the result was that, amidst uproarious cheering, Ki and Ann, fat, bow-legs, and all notwithstanding, took the cake.

This teased Ki even more than the walking had done. Nor was this all : it brought him suddenly up to the point of revolt.

When he went home that night his frame of mind was altogether unbecoming a Christian, not to say a Methodist.

Instead of going quietly to his cabin and to bed, as he should have done, he walked out upon the levee alone, and with head uncovered in the moonlight, while he mopped off his forehead, he swore that he wouldn't, so help him, "stan' one speck mo' o' dis cornfounded, doggorned, plague-taked nornsense !"

He had wept before he had stepped out into the arena with Ann to walk for the cake, and now, having done his duty fully, manfully, having amiably served as her "pardner" for the remainder of the evening, and courteously escorted her home, having deposited his own portion of the hated cake in the river, he wept again.

When Ki joined his companions in the field next day, there was something in his face which forbade any allusion to the incident of the night before. It was a new dignity, the dignity of a fixed resolve.

As he had walked alone at midnight on the levee after spending his emotion in tears, he had reviewed the situation with a calm scrutiny, and he saw clearly that there were but two honorable ways out of his dilemma.

He could not run away. The world beyond the community of the coast meant little more to Ki than the planet Mars. An open revolt would be a personal insult to the lady in question. To be forever freed from all association with this hated, detested woman, he must either marry—or die.

Life was sweet to Ki. Death, even palliated with the consolations of religion, had never lost its terror to him. Marriage, on the other hand— Ki actually giggled foolishly to himself as he contemplated it as an actual probability—had always been an inviting prospect, and so to-night, sitting alone beneath the stars, he registered a vow—a sacred vow *to marry*.

The resolution had no sooner possessed him, however, than he began to question himself as to whom, of all the girls he knew, he should select.

For one thing, she must be slim. If there was anything that in his present state of mind he hated more than everything else in creation, it was fat. He ran over in his mind the names of the several slender girls of his acquaintance, hesi-

13

tating and chuckling afresh over each at the idea of her actually becoming Mrs. Brown.

The enumeration complete, he found himself sadly lapsing into his old state of indecision. He would to-night, at the toss of a penny—or perhaps it would be better to say at the toss of her head—have been happy to wed any one of seven sweet dusky maidens, varying as to complexion, temper, and general character, but all willowy and slender.

A realization of his irresolution even now, in the extremity of his woe, filled him with dismay, but his desperation had carried him for once safely beyond the possibility of retreat.

If he could not in a moment make up his mind whom he most desired, he could at least resolve that he would not put his foot out of his cabin, excepting to go to the field, until he should decide.

Calmed with this resolution, Ki finally repaired to his cabin, and found forgetfulness in sleep.

A week passed, and another. In the evenings, seated alone upon his door-step, or within the broad crotch of a log of drift-wood that lay embedded in the outer levee beyond his gate, Ki still agonized in indecision.

The threatened failure of the old embankment had last year sent a new levee into the heart of the plantation, and for a considerable distance here it ran close against a nest of negro quarters. Ki's cabin, sitting somewhat apart from the others, at the point of divergence of the two banks, com-

manded an easy approach to both. The low land
between the two levees, a safe play-ground for the
children when the river was low, was now covered
with shallow water.

After a third week of painful indecision, Ki
made a little progress. *He decided that he could
never decide*—and of this decision was born a plan
of relief.

"Look lak I mus' be one o' deze heah reg'lar
Mormondizers, an' want 'em all," he had been
moaning to himself, when suddenly his reverie
began to take shape in this fashion: "Ef a man
go a-huntin' all day, an' can't meek up 'is min' what
bird he want ter shoot, he gwine come home wid
a empty game-bag ev'y time."

Then something within him had seemed to answer. "Yas, an' de bes' thing he c'n do is ter
stay home an' set a trap, an' pray Gord ter sen' de
right bird ter 'im."

It was an inspiration. Ki was so pleased with
the idea that he answered it aloud: "Dat's hit!
Dat's hit! Dat's des what I gwine do. I gwine
buil' me a—gwine buil' me a—gwine buil'—" and
he fell to meditating again. "Gwine buil' me a
fine fancified seat, right out heah on dis ole levee,
side o' dis lorg, an'—an' de fus' gal dat sets in it—
My Gord! whyn't I thunk about dis befo'? De
fus' gal what set down in it gwine be Mrs. Jessekiah Brown—*ef she do lak I say!*"

He was happier than he had been since the cake-
walk. Throwing himself down upon the grass, he

rolled over and over, chuckling aloud. The chair, a quaint affair made of pine saplings, and finished with arms of gnarled twigs, was the work of several mornings, and when at last it was finished, even to the not inartistic braiding of cross-twigs into an easy head-rest, Ki was as happy over it as a child with a new toy.

"Come 'long, Mis' Brown, honey. Teck yo' seat, my love, an' set down," he exclaimed, giggling foolishly as he moved back to his notch in the log, and glanced up at the imaginary occupant of the seat.

He felt almost as if his wedding invitations were already out ; and yet no sooner did he picture any special one enthroned beside him than his mind reverted with a pang to half a dozen others. His only safety lay in the sacredness of his oath. He had sworn, and called on God to witness his pledge, that he would ask the first woman who sat here to marry him, and he would do it.

For the first week after its completion Ki watched the chair from his window with a timorous nervousness, expecting, hoping, and yet fearing at any time to look out upon the future Mrs. Brown.

But a month passed, and she did not come, and although Ki managed to preserve a calm exterior, and had replied to all inquiries as to his retirement that he "had done got tired out o' s'ciety an' had done settled down," he was growing desperately weary of it.

The " settling down " had, however, by slow degrees resulted in a decidedly improved state of affairs at Ki's cabin.

When the little one-roomed hut had been only a place to keep his garden tools, to hang up his saddle, and to " turn in " himself as a last resort to sleep at night, it had been a small matter that the front yard was overrun with cockleburs and " jimsonweed "; that the rank, malodorous gourd-vine that straggled over the remains of last year's bean poles to embrace his mud chimney was a harbor for wasps, lizards, and the brilliant spiders that spun their filmy wheels in every available space. It hadn't mattered that the corners of his room and his mosquito-netting were decorated with this same delicate tracery, and that the high-water mark from the last crevasse had supplied the walls of his apartment with a unique dado of decay—a dado done in low brown tones, with strong stucco effects in green, close-clinging mosses.

It is, possibly, not exceptional that a very startling apparent incongruity should sometimes exist between a bachelor's apartment and the gorgeously-attired gentleman who goes forth from the same to enter the most exclusive inwardness of most exclusive society. A finely feathered he-bird has been known to take daily flight, joining a flock of very high fliers, from a roofless nest of mud and straw and unwashed rags.

It had been enough for Ki to know that the

pine press in the corner of his hovel held in safe
preservation his silk hat, dress suit, and the various delicate appointments of a gentleman's toilet ; that a cake of very strongly scented sweet
soap of a marbleized reddish color lay wrapped
in tin-foil beside a boot-shaped bottle of "hair-
ile" that for potency of perfume put both gourd-
vine and jimsonweed to shame ; and that his varied assortment of scarfs, scarf - pins, handkerchiefs, and the like was safe from wind or weather
in a shell-covered box made by one of his earliest
sweethearts.

Here also were a little folding-comb with a mirror within its handle—a vest-pocket convenience
for last toilet touches at church doors and front
gates—a gorgeous walking-cane, and cotton um-
brella. In fact, as to the matter of toilet furnishings, Ki was quite up to the requirements of a
finished society man, and he had, besides, what he
would probably have called an "innard" grace of
manner. It would have come outward and mani-
fested itself in *mannerisms* if there had been any
chance for it, but, as he himself lamented, "How
kin a feather-bed teck orn manners?"

Ki was too hopelessly fat to cultivate anything
more than the negations, so to speak, of manners
polite. His strength lay rather in the avoidance
of inelegancies than in the attempt to assume impossible graces.

A genial amiability is ofttimes a surer guarantee of social success than a figure of artistic pro-

portions, and yet Ki would have given all he owned or hoped to possess of personal attractiveness for the power to bend at the waist when he lifted his stove-pipe hat.

We have said that during the period of his retreat he had improved the condition of his home. Indeed, when two months had passed, the freshly whitewashed little cabin that sat smiling through a cool green garment of butter-bean and morning-glory vines, in the midst of a riotous mass of sunflowers, hollyhocks, and zinnias, was in no way recognizable as the recent neglected hovel.

While the trap to catch his bird was out upon the levee, Ki, with loving care, was getting the nest in order, and although he was eager at times for his mate, there were moments when the tortures of indecision were distinctly sharpened with a dread lest her coming should involve a life-long regret.

While he had chopped down the mud crawfish chimneys along his garden walk and strewed it with white shells, somehow he had been unable to think with pleasure of any other girl than Hannah Frierson, a willowy yellow maid, tripping up and down the walk; and yet, within the cozy corner of his porch, where he had placed a bench just broad enough for two among the vines, the brown, piquant face of another insistently and bewitchingly met his eye. She who seemed naturally to stand on the little step-ladder to gather butter-beans was a third. And yet another, by a strange persistency, struck his fancy as the dainty creature who should occupy the chair upon the levee. Her delicate, shapely wrist seemed in his imagination just fitted to lie over its rustic arm, and her slender foot would, he was sure, just about rest on the log where he sat.

He somehow had a feeling that maybe—he wasn't quite sure, but maybe—it would be pleasant to lay his hand upon her foot and pat it. Would that be lover-like? He doubted that it was exactly the correct thing to do; and yet, while he sat and looked at the end of the log, the impulse to reach out and touch the imaginary foot resting upon it always came·so irresistibly that he chuckled over the very thought.

Notwithstanding the fact that Ki was distinctly in a courting frame of mind, there were times when he would in desperation have retreated from his vow and started out again, hoping to make his choice, had it not been for his dread of meeting Fat Ann, and *that* he was resolved, with all the hitherto dormant decision of his tardy manhood, he would not do—*no, not if he died*. He hated, despised, abhorred the very thought of her with a morbid intensity heightened by solitude and long-suffering. Even yet, when he recalled the picture he and she must have made as they promenaded before the company arm in arm for the cake, cold chills ran down his back, and he talked bitterly to himself.

"De idee o' dat great big apple-flitter, what

'ain't got no mo' shape 'n a spinnin'-turtle, a-waddlin' by my side—matchin' fatness wid fatness! My Lord! De mo' I ponders on it, de mo' madder an' pervokeder I gits! De idee! A gal what 'ain't got no mo' wais'-line 'n a—'n a—'n *I is!*"

The summer was waning. Ki was now an acknowledged recluse. And though his little home grew prettier and more attractive; though his wages, untaxed by the demands of society, lay for the first time in his life a growing account to his credit; though his chair sat, clover-scented and picturesque, on the brow of the levee at his door, waiting to hold in its open arms the future mistress of the manse; though the nest grew daily more attractive and the waiting mate within it more eligible, never a bird had perched upon the limb prepared to entrap it.

A few of the settled married folk and some of the boys had strolled out, partly from curiosity and a desire for a friendly chat, but as Ki was rather taciturn they had been satisfied to consider this a last idiosyncrasy confirming his bachelorhood, and had not returned.

The girls missed him in an impersonal sort of way; but beaux, real marrying fellows, full to overflowing of direct sentiment, were plentiful, and so were skiffs and fishing-lines and blackberry patches. They hadn't time to think seriously of Ki.

At last it was an evening near the end of September. Ki, dispirited and sad, oppressed with that worst vacancy of the heart, a sense of having no one to care for him, had strolled out, following the old levee to the most distant point of its outward curve, and here he sat down.

He had seen several rowing parties start out in skiffs, and even now, though they were but floating black lines in the distance, he caught occasionally in a breath of wind the sound of laughter mingled with the witching notes of a harmonicon. He was desperately lonely and blue.

The sun was nearly down when at last he rose wearily to go in. He had proceeded some distance when the rustic chair came within range of his vision. The recent sunlight reflected from the river into his eyes embarrassed his sight somewhat, and bright spots were dancing before them, yet in a flash came the impression that there was something unusual in the appearance of the chair. The very idea startled him so that some moments passed before he dared confirm the suspicion by a second glance, and he was so maddened with a sort of stage-fright that he staggered a little when he did finally look again.

It was true. Some one was comfortably seated in the chair beside the log, taking the evening breeze. He could see the flutter of a flounce in the wind as he slowly and falteringly approached, his heart in his throat, breathing hard. Suddenly he stopped, leaned forward, ducked his head down, looked intently for a moment, and, falling like a log, rolled down the inside of the levee.

It was Fat Ann. Let us hope that his recording angel took note of the poor fellow's anguish of soul as, when he reached the bottom, he ejaculated, with a groan, "Good Gord!" If he did, the exclamation was surely not registered as profanity, but was rather entered as a prayer on the credit side of his account.

Ann, conscious only of unsuspicious friendly feeling, seeing him fall, hurried to the spot.

"Fur Gord sake, Brer Brown, huccome you twissen so sudd'nt orf de aidge o' de levee?" she exclaimed, breathlessly.

Ki lay still where he had fallen, at the water's edge.

"Po' Brer Brown done tooken wid a fit! Wait tell I come an' he'p you up," she continued, measuring the difficult descent with her eye.

This was a stimulant. Ki groaned aloud to show that he still lived. If she should come to him, he felt that he would die outright.

The girl, misinterpreting the groan as an indication of serious disaster, hurried to his aid. Somehow, in attempting the steep declivity, her foot slipped.

Whether, sliding like an irresistible avalanche, she carried Ki into the water with her, or whether she rolled clear over him, and he afterward fell in in his effort to rescue her, it is hard to say. Certain it is, however, that when after some time they reappeared arm in arm over the brow of the levee, both bore marks of a recent baptism.

That Ki was passing through another baptism of fire was evinced by the expression of dull despair that had settled over his face, as well as by a suspicion of incoherency in his speech.

Through it all, however, he had never quite forgotten that he was a gentleman and that Ann was a lady. Neither had he forgotten his oath, nor that he was a Christian—and a Methodist.

Now that it was, so far as she knew, all over, Ann, overcome with a sense of the ludicrous, shook with suppressed laughter. Her own effort at control fortunately kept her from realizing that Ki had several times distinctly sobbed, even while he made such polite remarks as he could command to the lady upon his arm.

"I 'clare, Miss—ur—a—Miss Ann, seem lak I los' my ekalubium. Dis heah levee ain't fitt'n' fur no plump lady—ur—a—I means hit ain't ter say fitt'n' fur nothin' but—but billy goats. I trus' you 'ain't fractioned none o' yo' dislocutioms, Miss Ann."

Ann had not yet found her voice. Still trembling somewhat from the shock, chilled with her wet skirts, and a bit hysterical withal, she shook so that when they reached the chair Ki felt impelled, by sheer courtesy, to steady her by laying his hand upon her shoulder as he bade her be seated. Then, moving off, he took his seat, not within the notch at her side, but astride the most distant end of the log.

"I 'clare, Brer Brown," said his guest, finally,

"I sholy is glad ter set down an' wring out my frock." And after a pause : "Umh! Dis heah cheer des fits me, lak you done had tooken my measure fur it. Was you studyin' 'bout me, Brer Brown, when you made it ?"

Ki, looking dazed, only blinked, and fortunately she did not wait for an answer. He sat wiping off his clothing with his handkerchief, while great drops of perspiration trickled down his face, and an occasional quiver like summer lightning played about the corners of his mouth.

Long after there was any need for it he continued to rub his trousers legs and the sleeve of the one arm that had been submerged. He was trying, with all the strength of a resolve grown strong by patient waiting, to bring himself to accept the conditions of his oath. He had prayed over this matter. He had trustingly begged the Lord in His infinite wisdom to send the right woman to him. And there sat Ann—the answer to his prayers—Ann, whom all his manœuvre had been planned to avoid.

After he had wiped his coat and she had wrung her gown until both acts were growing palpably absurd, and the silence was becoming momentarily more painful, Ki ventured to look up at the woman whom he must ask to be his wife. For a moment he was tempted to throw himself backward and roll into the outer depths of the Mississippi. The chill of its waters was still upon him, however, and, shivering at the thought, he turned from it to glance once more at his bride-elect. Of course she would accept him. Who ever doubts the descent of a dreaded and evidently impending evil?

Ki's proposal scene had been arranged for years, and he knew it all by heart from beginning to end ; but that old formula beginning with "Roses red" would never do now. He had fancied that when he should come to the "Sugar is sweet, an' so is you," the dainty little miss might be a trifle coy, and he should have to insist upon it. She might even protest, "I ain't no sweeter'n you is." But if Ann should say so silly a thing to him, he would scream—he felt it.

The moments were passing. He had several times taken off his hat and wiped it, only to be reminded that it had never been wet, and now he did so again.

Finally Ann spoke. "Yo' cabin do look mighty sweet, Brer Brown," she said. "Settin' whar it do, hit mus' ketch all de breezes an' be mighty cool. Ain't it ?"

Ki breathed fiercely. "No, Miss—ur—a—Miss Ann," he replied, swallowing a lump in his throat. "Hit's pow'ful hot ; an' — an' yit" — he could hardly control his agitation enough to speak— "an' yit I's afeerd ter leave de winders open o' nights, 'caze de lizards an' scorpions an' snakes is awful bad roun' my cabin—an'—an' rats ; deze heah grea' big fox-rats. Dey—dey des runs roun' my room at night lak squir'ls in de woods ; an'— an' skunks, too. Dey comes roun' reg'lar, a whole

passel ob 'em, an'—an'—ur—a—bats, an'—an'—
ur—a—squinch-owls, an'—an'—"

"De laws-a-mussy, Brer Brown, you ain't sesso!
An' does you sleep heavy wid all sech varmints
a-swarmin' roun' o' nights?"

"Sleep heavy? Who, me? I—ur—a—I—"
He was gaining time. "I nuver sleeps heavy,
Miss Ann. No, ma'am, I—I nuver sleeps heavy.
Yer see, mos'ly ev'y night I has de nightmares,
an'—an' sometimes I gits up in de middle o' de
night, an' seem lak I 'magines I hears robbers, an'
I des teck a stick an' whup ev'ything in de room.
I taken my bolster one night, an'—an' I beat it all
ter pieces 'gins' de side o' de bed in one o' deze
heah nightmares. I tell yer, I's—I's a dange'ous
sleeper, Miss Ann!"

"Umh! Look ter me lak you oughter have
some light sleeper ter stay wid you, Brer Brown,
an' teck kyar you."

Ki swallowed again. "B-b-but, yer see, Miss
Ann, I's afeerd I mought kill 'em 'fo' dey'd week
up, don't yer see? Dat's de onies' trouble. I des
tecks de load out'n my gun 'fo' I goes ter bed, an'
hides all de knives an' forks—'caze, yer know, a
pusson could job a pusson's eyes out wid a fork—
an' den I des lays down an' goes ter sleep. Dey
does say how sometime' a pusson do load a gun in
his sleep."

"Whee! You all but scares me, Brer Brown.
Don't you nuver git lonesome by yo' lone se'f,
Brer Brown?"

Here was a real opening. His heart thumped so that he heard it. He could hardly speak.

"Y-y-yas, 'm. I—I gits—I gits lonesome some nights—some nights when—when de—de dorgs comes onder my cabin an' howl—an'—"

"Dat's a mighty bad sign, Brer Brown. Is dey cry two times an' stop?"

Ki coughed. "N-no, Miss Ann. Dat what meek me fine it so strange. Dey say ef a dorg howl two times an' stop, hit's fur a man ter die; but—but deze heah dorgs dey keep a-cryin' three times an' stop—three times an' stop; dat's a sho call fur a 'oman ter die. Ef—ef I had air mammy—ur—a—any 'oman pusson stayin' wid me, I'd—I'd look fur ter lose 'er, sho."

"Umh! Dat's mighty strange. How long is dey been comin', Brer Brown?"

"Des—des deze las' few nights—an' I done tried ev'y way I kin ter get shet ob 'em—but dey won't go."

"My Lord! You done got me 'mos' too skeer'd ter go home, Brer Brown. But I mus' travel; hit's gitt'n' late." She rose.

"D-don't—don't go yit, Miss Ann." He began to gasp again. "S-set down. I—I des berginnin' ter talk ter yer good. I—I was des a-sayin'—"

She sat down again. Ki mopped his forehead.

"What was you sayin', Brer Brown? I 'clare, seem lak I kin see dorgs' shadders runnin' 'long de levee. I mus' be gitt'n' home. You done got me rattled."

"I des say—I say, don't hurry yo'se'f—I des—
I des a-sayin'—"

He mopped his forehead again, and his ears,
and the back of his neck.

"I was des a-sayin', Miss Ann, it's—it's awful
hot heah ter-night—des lis'n at me, ' awful hot !'
—I 'ain't got no manners. Hit's pretty toler'ble
warm heah, Miss Ann, ain't it ? I—I des a-pus-
firin' lak rain."

"Hit's cool an' winny ter me, Brer Brown.
Look how de win' blowin' my hat strings. I
'clare I mus' go. Hit's gitt'n' plumb dark."

"B-b-but I gwine tell yer, Miss Ann, dat of
co'se I—I does feel lonesome heah some nights—
an' I—ur—a—I feels—"

If he could only bring in the " Roses red " and
be done with it !

"An'—of co'se—sometimes I craves fur com—
fur comp'ny."

"I knows how you feels, Brer Brown, dat I
does ! I done been lonesome myse'f, an' I knows
de mizry ! I often 'lowed I'd come over beah an'
see yo' fancified cheer, what I done heerd de chillen all talkin' 'bout, an' talk wid you, but I 'ain't
had de cour'ge ter do so, tell dis evenin' I was
a-passin' by, an' I seen Betty Taylor a-settin' heah
lak a queen, a-fannin' herse'f—"

"Wh - wh - wh - what — what you say, Miss
Ann ?"

"I say, of co'se, when I seen Betty Taylor
a-settin' heah in yo' high-back cheer, big as life—

14

howsomever she ain't no thicker'n a stick o' sugar-cane—I 'lowed I could come too."

Ki never knew how he kept from falling at this juncture.

"Wh-when—when is you see Miss—Miss Betty heah, Miss—ur—a—Miss Ann?"

"She was heah when I come—when you was settin' orn de aidge o' de levee. When she got up, I sot down, an' I had des sca'cely tooken my seat when you was tooken wid—wid a some'h'n' 'nother an' done so cuyus. What was you sayin', Brer Brown, 'bout bein' so lonesome?"

Ki was grinning so he could hardly speak. "Who, me? I was des a-sayin'—I 'clare, Miss Ann, what was I sayin'?"

"You sayin' some'h'n' 'bout lonesomeness—"

"Is I? I 'clare I forgits. Who-who-who I say was lonesome?"

"You, yo'se'f. You say sometimes you feels lak— You ain't say what you feels lak."

"I—I 'clare, Miss Ann! Hit's so hot—ur—a—so col'—ur—a—I means ter say hit's so warm up heah ter-night— Look lak I done los' de thread o' my speech, Miss Ann—I—" And he actually giggled outright.

Ann was seized with a sudden panic. She felt sure that a spell of some dreadful kind was coming upon him.

She was afraid to stay, and yet she feared that if she started to go he might seize her, and beat her as he had beaten the things in the nightmare.

She was sure he would presently do something sudden. If he would only tumble down the levee again, she would be relieved, for then she could run and call for help.

It was quite dark now, and growing really chill.

Suddenly Ki sneezed. Starting as if she were shot, poor Ann sprang with surprising agility from her chair, and, facing round, started in a steady trot toward the quarters.

It seems too much that she should have rolled off the edge of the levee a second time, and really it would not have happened but for the darkness and the fright, which blinded her utterly.

Even after she realized that Ki was not madly pursuing her, she had fled in unabated terror from an imaginary pack of howling dogs, rats, and reptiles, fearing at each step the flapping into her face of the wings of owl or bat.

Her second tumble was perhaps a happy accident, for while for a moment it was as if the end of all things had come, she soon rallied, unhurt, to find herself safely in the road leading to her own door.

When Ki realized that he was alone, he threw himself on the grass again, and laughed until he cried.

It was perhaps two hours later, when, gorgeously attired in his dress suit, a zinnia and a sprig of mint in his button-hole, equally polished as to boots and beaver, and redolent of sundry perfumes of the toilet, he emerged from his embowered cottage, and started, clearing his throat and giggling ever and anon as he went, to the cabin where lived, with her mother, the umber lass Betty Taylor. Never once did his courage fail him, never did he falter, never look back. The string of Cupid's bow had been drawn nearly to the point of snapping, but now that it had sprung, the arrow sped without a waver straight to the mark. Looking neither to right nor left, nor behind him, nor yet within, fluttering and giggling only as the arrow whizzes from the very speed and directness of its flight, Ki proceeded to make his first unequivocal declaration of love.

There have been more graceful suitors perhaps than our poor hero. Others there have been more fluent of thought, more gifted in speech, but it is doubtful whether upon the ear of woman ever fell a more ardent avowal than that which greeted the surprised but not offended ear of the nut-brown mayde with the slender slender waist, who was seen in the tender moonlight that night to walk arm in arm with Ki up the levee and take her seat by his side in the rustic chair. And Ki sat in the crotch of the log.

And when he saw that her slim foot rested just where he fancied it would on the end of the branch beside him, he clasped his hands tightly behind his head until he could steady himself.

The announcement of the engagement created

a tremendous sensation on the plantation. The first one to whom Ki personally confided it was Ann. Somehow since his happiness his heart had gone out to her to a degree that was distinctly brotherly.

"I wanted ter be de fus one ter tell yer, Miss Ann," he said, in a tone mellow with friendly feeling, as they returned from the field together, "'caze you an' me's been des, as yer mought say, lak brother an' sister together fur so long—"

Ann laughed. "Dat's des de way I felt, Brer Brown, an' dat's huccome I went up an' sot in yo' cheer las' week ter tell you 'bout I gwine marry, but look lak you sort o' sca'ed me orf."

"How you say dat, Miss Ann? *You* gwine marry! Who — who you 'low ter marry, Miss Ann?"

"Is you tooken notice ter dat little slim yaller musicianer what play de bones at de cake-walk? He come f'om de Teche. He an' me been keepin' comp'ny ever sence."

"What! Hursh! You don't say!"

"Yas, I does say. You been stayin' home so close-t, fixin' up fur Betty, you 'ain't kep' up wid de news. But look heah, Brer Brown"—she lowered her voice—"co'se I knows you's a perfessin' man, an' you gwine do what's right, but—but is you tol' Betty 'bout—'bout dem nightmares?"

Ki hesitated, and there was a twinkle in his eye when he said: "I nuver has 'em on'y in de summer, Miss Ann, an' we don't 'low ter marry tell nex' month; but tell de trufe, I 'ain't kep' nothin' back f'om Miss Betty. But look heah! I's mo' tooken up wid yo' marryin' 'n I is wid me an' Miss Betty's. An' you say ever sence de cake-walk?"

"Yas, sir. He say when he seed me step out so mannerly an' taken yo' arm— But co'se he des run orn ter me dat-a-way."

"Well done! An' Miss Betty say dat same word ter me."

Both laughed.

"Is she? But Betty allus is liked de fat style; but fur me, gi' me de slim style! Hones', Brer Brown, I'd o' give all I owned de night o' dat cake-walk ef you er me, one, had o' been slim. I des dashed out reckless ter hide my feelin's. Ef air one of us had o' moped ur stepped heavy, dey'd o' had de laugh on us!"

"Dat's so; an' look lak de laugh on our side now. Well, Miss Ann, I wushes you joy, an' I shek yo' han'."

"An' I shek yo' han', Brer Brown."

CRAZY ABE

CRAZY ABE

THE suggestions of the place, the hour and the season, were all of repose—the place, the broad, breezy gallery of an old plantation house; the hour, after breakfast; season, the late summer.

The vine-clad gallery, itself an invitation to shade and rest, held inviting accommodations in the way of willow chairs and hammocks, all languidly swaying with an air of nonchalant hospitality.

The after-breakfast hour, usually a contemplative one from which one surveys the day's duties, was here, from the very promise of an idle day which the prospective view afforded, especially an hour of rest.

Gastronomically speaking, it was the interval between waffles and watermelon, while the breeze, with the fragrant coolness of the night still in it, was shaking the lace curtains all over the house, chasing out the breakfast odors, before the little darky in homespun made her first tour with cold water from the spring which she served from her brass-bound bucket, with dipper and dipping courtesy.

How sweet everything was!

There was nothing to dissipate the idea of rest. Even the sewing-machine in the corner of the hall hid its suggestion of labor beneath its cover, and became a holder of palmetto fans, recklessly lending its treadle in a creaking song to any child who cared for the holiday measure.

It was the waiting time on the plantation, the growing season, and, of all nature's activities, what is so restful as the unconscious energy of growth?

"Behold the lilies, how they grow!" So the cotton-fields spreading out before me grew. They toiled not, neither did they spin, but wore an aspect of serene repose, in restful ignorance of the vigor that was transforming their juices into the bone and sinew of the natural body of a giant king of commerce.

Across the fields, the negroes lounged about the doors of their cabins or rolled on the grass, smoking, gossipping, sunning themselves—yielding to the drowsy influences of the hour and the season.

Everything in view was removed from the intense. Even the gleaming plaids of the blacks, in whose costumes we look always for a pronounced bit of color, were subdued into soft tints by nearly a year of weather and wear.

The roses blooming along the walk to the gate were the listless, softly-tinted, faintly-perfumed teas; and from the vine about the gallery hung scattering sweet honeysuckles, bending and swaying — holding no opinion against a breeze too gentle to compel acquiescence, but which played lazily at will with the ever-assenting crêpe-myrtle blooms, the most frivolous little gigglers that ever compromised the dignity of a stately tree.

There was surely nothing that offended me in this first view of the old plantation.

I had come here to rest, and I felt sure I had come to the right place.

The overseer's family, who occupied the house, I soon found to be quiet, uninteresting, and, fortunately, unobtrusive people, who contented themselves with ministering to my material comfort, wisely ignoring the question of my further entertainment.

This gave me just the freedom which I craved, and, in a big square room, with a huge dormer-window looking out upon the roof, I soon found the most delightful of summer retreats where, safe from intrusion, I could read, or think, or dream, undisturbed by the world, the press, or the devil.

As I am a newspaper man, these terms will be recognized as designating the fiends who pursue the busy man of my profession.

Although this old place had belonged to my grandfather, it had passed out of the family, excepting the small interest which I still held, many years ago; and so I congratulated myself that there was probably no person living there now who would feel any special interest in my grandfather's grandson.

To have discovered even a devoted old slave

who would entertain me with reminiscences of my revered grandparents, would have been objectionable as an intrusion upon my rest.

It pleased me better to lounge upon my grandfather's old, heavy mahogany bed—to count the very blue, very double, and very regular roses that bordered its paper tester, and to wonder if he never wished the roses were red.

Was he satisfied with the appointments of this apartment, artistically considered? Was he of the same sturdy sort as the old four-posted, unwieldy bed? I rather fancied the idea that he was, and then it pleased me to observe that the bed was solid and not veneered, as even good old things sometimes are.

These were restful wonderings—restful because there was no danger of their being confronted with answers.

I did, indeed, seem sometimes almost to read a solution of my queries in a certain stern look which I perceived in the eyes of an old, faded portrait of my grandfather, which hung over the mantelpiece, but I soon discovered that this glance of severity was perceptible only from this one point of view. The light from the dormer-window, falling upon my grandfather's face, made him frown upon me whenever, during the day, I lounged upon his bed; but the same eyes beamed with mild approval when, in the opposite corner of the room, I amused myself by taking down from a lofty old bookcase the cobwebbed remains of his ancient library.

Thus encouraged, I found myself frequently pouring over these musty old volumes.

It was when thus engaged that the thought came to me that possibly, in the perusal of these works, I might form some estimate of the mental status of my grandfather; but, somehow, I did not find the old volumes deeply interesting.

As relics, I revered them; and I was pleased to realize that, being bound in calf, they were substantial, like my grandfather's bed, and, I was assured, like himself; but when I opened one of them, and read on its title-page "History of Chronic Phlegmasiæ," I felt that it would be tedious.

I was glad to reflect, however, that my grandfather, who was not a physician, must have been a man of considerable intelligence to have cared for this book.

Perhaps he studied medicine, and treated his own slaves. If so, I wondered if he ever gave them bread pills; but one look at his honest face satisfied me on this point.

He was not a man of shams.

I wondered, then, if his negroes had been subject to "phlegmasiæ," and did he treat it successfully?

All of these, it will be perceived, were surface reflections, so far as the book was concerned.

There were a few Latin books in the collection.

It seemed to me that my grandfather smiled upon me with something like conscious pride as I glanced from the page of " Cicero Delphini " to his face.

The bond of sympathy between us here was again superficial, however. It lay merely in my appreciation of his appreciation of Cicero.

Most of our middle-aged men of to-day spent their college years in the army. I fought under Lee. A man can't have everything. I am glad, however, since my grandfather died before Lee's day, that he knew Latin.

I finally took down a well-worn volume.

Here, I said, is evidently an intimate friend of my grandfather.

I hoped, while I brushed the accumulation of dust from its cover, that this friend might not also introduce himself to me in an unknown tongue, and so I was quite happy when I perceived it to be Fielding's " History of a Foundling."

I had heard much of Fielding's pure English, and so I proceeded with delight to cultivate my grandfather's friend on this high ground of literary excellence.

I am both proud and sorry to say that I did not like this book, and as I glanced frequently from its pages to my grandfather's face, I found myself wondering if he could have sifted this English of all sense and taken it only *as English*.

I confess I found it difficult to do so, and as I progressed in my reading, my grandfather's approving smile grew irritating to me, and so, that I might retain my reverence for him while I familiarized myself with this classic, I crossed the room, and, throwing myself across the bed, finished the book beneath his frown of condemnation, which, of course, I appropriated to the objectionable sub-stratum, which lay ill-concealed beneath a luxuriant but transparent growth of choice words.

My room was never lonely. When I grew tired of the library, or of the grandparental eye, or of a certain enormous hair sofa, with neck-breaking bolsters fitting into its ends, I drew my chair into the cozy little alcove at my dormer-window and dreamily surveyed the landscape.

There was an insinuating young lizard that came every day to my window, and as he nimbly sprang from the wisteria vine that hung about the sill to the brown shingles of the roof, I was amused to see him change his color to suit his support—or, his constituency so to speak—and so I often fell into reflections on politics and various things.

The ways of a lizard have many counterparts in every-day life.

The scene from my dormer-window was extensive, commanding a pretty view of spreading fields in front, while to the right extended cornfields, orchard, and vegetable garden—the immediate appointments of the homestead.

It was from this vantage-ground of vision that I first became interested in Uncle Abe.

Looking in the direction of the cornfields, my

eye naturally fell upon his lonely figure, as he sat from early morning until night on his narrow, vine-clad cabin porch.

The fact that he was commonly known on the place as " Crazy Abe," and was evidently a helpless paralytic, served to label him as an unconscious, semi-animate object, just valuable, in the pretty sketch which my window framed, as a bit of local color.

Knowing that he was the last one of my grandfather's old slaves, I regarded him pictorially as a forlorn and expressive tail-piece to the last chapter of the old *régime*.

Some day he would not be there, and the book would be closed.

This invested him with a sort of pathos apart from his personality.

As I regarded him from my window day after day, I found myself desiring the thing which I had dreaded. I wished that he might recognize me. It would have been pleasant to hear him say: "Your grandfather used to do thus or so," or " your grandmother was gentle, or haughty, or merry." I sometimes contemplated visiting the old man, and knocking at the door of his memory, but the indications were not inviting.

The old woman who tended him pronounced him " clair 'stracted," and assured me that he would " a heap 'd ruther talk ter varmints 'n ter argify wid humans." And so, in my morning walks, I found myself instinctively avoiding his cabin.

Often, as I sat inside my window, I saw him talking, apparently to himself, and his merry laughter floated up to me more than once.

It was to me like the last fitful flicker of an expiring candle.

I found myself growing somewhat sentimental over the old fellow, and had already resolved that I would visit him and try the effect of an introduction, when one morning I was unexpectedly called to his side by discovering him to be in great distress.

Looking down, I perceived that he was weeping violently, while a negro man, rapidly cutting the weeds with a scythe, was approaching quite near the little cabin.

It was curiosity, perhaps, as much as sympathy, which led me in haste to the scene.

As I neared the porch, the overseer stepped forward and explained that "nothing was the matter."

"I have ordered these vines and weeds cut away from the old fellow's porch, and he's making a fuss about it ; that is all," he said.

I glanced at the trembling, weeping figure in the corner of the little gallery.

It was the impersonation of weakness and distress.

"Why do you insist on cutting the weeds ?" I asked.

15

"Why shouldn't I?" was the answer. "The fact is, I have humored the old creature in this nonsense until he thinks he can have everything his own way."

"Humor him once more, won't you?" I asked. "It is a negative sort of indulgence, to say the least of it, and, from his appearance, I hardly think he will trouble any one long."

I gained my point.

"How long has the old man been helpless?" I asked, as we walked away.

"I don't know," he said, "they say he was taken suddenly while ploughing, and that he had been one of the best hands on the place. He was as you see him when I came here four years ago."

"Paralysis, is it?"

"Paralysis. You'll find a few like him on almost all the plantations. We always look after 'em, when they peg out."

On the morning after this, I was sitting in my sanctum, when a little negro girl came to my door, and said, timidly:

"Crazy Abe say how he crave ter see yer, ef 'tain't no trouble; ef yer please, sir."

"'Crazy Abe,' did you say?"

"Yassir. He say, ef 'tain't no trouble; ef yer please, sir," she repeated.

"I'll be there, directly," I said; and, curious to know the meaning of my invitation, I hurried down forthwith.

I shall never forget the picture that greeted me as I approached the old man.

Laughing nervously, while big tears rolled down his cheeks, he extended both his trembling hands toward me.

It was a moment before he could command his voice.

"An' dis is Marse Torm's chile!" he began, finally. "Did I ever 'spec' ter see de day! Bless Gord fur de sight! Set down, honey, set down!"

Mute with surprise, I drew a chair from his room and obeyed.

Leaning forward, the old man surveyed me critically.

"De name an' de voice an' de likeness!" he said, continuing his inspection. "Look like my yo'ng marster done come back f'om de sperit lan' an' stan' 'fo' me ag'in!"

"And so you think I look like my father?" I asked.

"'Tain't lookin' *like* 'im, Marse Torm. Seem like yer *is 'isse'f!* Even ter de name! Look like my heart was stirred ev'y time I seed yer cross de yard; but I 'ain't seed yer close twell now, an' when I heerd yer voice istiddy, look like all my white people riz up like ghos'es an' pass 'fo' my eyes! All night long I been a-studyin' over de soun' o' de voice, an' 'ain't place it, and dis mawnin' I ax Mr. Smiff who you is, an' when he say yer name, I knowed yer was Marse Torm's baby, an' I sont fur yer.

"I knowed yer'd come when I sont fur yer! I knowed yer'd come!"

He here asked me a few questions about my family, which were soon answered.

I was mystified beyond expression. His mind seemed perfectly clear, and his memory was true and strong.

"I driv yer pa an' de bride down ter Camden in de ole ca'yage de day dee ma'yed. How it comes back ter me, a-lookin' in yer face, Marse Torm! Yer see, in de 'vision o' de prop'ty, I fell ter yer oncle Edwin, an' I grieved, 'caze I wanted ter go wid yer pa, 'caze I set de heapes' sto' by him, an' dee lemme drive de ca'yage ter sort o' cornsolate me, 'caze I warn't a-gwine 'long wid 'im. Yer see dem days we had ter trabble a day an' a night ter git ter Camden, an' de big ca'yage goin' froo de woods looked like a cha'yot wid de big lights on de sides, an' heah berhindt come 'long de waggin-load o' niggers dat was a-gwine wid Marse Torm, an' berhindt dat ag'in de waggin-load o' trunks.

"Seem like all de lightnin'-bugs in de woods come out dat night an' swarm roun' us, ter glorify de percessiom wid light. Look like we was travellin' 'mongs' de stars, an' I claimed dat de bride an' de groom was de sun an' de moon.

"I tell yer, dat was a glorious night. Marse Torm call-t back ter de niggers in de waggin dat dee could sing ef dee want ter, an' I tell yer dee made dem ole woods ring! I b'lieve dem lightnin'-bugs come out ter heah de music—dee say varmints got a yeah fur chunes—an' I know, when I fus' sot heah on dis po'ch, dey was a little lizard what 'd come out 'n meander roun' me quick's I'd whistle."

I regarded the old man with increasing wonder. Was this "Crazy Abe," the old creature whom I saw laughing at the winds and talking to himself every day? I remembered his distress of the evening before, and resolved to touch upon the subject which occasioned it, though I approached it with caution.

"I see you have a nice shady place here, Uncle Abe, but isn't it too close for you?" I asked, by way of introduction, as I glanced at the heavy bamboo vine that formed a thick bower about him, while around the gallery grew a dense bed of weeds, conspicuous among them the wild sunflower and bitter-weed.

A change seemed to pass over the old man's face as he answered:

"Dee's all I got lef', Marse Torm!"

I felt sure I had touched his weak point. It was a mistake. His insanity was in some way connected with the weeds.

While I was searching for a diverting remark, he turned his feeble eyes upon me and said:

"Marse Torm, kin I talk ter you?"

"Why, certainly, say anything you choose to me."

"I nuver talks ter nobody, but 'cep'—but 'cep'—

I'll have ter 'splain it out ter yer, Marse Torm. Yer know dee calls me Crazy Abe, an' I 'ain't blame 'em.

"When a ole 'cripit crittur like me *commence* ter teck on ter 'isse'f, hit's 'bleege ter look dat-a-way, but I's pass a keerin' fur de way I looks, Marse Torm.

"I's de same as gone f'om de worl', an' I done set my face todes de far shore, but I gwine tell yer 'bout de way I bides my time.

"Yer see, Marse Torm, I been a-settin' out on dis po'ch, dis is five summers, sence de mizry stricken me in de laigs an' I kyant walk, an' de fus' summer I sot heah, de sperit warn't squenched in me good.

"Seem like I wanted ter git up an' go; an' den I couldn't, an' den I pass froo a long, dark day o' lonesomeness. Seem like I longed fur folks ter come an' see me an' talk wid me, an' sometimes dee'd come, but mo' times dee 'ain't come.

"Yer know folks is got plenny ter do 'dout foolin' wid ole 'cripit folks like me. An' den, when nobody 'ain't come, an' de days come an' go so slow, I couldn't do nut'n but ponder on de ole times; an' whilst I was lonesome like an' sorrow-ful, one day one o' dese heah little hummin' birds come a-buzzin' froo de vines—purty an' little an' shinin'. I d' know how 'twas, Marse Torm, but all on a suddint hit 'minded me ob a little yaller wife I had, when I warn't no mo'n, yer mought say, a boy.

"Hit was so peart an' little, an' nuver stay in one place, an' seem like hit warn't made fur no cage.

"Well, hit sot me ter noticin', an' I'd watch fur it ter come back, an' I call-t it Silvy, ter myse'f.

"Dat was Silvy's name, an' de mo' I studied it, de mo' seem like hit favored Silvy.

"I nuver will forgit de day ole boss bought Silvy an' brung 'er home. Dey warn't a yo'ng buck on de place what had any sense lef', quick 's he looked at 'er, an'—I d' know huccome—but some way—womens is notionate—she tuck me !

"An' Gord, how I loved 'er ! I was clair sp'iled wid she a' choosin' o' me, an' I *com*mence ter speculate 'bout my looks, an' I'd meck 'ten' like I had business wid ole boss, an' meck up all kine o' 'scuses ter go up ter de house, jes' so I c'd peep in de hack-rack look'n-glass an' see Silvy's ch'ice.

"I wouldn't o' let 'er do a turn o' work ef I c'd o' saved 'er, an' when I'd see 'er in de fiel', a-hoein' in de rows wid de big black wenches, an' she so purty an' sweet an' shinin', I 'lowed ter myse'f dat dem little roun' wris'es warn't made ter fling no hoe.

"Ef I could o' did de way I wanted wid 'er, I b'lieve I'd o' sot 'er up in one o' dese heah glass sto'-cases, wid a satin-silk-velveck dress on, an' flung lumps o' sugar at 'er. Yer see, I loved 'er a fancy fashion.

"Well—but, Marse Torm, you's a-gittin' tired!"

"No, no! Go on! I am interested," said I; and in truth I was.

"Well, lovin' 'er dat-a-way, hit nachelly struck my min' ter buy 'er free.

"I jes' longed ter see 'er come an' go, any way de notion teck 'er, an' so I axed boss, an' he was mighty good.

"He see de way I was all bruck up wid lovin' 'er, an' he 'lowed dat he'd meck it easy fur me— dat payin' me fur wuck 'fo' hours an' arter times, I mought buy her free fur two hon'red dollars less 'n he guv fur 'er.

"You see, Silvy warn't much good ter ole marster.

"He bought 'er fur a sort o' house-gal an' hair-dresser, an' dee say she sassed de white folks reg'-lar, an' I don't 'spute it, 'caze she had a lively tongue, git 'er started, an' dat's huccome dee sont 'er in de fiel', an' I reckin boss would o' sol' 'er 'cep'n fur me o' marryin' 'er.

"Ole marster nuver done sech as dat.

"Well, I wucked 'long fur fo' years, an' I had mos' 'nough ter buy 'er, an' I was happy tell I was mos' drunk wid happiness; an' Silvy, she was powerful sot on freedom, an' 'treckly, 'bout dis time, heah come de prormus dat Gord gwine ter sorn us a little baby, an' I was dat mixed up wid joy an' sorrer dat I 'ain't knowed what ter do.

"In cose, I was 'joyed like any human, but I

was sca'ed dat ef boss knowed it, he mought back out o' de trade an' raise de price on Silvy.

"An' Silvy, she was a-hurryin' o' me, yearly an' late, ter wuck an' save ter meck up de money, so dat when de baby come, hit mought come free; an' jes' 'bout dat time, Silvy upsot a kittle o' bilin' water an' scalted her foot, an' had ter lay up in de house; an' yer know, Marse Torm, she 'lowed ter me dat she done it a-purpose, 'caze she knowed dat ef she kep' a-gwine in de fiel', folks was gwine ter talk.

"Well, dat time I had all de price, lackin' twenty-five dollars, an' I knowed I didn't had no mo' 'n 'bout three mont's ter git it, an' so I'd wuck, sackin' cotton seed an' sech, all night, some nights, an' —well, Marse Torm, de evenin' I tuck de money up ter de house, ter ole marster, I 'ain't seed de way I put my foot. Seemed like I was blinc, an' dizzy, an' my cornscience stricken me, too, 'bout foolin' ole boss, 'caze seemed like I was a-stealin' f'om 'im, 'caze I knowed dat he nuver s'picioned 'bout we's baby on de road ter freedom, stid o' b'longin' ter him.

"I b'lieve I'd o' up an' tol' 'im, but Silvy, she'd teck on ef I named it, an' call me a fool an' sech.

"Silvy knowed a heap o' names ter keep a feller down, so I 'ain't named it ter boss, on'y gi'n 'im de money, and he call-t in ole Miss an' de overseer ter witness dee names ter de paper, an' dee signt 'em down, an' I started out wid de free-paper.

"I was proud as de President o' dese Nunited

States, but feelin' sort o' mean 'long wid it, same
's a man mought feel wid a chicken hid in his hat,
on'y wuss.

"Well, treckly I started out, boss, he call-t me
back, an' I see him whisker somch'n in ole Miss's
ear, an' ole Miss she brung me a little bundle, an'
she say: 'Heah, Abe', she say, 'Heah's a little
present fur Silvy.'   An' she ain't said no mo',' an'
when I got ter de kyabin an' me an' Silvy git done
laughin' an' cryin' an' j'icin' over de free-paper, I
'membered 'bout de little bundle what ole Miss
gi'n me; an', Marse Torm, what yer reckin hit
was?   Gord!   Yer could o' heern a pin drap
when we opened dat bundle!

"Hit was a whole passel o' ole Miss's baby-
cloze.

"I tell yer, Marse Torm, my white folks was
Gord's own people.

"Seem like ole Miss was a-sayin': 'You po'
chillen 'ain't need ter hide yer baby; teck it—you
welcome ter it.'

"I jes' nachelly sot down an' cried, I did, Marse
Torm, an' love my white folks mo' an' mo'; but
Silvy 'ain't cried none, on'y jes' count de tucks in
de long dress an' hol' up de lace 'g'inst de light an'
laugh.

"But Silvy 'ain't claim ter have 'ligion.   She
was a proud little gal.

"But I cried good, an' my heart went out strong
ter ole Miss Heah Silvy been wropped up in big
shawls, claimin' ter be chillin', an' mos' a-sweatin'

ter death ter keep de secret, an' a scratchin' 'er so'e foot ev'y day ter keep out 'n de fiel'.

"Well, bimeby de baby come—a purty little yaller gal-chile, jes' like 'er ma, an' I was proud as a king, an' den, one day, ole marster axed me ef I ain't a-gwine ter buy myse'f free, an' I laugh an' say: 'No, sir, I ain't a-cravin' arter no freedom. I ain't nothin' but a reg'lar nigger.'

"I heap'd ruther teck all de extries ter buy fineries fur my two purties, an' I done it, too.

"Well, time passed 'long. Dee say time fly—look ter me dem days like she travel in a blue streak like de lightnin', an' 'fo' I knowed it, de baby was a-stan'in' 'loney, a-holtin' on ter de cheers, an' growin' purtier an' purtier ev'y day, an' 'long 'bout dis time—I hates ter tell yer 'bout it, Marse Torm—'long 'bout dis time dey was a tall, yaller, free-nigger preacher what come ter preach in de Baptis' Chu'ch.

"I 'ain't liked 'im when I fust sot eyes on 'im.

"He was one o' dese heah long-face, long-coat-tail, long-laig, long-pra'r preachers. He was tall an' slim—he was dat slim tell he was narrer, an' sort o' cock-eyed. Look like he kep' one eye on Heaven, an' helt on ter sin wid de yether one, an' he was powerful sot on visitin' 'mongs' de sisters.

"'Tain't no use for me ter talk 'bout it, Marse Torm ; but one night, whils' Silvy was gone ter meetin' at de cross-roads, an' I was a-teckin' kyar de baby, de little gal tuck ter croupin'. All de white folks, an' my own color, too, dee done de bes' dee could, but 'twarn't no use.

"When Silvy come back, an' I heerd her say good-night ter de preacher at de do', she come in an' see de little gal a-layin' in my arms—daid.

"'Twarn't sick mo'n 'bout fo' hours.

"Well, Marse Torm, in cose I was all tarrified wid grief an' bruck up 'bout losin' de little gal, but I had Silvy, an' I blessed Gord fur what was lef'.

"Seem like my sperit was raised ter Heaven, like, an' Silvy look like she got 'ligiouser an' 'ligiouser, an' mo' sot on de preacher, but I 'ain't s'picioned nothin' tell one night she 'ain't come back no mo', an' when I look, I see she done had tuck all 'er cloze an' gone—she an' de preacher claired out in de night.

"I 'ain't nuver follered 'em. He was mo' her sort 'n a black wuckin' nigger like me; but I knowed ef I sot eyes on 'im, I'd o' kill-t 'im, but 'twouldn't o' bettered me none, an' I 'ain't blamed 'er—an' I 'ain't begrudged buying her free, nuther.

"She warn't none o' yer cage birds, she warn't!

"Look, yonner she come!"

I turned quickly. A little humming-bird fluttered, hovered over the flowers a moment, tasting here and there, and was off across the yard to the crêpe myrtles.

The old man smiled as he watched it.

"I 'ain't got nothin' ag'in' 'er. 'Twas jes' in nature. She warn't my kine!" He spoke meditatively, and suddenly his face brightened, as pointing to a little yellow butterfly, he exclaimed : "Look, Marse Torm, yonner de baby ! She comes ter see me mos'ly ev'y day.

"De fus' time I reconnized 'er, hit sot me ter mos' cryin'. I 'membered how I used ter love 'er an' play wid 'er an' dance 'er on my foot ; an' whils' I was a-studyin' on it, bless Gord ef de little yaller thing 'ain't come an' pyerched on my ole daid foot a minute, an' den riz up an' flied back. ter de Kingdom."

"The Kingdom ?" I repeated, questioningly.

"I forgits you don't know, Marse Torm. All my people's done gone inter de Kingdom but 'cep' me, an' seem sometimes like dee's onpatient an' calls me ter come ; an' when I looks over yonner 'cross de fence an' see de corn tassels a-wavin' an' a-beckonin' at me, seem like dee's my folks what done crossed over, an' dat's huccome I calls de corn-fiel's de Kingdom.

"Look at 'em now, Marse Torm, jes' seem like dee's a baigin' me ter come.

"I d' know how 'tis, 'caze in cose dis is all in my min', 'caze Gord's sperits ain't flyin' roun' in butterflies an' sech ; but dat little yaller one what I calls de baby, hit 'ain't nuver is come f'om no place but de Kingdom, an' fly back de same way.

"Seem like Gord was so min'ful o' me in my lonesomeness, like He wants ter lemme see dat de baby 'ain't forgittin' me, but dat she b'longs ter de Kingdom an' 'bleeged ter go back ag'in."

I was assured now that the old man was not insane, and so I ventured to ask, "And what about these weeds, Uncle Abe?"

He laughed. "Oh, dee's all my little fambly—dee jes' nachelly b'longs ter me.

"Silvy an' de baby dee 'ain't nuver 'zac'ly b'longed heah, nohow, an' dee comes an' goes.

"Silvy, she jes' come ter me fur a little spell, 'caze I was strong an' willin' ter holp 'er—same as de hummin'-bird teck what she want an' go—an' de baby, she b'longed ter de Kingdom.

"Gord on'y loaned 'er fur a season. But deze heah little black haids, roun' heah," he chuckled as he said it, "dee jes' nachelly growed up roun' my foots."

The sound of the dinner-bell, and the simultaneous invitation by a little white-shirted, black-legged chap who ran up to the cabin shouting, "Dinner radcy!" put an end to my visit.

I left the old man with a feeling very different from that with which I had approached him; but bidding him good-by and promising to come again, I followed the little negro into the house.

I needed no reminder of my promise to repeat my visit.

Next morning, having seen from my window that he was in his accustomed seat, I stepped over to Abe's cabin, taking him as a treat a dozen of my best cigars.

To my surprise, he declined them, though evidently pleased with the attention.

"No, no, sir," he protested. "Ef I sot up heah
puffin' a *ciggar*, I'd git ter 'lowin' I was white,
sho' 'nough !

"I's sp'iled 'nough now, a settin' up heah ringin'
a bell whensomever I wants a drink o' water,
same 's white folks."

"I've come this morning for some more of
your story, Uncle Abe," said I, drawing up my
chair.

"Yer wants me ter 'splain 'bout all dese yo'ng
black haids, does yer?" Glancing at the weeds,
he laughed as he had done before, but as he began, his face took on a tinge of sadness.

"I tol' yer, Marse Torm, how watchin' fur Silvy
an' de baby comin' an' goin' started me ter huntin'
'bout fur company.

"Well, I has ter tell yer how 'twas arter
Silvy lef' me. I jes' nachelly wilted down, like
—same as a plant de fros' done struck — an',
in cose, I bruck up in my kyabin an' I went back
an' live wid my daddy. He was livin' den, an'
him an' he's wife, an' he's wife's gal, Dorcas—
what she had 'fo' she married my pa—dee lived
togedder.

"I allers call-t Dorcas sister ; howsomever she
warn't no kin ter me, no mo'n our mammy an'
daddy dee married, but we was riz f'om chillen
togedder.

"Dorcas, she was one o' dese heah plain, brown,

straight, strong-arm, strong-han', reg'lar wuckin'
gals, dat go an' come an' 'ain't say much ; an'
when I come home all bruck up, like I was,
Dorcas show dat sense not ter name my trouble
to me ; but jes' look like she 'ain't nuver forgittin'
me, a-men'in' my cloze, an' dee was a-needin' it,
too—'caze Silvy, she didn't had no men'in' ways,
somehow, not sayin' nothin' ag'in' 'er—but Dorcas,
she 'tend ter me same 's a good sister, an' cook
my victuals reg'lar an' nice, ain't nuver guv me
no druggy coffee, and keep my flo' all a-shin'in'
an' white, wid lye she meck in de hopper—she
'ain't use dis heah cornsecrated lye, like Silvy—
an' she jes' nachelly looked arter me, an' when I'd
'gin ter mope roun', she'd meck 'ten' like she ain't
seein' it, an' maybe pop corn ober de fire ob a
evenin'.

"But I was dat se'f-conceited, I tuck it all,
same as I'd teck de sun an' de rain, an' 'ain't see
it, an' a year pass dat-a-way, an' a heap o' de
boys come a-co'tin' Dorcas, but look like she 'ain't
crave ter marry, an' I 'ain't s'picion nothin' tell
one Sadday night.

" Ev'y Sadday night Dorcas kill-t a chicken fur
my Sunday dinner, an' I knowed she sot a heap
o' sto' by dem chickens.

"Well, one Sadday, she done had kill-t all but
'cep jes' two, an' dee was sort o' pets, pickin' an'
eatin' roun' de house, an' know dey names, an' she
say ter me, she say, 'Abe,' she say, ' which is de
purties' hain, Yaller-laig ur Speckle ?' An' I say,

'Speckle heap de purties',' an' 'fo' I knowed it, she done had kill-t Yaller-laig, an' 'ain't kill-t Speckle jes' on de count o' me a-praisin' 'er.

"Well, dat open my eyes, 'caze yer know, Marse Torm, gals dee don't bodder long wid seeh as dat fur no brudders.

"Well, yer know folks kyant grieve fo'ever— dee jes' nachelly kyant do it—an' so bimeby Dorcas an' me, we tuck up an married; an' now, when I looks back, seem like all my life b'longs ter Dorcas.

"She was strong an' kine an' nuver-forgittin', an look like I was 'pen'in' on 'er fur ev'ything 'fo' I knowed it.

"Well, we had a whole passel o' chillen. An' now, whils' I was a-settin' heah, bidin' my time, waitin', yer mought say, an' noticin' fust de hummin'-bird an' den de baby, one day I was a-lookin' up in dis heah vine, an' a long branch seem like hit was a-reachin' ter me, quiet like, an' gentle an' strong, an' I see de vine was a-holdin' de sun out'n my eyes, an' a-temperin' de win' on my back, an' all on a suddint, seem like hit was Dorcas, jes' standin' by my side an' watchin' over me 'fo' I knowed it—jes' de same way I 'skivered 'er in de flesh.

"An' when de vine growed down ter touch my haid, seem like hit was sof' an' strong like Dorcas's han', an' I put it froo de back o' my cheer, an' I baiged 'em tell dee nailed de cheer ter de flo', so's dee kyant breck it orf a-movin' it; an' now it done growed stronger an' stronger, tell I

16

c'n lean my haid ag'in' it, an' seem like hit's Dorcas, hit so stiddy an' 'ain't nuver leave me.

"Well, seem like I was happy wid findin' Dorcas, an' bimeby I *commence* ter notice two o' deze yaller flowers, like yer see yonner, two o' dem. black-face 'nigger-haids' a-growin' on one stem, right heah by my side, an' dee 'minded me ob a pair o' twin babies Dorcas an' me had ; an' f'om dat I jes' nachelly *commenced* ter pick out all our little fambly roun' de po'ch, an' dee comes ev'y year.

"Yer see dat thistle growin' dar, Marse Torm. I was wantin' ter pull it up, 'caze seemed like hit 'ain't b'longed ter my little crowd ; an' I reached, an' reached, an' I couldn't git it, an' I was a-feerd ter ax anybody else, less'n dee mought pull up some o' de chillen, an' so I lef' it 'lone tell de fros' come, an' when de win' commence ter teck it orf, same as goose fedders, tell hit was mos' gone, I knowed hit come ter 'mine me ob a little ejiot chile o' ourn.

"Hit growed up purty an' peart an' fine, tell seem like de blight stricken it, an' same as de thistle-haid go ter de win', all he's little senses look like dee blowed away.

"An' when I knowed de thistle come to 'mine me o' him, I was glad I 'ain't pulled it up, 'caze he's got the same right as the res', an' I knows when I meets 'im in the Kingdom he'll be whole an' soun' like de balance.

"Look at 'im now, Marse Torm.

"He was jes' dat-a-way 'fo' de blight teched 'im."

The old man looked with an expression of simple fondness upon the handsome purple bloom just opening at his feet, and seemed for a moment to lose himself in contemplation.

"What about these over here?" I asked, pointing to a row of pot-plants on the opposite end of the gallery, conspicuous among them a gorgeous red geranium, aggressively brilliant now in its scarlet bloom.

"Oh, dee's de white folks!" he replied, laughing. "Dee's de quality—all but 'cep' dat big rade geranejum in de square box, I calls hit Mr. Meyers!"

He laughed heartily here, and in response to my look of inquiry, proceeded to explain.

"You d' know nothin' 'bout Mr. Meyers, Marse Torm. He was a rade-haid, rade-face overseer what we all had indurin' o' de wah what 'ain't done nothin' but jes' spit terbacker an' cuss.

"I d' know huccome dat geranejum 'mines me o' Mr. Meyers.

"Seem like hit look at me biggoty-fied an' 'ain't hol' itse'f in, an' I don't call it nothin' *but* Mr. Meyers, jes' fur granjeur ; an' some days when de win' strack it an' look like he go ter teckin' on *too 'bove-ish*, I cusses 'im—jes' doggon' an' sech—but I 'ain't mean no harm.

"Some mornin's, when yer hears me a-laughin' out heah, I ain't doin' nothin' but a-devilin' Mr.

Meyers, jes' ter pass de time, 'caze I knows he kyant cuss back, but I 'ain't mean no harm—jes' a-passin' de time."

I looked at my watch and rose to go, expressing, as best I could, my pleasure in the visit, and as I started away I added, hardly measuring my words :

"I hope you'll be better soon, Uncle Abe."

"I ain't sick !" he answered quickly. "I's on'y stricken fur a warnin', and when the time come, I don't look fur no pain.

"Seem like hit'll be jes' de same way as de warnin' come—like now I's heah and now I ain't, but I's radey, bless Gord, whensomever de call come.

"Good-by, Marse Torm, good-by ! Come an' see me ag'in 'fo' yer go. Good-by ; Gord bless yer !"

And a tremulous shake of the half-palsied hand, a smile and a tear were the last I saw of Uncle Abe.

It was perhaps an hour after this that, looking from my window, I saw a crowd, negroes and whites, rushing toward the little cabin, while a voice called out in alarm :

"Come quick ! Crazy Abe look like he done daid !"

I was there in a moment.

It was as he had prophesied.

There had been no pain. The same smile rested on the peaceful face, but the tear was dry. The head, fallen back, rested on the softly matted ten-drils of the faithful vine.

As I approached, a little yellow butterfly rose from its resting-place in the white hair and flew over to the cornfields. I watched the pale yellow wings until they finally disappeared in the waving field.

Stirred by a sudden breeze, the corn-tassels threw up their heads ; long, green leaves raised themselves, like joyous arms, and flapped in the wind.

The figure was finished.

There was joy in the Kingdom.

QUEEN ANNE

QUEEN ANNE

IT was late in the evening, and I was driving
in leisurely fashion over the picturesque road
that lies in Arkansas between the good old towns
of Washington and Columbus. Sensitive to the
beauties of wild nature, as most city-bred people
are, I had enjoyed every foot of my drive, and
now, when a shaft of sunlight from low in the
west suddenly penetrated the wood about me, I
drew rein, that I might enjoy the scene for a
moment.

Autumn tints, barely visible before, seemed suddenly to burst into living flame, sumach, maple,
and sweet-gum glowing with their respective fires,
while here and there a vivid buckeye sent up a
burning torch of scarlet bloom. And behold rev-
elations of life on every side! The *bois d'arc*
hedge, from whence a moment ago came only
suspicious twittering, was now alive with fluttering gray figures.

On a gray branch just above me perched a
plumed squirrel, while a brilliant green snake
twisted himself in and out of a clump of leaves
so like himself in color that no less a detective
than the sun would have betrayed him.

A cloud of autumn leaves, crisped and sere from early frost, rose on a sudden breeze and crossed the road, and lo, as they fell before me, I perceived among them a covey of partridges. Another gust—leaves filled the air again, and when they fell once more, the partridges, too, were gone.

And now, just at my side, leaning against an old charred stump—how strange that I hadn't seen her before !—was a little plantation darky.

Only a "little nigger" standing beside a country road, as natural a feature of the landscape as the *bois d'arc* hedge behind her, or the cottonfield beyond, quite as ubiquitous a variety of life here as the band of guinea fowl that played their metallic music in rivalry with the cow bell's a stone's throw away, or the scrub outdoor hog that upturned a molehill within reach of her arm.

A round little face, black as a raven's wing—a mop of sun-burned hair, red as a fox's brush—a diminutive figure, erect, and in slenderness like a bamboo reed—nervous bare toes that burrow in the sand—a tattered garment of faded homespun—how the sun revealed it all as she stood there in its full glare by the roadside !

"And who is this?" I asked, smiling, as soon as I could recover myself, for in truth the sudden revelation of this near human presence surprised me greatly.

"Name Queen Anne," she answered directly, unabashed and serious.

"Queen Anne! And what are you queen of, pray?" I asked, laughing now.

She looked at me curiously a moment, and shrugged her shoulders.

"I don' know, sir, less'n I des queen o' de wilderness."

Her utter lack of self-consciousness attracted me.

"And what is your majesty doing, wandering out unattended, so late in the evening?" I continued, playfully.

"I d' know nothin' 'bout no majesty," she replied with naïve directness. "They ain't nothin' b'longin' ter me roamin' roun' heah as I knows on. Ain't no pusson heah but 'cep' me an' granny."

Following her glance, I now saw, lying in the shadow of the stump, an aged negress, yawning and stretching—waking from sleep.

"Your grandmother?" I asked.

"Yas, sir. I fetches 'er out ev'y day ter see folks a-passin'. She des foolish in de haid f'om ole age, an' I has ter min' 'er."

The old creature, perceiving me, began a high-noted harangue, unintelligible excepting for the word "bacco," which, with her outstretched hand, served to interpret the whole.

I was sorry to have none of the weed with me, but I threw her a coin, and promising the child to bring some tobacco on my return, I started on.

Before turning into the deep wood beyond, I drew rein again for a moment, and looked back.

There was something in the extreme youth and diminutiveness of this little child, out of sight of human habitation, holding guard over her irresponsible charge, that attracted me rather painfully.

They were crossing the road as I looked back, the old creature supporting herself on the little girl's shoulders.

It was a pretty picture. How vividly it comes back to me to-day!

If this had been all; if I had never come back that way, little Queen Anne and all her unconscious picturesqueness would have remained only a central figure in a casual memory sketch, but as it is, I feel like taking off my hat in the presence of the memory of the simple-hearted child who stood barefoot in the road on that autumn evening.

Business detained me, and it was several weeks before I returned.

Ere I realized my proximity to the spot, I perceived the child standing again in the shadow of the same stump by the roadside.

Drawing from my pocket the package of tobacco, to which I had added some candy, wondering the while if Queen Anne would remember me, I turned to address her, when I perceived that she was weeping.

"Granny done daid!" she exclaimed, sobbing aloud.

Had she discerned a note of sympathy in my

previous interview with her, that she waited here to tell me of her sorrow?

I was much moved by the insignificant, grief-stricken child, and exclaimed, impulsively, "Why, why, why, I am very sorry. And what are you doing with yourself, child?"

"Marse John seh he gwine look out for a kine pusson to teck me—you seems lak a kine pusson. Does you know air kine lady wha' need a handy lill gal ter wait on 'er?" Thus, between sobs, she told me why she hopefully awaited my return.

I did know a certain kind lady at home, and a certain baby who needed just such service, but yet I hesitated.

What did I know of this wild, wayside weed? What did her guardians know of me?

"And who is this 'Marse John'?" I asked, evading the appeal.

"He we'all's new boss. He seh he'd teck me 'issc'f, but he's one o' deze heah ole-yo'ng-bachelor mans, wha' ain't married nur nothin'—dey don't need no handy pusson roun' 'em. Yon' 'e come now!"

Glancing down the road I perceived, approaching, a man on horseback. He was apparently young, though his hat was drawn down so as to obscure his face.

Something strangely familiar in the pose of the man attracted me, and when he came up, halting in the shadow of the buggy, he raised his hat.

"John!"

" Ben !"

How delightful are these unexpected meetings !

My room-mate at college, my chum, my best-beloved boy-friend, John Goodwynn, was at my side, looking into my face, grasping my hand.

When last I had heard of him, five years before, he held a professorship in —— College, and had pledged his life to science.

Explanations came quickly.

" Eyes gave out—inherited this old place—came here for rest—but pshaw !—when a man loves a thing—going up to the house now for a microscope—digging a pond for my cows—I find study for a year. Come on up to the house, old boy ; got a lot of curios there. The sight of you is better to my eyes than a year's rest. Married, are you—you wretch ?"

" Yes, and happy as June-bugs, we three !"

" Three ! Ha, well, and this third party ?"

" Ben, junior, of course, and in need of a handy little pusson, des like Queen Anne here, to wait on him. You see I've been making friends with her majesty."

" Say, Ben, are you in earnest about that ?" he asked, as we started to the house, " for if you are, it's all right. The little pickaninny hasn't kith or kin to interfere, and I know she'll be safe with you, old fellow."

And so, after talking the matter over, it was decided.

And this is how we got Queen Anne.

The child never appeared so diminutive as the day I led her in to meet my wife.

"Allow me," said I, with mock ceremony, "to present to you her Majesty, 'Queen Anne,' queen o' the wilderness, alias 'a handy lill gal to wait on a kind lady!'"

Taken by surprise, but in no wise abashed, the child responded with a ducking courtesy, as she said, "How yer come orn, lady!"

My wife laughed outright, though she cordially extended her hand, and pleasant relations were forthwith established.

Our year-old boy, with childish intuition, held out his arms to her at once, to her infinite delight, and from that moment never had veritable queen more loyal subject than he.

Queen Anne's resources as an entertainer were unfailing, and her fund of song, dance, and story as inimitable as inexhaustible.

The religious instinct, so strong in her race, seemed to dominate her every other sense, and, though gleaned from ignorant and superstitious teachers, her ideas had all a substratum of truth.

Most of her plays were artless imitations of religious services, of one sort or another.

I recall a verse which seemed a favorite with her, and which she truly excelled in singing. It ran like this:

> "Yo'ng chillen, you should love de Lord,
>   An' keep yo' giarmints clean,
>   Fo' fear dat you should fall in sin—
>   An' jedgmint roll between."

This seemed essentially an emotional performance, and begun in a low, vibrating tone, rose tremulously and swelled to the last line, when all things awful seemed in order, her hands began to clap, body to sway, and when "jedgmint rolled" from her lips, over she rolled bodily— limp, insensible.

There was no ridicule in this. It was mere imitation, pure and simple.

Her wide-eyed wonder over the novelties of the city was as amusing as refreshing ofttimes, and her alacrity in grasping new ideas led her occasionally into queer little mistakes.

On the occasion of her first receiving a card from one of two lady callers, she turned immediately to the other, and asked, "Did you come in widout no ticket?"

A favorite pastime with her was standing at the gate "choosing ladies" from gayly dressed passers.

Standing thus, one day, she called to the servant next door, "Oh, Tildy, is y'all got a pianner over to yo' house?"

"Yas," came the answer, "We got a upright piano. What sort is yo' madam got?"

"We'all got a downright one," she replied, unhesitatingly, but quickly slamming the gate, she indignantly came in.

One warm day, my wife having taken her down town, gave her a glass of soda-water.

She had never seen the effervescent drink before, and drank it with childish delight, but in a few moments she grasped my wife's arm in terror.

"Oh, Miss Mar'gret, I sho'ly is pizened!" she exclaimed. "Dat fizly stuff is a-shootin' me in de nose!"

But why recall more of the little girl's blunders? She was with us for three years, and we never saw the shadow of a lie in her honest black face, nor touched a disloyal chord in her affectionate heart.

"Miss Mar'gret" was in all things her ideal lady, "Marse Ben" her model gentleman, the baby her constant loved companion, I had almost said her idol.

One day our baby waked up with flushed face, and the following morning the doctor said that dread name, "scarlet fever."

Unwilling to have her unnecessarily risk contagion, we sent Queen Anne to a neighbor, though she pleaded piteously to remain.

On the fourth day, the crisis of the disease was approaching, and the doctor's cab was at the gate many times.

While we sat in the early twilight, anxiously watching the little sufferer, the door opened so softly that we did not know she had entered until Queen Anne knelt at the cradle between us.

"P-l-e-a-s-e, Miss Mar'gret, don't sen' me away," she begged. "I 'ain't nuver is disobeyed you befo', an' I ain't afeered."

We could not send her back. No one would have taken the risk of receiving her.

And so she stayed. She was but a little child, and in an hour was fast asleep on the floor, but during the long days of tedious convalescence following she was untiring in her childish devotion.

The first evidence of returning consciousness that our baby gave was in following her with languid eyes about the room, even before he raised his feeble arms to her.

He was playing about the room when Queen Anne took the fever.

We nursed her as we had done our own, but the doctor said from the first that there was no hope.

It was pitiful to hear her laugh aloud in her delirium, the same gushing laughter that in health told of a happy heart, and the little convalescent at her side would echo it, delighted, and perceiving our serious expressions, looked in questioning wonder from our faces to hers.

She had been in a stupor all morning of the day she died, and in the evening, while we sat watching her, she started up suddenly, a bright smile illuminating her face as she began feebly to sing her favorite song :

"Yo'ng chillen, you should love de Lord—"

Her voice broke several times over the words, "keep yo' giarmints clean," and her breath came slowly.

We opened the window to give her air, and a last ray of the evening sun covered her for an instant, and when it went out it carried with it the pure spirit of little Queen Anne.

She had gone with clean garments into the Master's presence.

CAMELIA RICCARDO

CAMELIA RICCARDO was a belle in her set.

If you had seen a picture of her fair face, separated from its surroundings, you would have said she might have been a belle in any set; that is, if soft black eyes, cheeks like damask roses, hair long, black, and braided, and lips made up of rosy curves, go to constitute that feminine attraction commonly so called. Taken with the limitations of a most circumscribed environment, however, her possibilities of "belledom" narrow down to a single set; and that this "set" was rather far down in the social scale, we perceive at a glance by the very tokens that augment both her attractiveness and her opportunities within this limited circle.

Could anything be more picturesque than her unconsciously æsthetic dress of red merino, shrunken through constant washing to undue shortness of waist, and lengthened, regardless of aught save modesty, by a flowered flounce of antique design, while about her neck gleamed the gaudy colors of a brilliant green-and-red figured cotton kerchief? Could anything be more piquant than her ever-changing attitudes, each expressive of some vivacious emotion, and each a marvel of uncultured grace? At a distance of several feet to left, to right, and above her, hung, in artistic alternation, orange-branches fruit-laden, pineapples, bananas, plantains, cocoa-nuts, and every fruit that lends itself to suspension by stem or hair; while beneath these lay, stacked on shelves in pyramids or ranged after the fashion of mosaics in conventional designs, a tropical profusion of the smaller fruits.

The fruit-stand was hers, and she was belle—of the French Market.

The elaborate decoration of her stall—the prettiest in all the market—was her own handiwork, and if you said one day that the arrangement was perfect, on the morrow you would think it plain, in contrast with the new design of the morning.

And she was smart! Ask the butchers in the market or try to take advantage of her in a trade! She would sell to half a dozen customers at once, giving each his correct change, while she smiled on a seventh; and no one of them all would pass on without receiving a twofold favor, *lagniappe* and a smile, either of which would insure his return. If you but stopped to look at her oranges, she threw two or three into a dainty paper sack and put it confidingly into your hands, while the pretty lips said—in a voice as musical as an ideal "tra la !"—" Fi' cen' !"

Did you hesitate, another orange was recklessly

dropped in and the same voice said "*lagniappe*" in two more music notes and with an air that seemed to say, "Since it's you!" You bought the oranges, of course ; or, if you didn't, the man behind you did, and so—what was the difference?

Diagonally across from Camelia's stand was that of a young Sicilian, Immanuel Prebasco by name, known throughout the market as "Dago 'Manuel," to distinguish him from a fellow-countryman of the same name, who "would fight any man who called him a Dago." The other one was an "Italian bawn," he would have you know, and would "tich-a you weeth-a wan *blague eye* who you call-a wan-a Dago !"—as he was wont to say upon provocation ; and his sturdy fist, raised menacingly, gave emphasis to his threat.

This 'Manuel was not so proud. He often said, with amiable philosophy : "W'en some*body* call-a me wan-a Dago, s'pos-a I break-a he's head—w'ad's the differend? I am wan-a Dago, all-a same !" And his lounging attitude, as he yawned and stretched himself, exemplified with equal truth the genuineness of his sentiment.

Dago 'Manuel's one strong point was his love for Camelia. She was his vision of the night, his day-dream ; and, unfortunately, half his days were spent in dreaming, for his business partook of the gentle spirit of his philosophy. It was comfortable, but it was slow. Needless to say, 'Manuel was lazy. Basking in the sunlight of accidental propinquity, he lived happy days in gazing fondly upon the materialization of the image of his dreams, and took no thought for the morrow. Camelia was near him—it was enough. He could even talk over the heads of her customers to her, *when she had time to listen*, for, it must be understood, she was a woman of business.

"Loan-a me wan-a bunch-a banana, 'Manuel!" she called out to him one morning. "I am all-a sell oud!"

"Take-a my whole shorp!" he answered, and, lowering his tone as he hung his best bunch up in her stall for her, he continued, tapping the bosom of his checked flannel shirt: "Take-a the boss too, eh, Camelia?"

"W'ad I wan' weeth-a you, 'Manuel?"

He leaned against the end of her stall on his folded arms, getting his handsome face very near hers, as he answered: "I lorv-a you! Tha's nod-a good rizzen fo' mague you wan' me, eh, Camelia?"

She stepped aside to serve a customer, but was soon back again. It was late, and the morning rush was over.

"'Manuel, I wan'-a ass-a you sometheen," said she. "You theen thaz a good-a rizzen fo' me to marry weeth-a you?"

"'S the *bez* rizzen, Camelia!"

Another customer came and went, buying more of the borrowed bananas, but Camelia had soon resumed her place. The subject seemed not very distasteful to her.

"You say thaz the *bez rizzen*, eh, 'Manu*el?* If thaz the bez rizzen, then I muz-a ged marry weeth abou' twenny-fi' young mans. Every wan mague me thad *sem rizzen!*"

She shrugged her shoulders and laughed ; but 'Manuel frowned visibly and straightened himself, as he replied : "Thing you god-a mo' senz, blif everytheen all-a them fool-a mans tell-a you, Camelia. God-a no business tell-a you sometheen ligue thad !"

"Ees thad so, 'Manu*el?* You theen thad business ees just-a fo' you, eh ?" And she ran off, laughing, to meet a crowd of buyers ; and the coquette was for the moment merged into the keen little woman of trade.

'Manuel was out of spirit. He strolled moodily across to his own stall, hesitated in front of it, then, languidly selecting a specked apple from a picayune pile, threw it, with indolent force that told of reserve strength, across the levee. It rolled and bumped and bounced along the wharf until suddenly, disappearing in a hole in a broken plank, it fell into the river below. Another followed, and another, all sharing the same fate.

"Throw-a yo' prorfit in the riv' poody straight, eh, 'Manu*el?*" said a neighbor Dago, by way of pleasantry.

" 'Manuel ees-a good-a short, yas ! Keel every time-a ! Blif 'e ged mo' ridger shoot-a dork 'n sell-a banana," another added, laughing.

'Manuel was in no mood for retort. Folding

his arms, he strolled leisurely around to the opposite side of his stall, abstractedly re-arranged a row of pyramids of black-edged bananas, and finally, drawing out from under the lowest shelf a box of lemons, he seated himself astride its extreme end, so that its contents were beneath his hands ; and now, taking their stained wrappers from the decaying lemons, he proceeded deliberately to re-wrap them in fresh papers. It was the work of an hour, during which time he rose occasionally, exchanged a pile of bananas for a nickel, and returned moodily to his task.

Finally, having finished, he pushed the box back with his foot, and calling to a neighbor, "Mine-a my shorp for-a me !" he strolled through the market and seated himself on the last of a row of stools at a coffee-counter.

It was near noon on Sunday morning. The half-past eleven-o'clock bell had rung nearly half an hour ago. Butchers on all sides were scraping stalls, opening ice-boxes, and packing up, preparatory to leaving when the noon gong should sound its command. A few who did not care to wait for the chance custom of tardy marketers, had already closed their shops and were hurrying away.

Camelia had cleared and boxed in the lower shelves of her stall, and piled the remaining fruit on the top, intending to go home as soon as her little brother should come to take charge. She sat now, with a wooden cigar-box, her "cash drawer," open upon her lap, while she hastily counted the receipts of the morning.

"Severty-fi', eighdy, eighdy-fi'," she counted aloud, as she added nickels to the sixth dollar of fractional coins that lay in her red-merino lap. She was so intent on counting that she seemed not to notice that a man had seated himself at her side. When at last she did look up, however, it was evident from her unchanged expression that the man was no stranger.

"I thing, me, yo' lill han' is too pritty fo' coun' money, Camelia," he said ; "'twas nod made fo' thad."

"Tague-a yo' han' a-way, M'sieu François! I show you terregly for-a w'ad my han' ces mague!" and she raised her palm threateningly. "You mague me *fo*'gid all-a my cound," she fretfully added.

"I know yo' coun', lill gal, five dolla' an' eighty-five cen'. I mague, me, deze mornin', nine'y cen' more as you, on nutting bud mutton chorp. Al-togedder, deze week, mague 'ondred an' twenny-five dollah cleah prorvit." And he rattled the silver contents of a little white canvas bag and laid it at her side.

"I theen-a you muz-a be gedd'n verra reech-a, M'sieu François."

"I got 'nough, theng God!" he answered, and then he added, tenderly, "Got 'nough *fo' two*, Camelia! W'ad you say?"

"Well, of coze I say geev-a me wan-a 'alf,"

and she playfully laid her hand on the canvas
bag.

His head bent lower.

"You can 'ave 'alf, lill Camelia! H'only the
'alf w'ad you tague muz draw wan prize, an' you
muz 'ave to tague the prize ad the sem tam!"

Camelia seemed very obtuse. "Tha's-a mo'
bedder yed. *W'as-a* the prize, M'sieu François?"

The Gascon rose and looked about him. There
was no one near. He made a profound bow, and,
with his hand pressed against his breast, said im-
pressively: "François Leboeuf, ghrade-ghran'son
of Alphonse Leboeuf, w'ad 'ave that sem stan' in
the Frenge Moggit w'en General Jackson fighd
wid doze cotton-bale, *h'offer 'imselve to you!*"

"W'ad I god-a do weeth-a Genera' Jackso'?"
she answered, pettishly.

"N-u-t-t-i-n-g! I h'only wan let you know *oo
eet ees* w'ad wan' marry wid you."

"Of coze, M'sieu François, I know you ees
wan-a gread man! I know you ees the fines'-a
man een the Frenge-a Mogged, bud— M'sieu
François, you know some-a-theen?"

"W'ad ees thad, lill Camelia?"

"You don'd-a *sude me*, M'sieu François!"

The Gascon was furious. "Thaz all you god-a
say to Jean François Leboeuf, w'ad 'ave so far
*fo*gid ees phride to h'ass you marry wid eem?"

"Thaz all, M'sieu François. Thaz-a the only
rizzen I won' marry weeth-a you. 'F I thoughd

you would-a sude me, I would just-a soon marry
weeth-a you 's weeth-a some orther mans."

Her tone was gentle, apologetic, humiliating.

"Thing w'ad you say ! 'Tis yo laz chanze, Camelia ! The ghrade-ghran'son of Alphonse Leboeuf *don' wan' be fool wid, no !*"

"I don'-a fool weeth-a you, M'sieu François.
'F I thoughd you would-a sude-a me, I wou'n care
northeen 'boud-a Genera' Jackso' an' doze cotto'-
bale w'ad fighd weeth-a heem. Would marry
weeth-a you all-a same."

"Sacra— W'ad the dev' ! W'ad you talk
aboud, Camelia ? General Jackson an' doze cotton-bale *'ave nutting to do wid me !*"

"Then for-a w'ad ees you spik aboud them
every time you ass-a me marry weeth-a you ?"

"'Tis my phride ! Il'all doze family of Leboeuf 'ave ghread p-h-ride."

Camelia rose, tied her hat-strings, and, in the
most unemotional way possible, said : "My money
ees all-a cound, M'sieu François, an' my brorther
ees - a come. Goo' - by !" and, quietly turning
away, she left him—left Jean François Leboeuf,
the richest butcher in the market, standing, in the
midst of his harangue, as she would hardly have
left the humblest suitor—left him rejected—indignant.

He stood gazing after her a moment, muttered
something about "the dev'," but finally, recov-
ering himself, he shrugged his shoulders and
laughed—actually laughed, as he drew from his

breast-pocket a package of cigarettes, lit a match
with one stroke down the side of his trousers,
puffed once, twice, and walked off.

Besides being the richest, François was also the
handsomest butcher in all the market. Tall, dashing, heavily moustached, and be-diamonded, he
was as thoroughly lionized in his set as—an English cotton-buyer or a popular leader of the german in another. "Monsieur François" seemed to
his admiring neighbors to have all the elegancies
of a man of the world. He threw into the open
basket of the Sister of Charity, who paused at his
stall on her daily rounds, cutlets that would have
sold for much, with a reckless nonchalance that
must have delighted the ghost of his "ghrade-
ghran'fodder," and made his soul repose in peaceful pride. Men who have grandfathers of whom
they are proud should always give to the poor
with a loftiness of mien that makes the gift seem
to be reminiscent of generations of bounty. Monsieur François realized this, and, in a different
way, the Sister of Charity realized it too from
her opposite standpoint, in the less blessed office
of receiving. She, at least, realized something
which made her smile very appreciatively and
bow very low, as she did not smile and bow to
the rest of the butchers. Whether it was the
presence of greatness which she perceived in the
oft-resurrected *grandpère*, at which she smiled, as
does the babe who sees an angel in its sleep, or
whether she was sordid and earthly enough in her

heavenly vestments to defer thus to the greater quantity and better quality of the alms, we cannot say. The thing visible was more meat, more smiles—but let us not judge. Monsieur François's rôle in it all was that of My Lord Bountiful, and it was becoming to him.

There were other aristocratic points, too, about Monsieur François. For one thing, he lived in his own house, an inherited home, and — his sisters played the piano. No firemen's ball or Sunday picnic of the French quarter, that thought much of itself, was *en règle* without his name on one or two of its important committees. Those of his *confrères* of the market who enjoyed the honor of knowing him socially considered him somewhat incomplete as to appearance without a badge of some such distinction on his breast.

Camelia Riccardo was not in his set. She lived humbly, very humbly, in a lowly-squatting, heavily-shedded oyster-shop, near the market. Its two windows, one of which was nailed up for the accommodation of inside shelves, looked out from under the shed roof like a pair of bad eyes from a scowling face, which seemed to bear a family resemblance to the Riccardo *père*, who was one-eyed, dark, and grim.

Besides selling oysters and fruit at home, Nicholas Riccardo peddled vegetables and small fruits from his wagon through the streets, but there was a pathetic languor about all he did. It was pathetic in its opposition to anything like enter-

18

prise, in its contempt of success. You caught it in the minor key in which he drawled out: "Swee' po-ta-ders—ten—cen'—a—buck-e-e-t;" in the slow, rickety movement of his unwashed wagon-wheels; in the sunburnt, unkempt coat and mane of his uncurried pony.

Camelia had the energy as well as the beauty of the family, and since she had gone into the market as bread-winner, they were seeing better days. Still, they were poor. Their front room, festooned with strings of garlic and pepper-pods, and furnished with counter and shelves, was shop, restaurant, and parlor combined. The corners of its floor were filled with piles of onions and potatoes, and as you approached its one door, you were greeted with the smell of garlic. It was like the father's breath. Outside the door was the fruit-stand, and here, tending shop, while her father took his *siesta*, Camelia spent her afternoons. If sales were slow, and they generally were, she filled the intervals industriously, knitting the broad cotton lace that adorned the Sunday frocks of the entire family feminine — her mother, self, and five little sisters.

Every one in the market knew that François was not the least ardent of Camelia's suitors, and he was pronounced her "bez chanze" by all. There was that in the manner of this eligible *parti*, however, which offended Camelia: it was a lack of deference. She could have defined it in no better way than she expressed it to himself, when she said, "You don'd-a sude me."

He *did not* suit her. Dago 'Manuel, on the contrary, was all respectful devotion. He worshipped her. The day after her rejection of François, 'Manuel came and talked to her again. He hated his dashing rival as only those who love can hate.

"Seem to me, Camelia, thad-a fool Gascon's god plenny cheek, yas—talk every day weeth-a you," said he, when for the first time that morning he found her at leisure.

He had strolled across to her, as was his wont, and stood now lazily pressing the blade of his penknife in and out of its handle against the end of her stall. He spoke with marked indirectness, gazing into space—an uncultured way of approaching an embarrassing subject by an assumption of carelessness.

Camelia took the cue. She could be indifferent, too. Seizing an improvised dust-brush—a bunch of turkey-tail feathers tied together—she began in nonchalant manner to dust the top rows of fruit, while she replied:

"'S-a very nize young man, 'Manu*el*. 'S-a very ridge-a."

'Manuel lifted his glance from space and focused it directly into her face as he said: "Ridges don' mague some*body* 'appy, Camelia!"

She stopped dusting, folded her arms, and, tapping her left shoulder nervously with the brush, said slowly: "Know sometheen, 'Manu*el?* Thad-a

man wa's goin'-a ged marry weeth-a me, 's god-a
mague plenny money, yas !"

She even ventured to look into his face, as she
added : " I am *ti*', me, of bein' po' !"

'Manuel was almost savage now as he asked :
" You goin' marry weeth-a François, Camelia ?"

She dusted her own skirt - front abstractedly
with the turkey-tails as she answered with naïve
coyness : " 'S god-a nize houze, 'Manu*el!* Sez to
me, sez, ' Camelia, I goin'-a geeve-a you wan-a fine
piano.' "

" Piano ! Holy Sain' ! W'ad you goin'-a do
weeth-a wan piano, Camelia ?"

She laughed. It *was* ridiculous. Dropping the
duster on the shelf, she raised both hands and
looked at them, turning them over, showing now
their dimpled brown knuckles and now the red
palms.

" Sez to me, sez, ' Camelia, yo' lill-a han' ees too
pritty fo' coun' money. 'S just-a nize fo' diamon'
ring an' a play piano.' "

'Manuel scowled. " 'F 'e say some-a-theen ligue
thad to you 'gain, 'm goin'-a *kill 'im!* 'S god-a
no business loog ad yo' han'."

She had gone far enough. With a pretty
movement, she lay her right hand close beside
'Manuel's, that rested its dark length now on the
edge of her stall. His looked ugly, sinewy, masculine, *strong*, against the plump little one beside
it. She held it there a moment in silence ; then,
regarding 'Manuel with a strange, half-serious air,
she said :

"Thing yo' han' loog-a mo' stronger than-a mine, 'Manu*el;* bud thing mine mague-a mo' money than-a yoze."

'Manuel made no reply, and she continued: "Seem to me, 'Manu*el, thad* han' muz-a nod̦ egspeg *theze-a wan* to work for a-heem!"

"Fo' God's sague! W'ad-a you talk, Camelia? Theez-a han's willin'-a work fo' thad-a wan! Tol' eem so, tousan' o' time!"

There was silence for a moment. Finally Camelia spoke again. "W'en *thad-a* han' beat *theze-a wan* mague-a money, *can 'ave it!*"

Then, laughing and blushing as if she had said too much, she ran off to the other end of her stall. But 'Manuel had caught her serious tone. He followed her with eager eyes, as one dazed, for a moment; then crossed over to his own stand.

Later that day François came again and talked with Camelia. He was in love with the beautiful girl, and, besides, her indifference piqued while it surprised him. Camelia, nervous and excited over the thing she had just said to 'Manuel, now flirted recklessly with the Gascon.

'Manuel looked at them, and saw, but did not perceive, them. His heart was too full of new sensations to admit a jealous pang. There comes a time to most of us—and woe to him to whom it never comes—when we first seem to meet our *Selves,* face to face; when we are humiliated and confused by the contrast between this real self and the ideal self that had made us self-respecting.

In our consciousness of endogenous growth, from the heart outward, we had felt sure of our development, for had not our hearts gone out of us with each aspiration? As the banana-stalk, conscious only of the perfect leaf sent heavenward from its heart, is shocked when it beholds its garment of rags mirrored in the stream, so we, in this first startling interview with self, are chagrined at the ultimatum of our heart's best impulses. We blush to see that they had scarcely risen above our heads before they were riddled by the first passing breeze, and the ideal character in which we fancied ourselves clothed is but a wind-riddled, rusty fringe of broken resolutions.

'Manuel had no formulated standards. He had not so much as a vague conception of an ideal, and in this first moment of self-consciousness—of real living—he could not have given his experience a name. He only knew suddenly that he was a lazy, miserable, good-for-nothing dreamer, and he did not know this quite clearly; yet this knowledge, imperfect as it was, this picture, darkly seen, of his real self, was quickly offset by another—a *possible self*—the self whose manliness Camelia had challenged; and thus, from his first introspection, began to evolve his first ideal—an ideal with strength corresponding to the weakness which he saw in the real picture.

He sat with his back to the market, facing the river, and there was a strange new look in his classic face. He held his strong right hand out before him, opening and closing it with such force as to bring all its powerful muscles into play. Then he stretched out his long, sinewy leg, doubled his fist and struck his hard, muscular thigh, as he muttered between his clenched teeth:

"My God! My God! The dev' ain' got no shame! 'F I was a *man*, I wou'n-a had-a face to lorv' 'er! Gred, big, lazy loafer! W'ad for some*body* ain'-a *kill* me? My God! I swea'—yas, I swea' *am a man!*"

Then he suddenly rose to his feet, and, looking neither to right nor to left, walked out on the wharf toward the river, leaving his fruit-stand without guard. He was living his first joyous birth-moment of spiritual life—the life that was stirred within him by one glimpse of a woman's love! What were material values in a moment like this—the loss of a customer more or less? Camelia loved him—loved him as he was—for what he might be.

He continued his walk until he reached the river's edge and there stood, looking down upon the deep eddying water and seeing nothing. He recalled Camelia's words; saw again the love-look that had risen unbidden to her eyes in one unguarded moment; saw the little hand that lay beside his; heard again her challenge, her promise! Tears rose to his eyes. "I swear—I swear! Before God, I swear!" These were his only spoken words, and here, alone with his heart, he spoke them in Italian.

He lingered a long time at the water's edge ; when he returned to the market, Camelia had gone, and he, too, gathered up his fruit and went home.

Next day 'Manuel did not appear in the market, and on the next his stall was empty. He had come in the evening with Raphael, his young cousin, a lad of thirteen years, and taken away all his remaining stock in trade. He had made no explanations. He lived "away up in Bouligny," several miles above the market, and his coming or going was not deemed of sufficient importance to warrant a journey of inquiry thither, though there were surmises in regard to his absence, and jests—enough of them. Days passed, and yet he did not come, and everybody laughed and looked at Camelia. François waxed especially facetious over it, and one morning he perpetrated a joke at the expense of the absent, which caused no little merriment, and threw Camelia somewhat off her guard. Improvising a placard from the top of an old pasteboard box, he hung it over the deserted stall. It bore these words : *" Cloze for repare."*

Camelia could not read the words, but she caught their spirit of ridicule, and the sign had hardly swung when she climbed up, tore it down, and threw it—in the Gascon's face ! Then, without a word, she turned and went to her own stall. This exhibition of loyalty to 'Manuel was

taken as a betrayal of tender sentiment, and the
little crowd that had gathered about François
looked at each other with surprised glances,
and there were exclamations :

"O—ho !"

"Spunky lill gal, yas !"

"That's what's the matter, eh ?"

And one facetious young butcher touched
François under the ribs and said : "Might 's
well give up, young man ! B'lieve you got no
chance."

But no one asked Camelia any more questions
about 'Manuel. She wondered, as did every one
else, as to the cause of his absence, but she concealed her anxiety so well that every one thought
she knew.

'Manuel lived in a small corner hovel up in the
sixth district, and kept, like most of his country-
men, a little fruit and oyster shop. Raphael
tended shop during the mornings, while 'Manuel
sold in the market ; and in the afternoons, while
'Manuel took charge, the boy hawked the perish-
able wares through the streets.

The first few days that 'Manuel spent at home
were passed in deep thought. He had sworn an
oath, sworn it with all the strength of his resur-
rected manhood, and he swore it again twenty
times a day, as the memory of Camelia's little
hand beside his own, and of the one brief glimpse
into her heart that her womanly words had given
him, recurred to him. He would prove himself

worthy in the one material way in which he had been lacking. He would make money *like a man*, and Camelia should use it—like a woman, yes, *like a lady!* And he would begin *now*. He walked up and down, up and down his little shop —out through the narrow, dirty back yard, between piles of empty barrels and boxes—thinking, thinking.

It is easy to swear. Ah, and when one is filled heart and soul with an indomitable *will*, it is easy *to do*. The question in 'Manuel's mind now was only "How?" He looked about him, upon the picture of waste and dirt, as at a blank wall. There seemed no answer to his demand for success in the dilapidated piles of lumber, in the paltry stock of over-ripe, decaying fruit, in the inquiring face of the dependent boy at his side.

But soon, under the force of his resolve, the elements of failure round about him began to rearrange themselves, and the combination assumed, vaguely at first, the form of a new word —Success.

And the first letter of the new word was wrought in cleanliness. Load after load of trash was carted away from 'Manuel's back yard, to make way for a new guest, whose name was Thrift. 'Manuel had formulated his plan, and found relief in the labor it involved. All day long he worked with the plane and saw ; and soon disreputable-looking contributions of the old lumber-pile began to shine beneath his hand as fresh planks, adorned, as the work progressed, with points and scallops. Before a week had passed, there stood in his back yard a handsome set of shelves in pyramidal form. It was twice as large as his present stand in the market, and from its top arose a canopy, spreading, umbrella-fashion, over the whole, and the canopy was bordered with points and scallops, the embroidered planks of the lumber-pile.

Then came the painting—green and white and red, Italy's own colors. The red, too, was the tint of Camelia's cheek, the white was the ivory of her teeth, and the green was the hue of the kerchief that lay about her neck—and 'Manuel was satisfied.

Raphael had assisted 'Manuel as he could ; and while they worked, the two were frequently in close conversation. 'Manuel was often emphatic, always serious, but Raphael would frequently shake his head and scream with laughter. He was a beautiful boy, and his life of trade had made him shrewd and quick. If 'Manuel had possessed his young cousin's energy, things might have progressed more smoothly between him and Camelia from the first.

Finally the work of art—and love—was finished. At midnight 'Manuel and Raphael put it on a wagon and took it down to the market, and when the sun rose across the river, its beams fell on a structure the like of which had never been seen in the place ; and 'Manuel was not there to explain. He and Raphael had packed the *débris* of the old stall into the wagon and carried it away, before day.

The sudden appearance of a marble front on Fifth Avenue would hardly cause more consternation in the world of fashion than did Dago 'Manuel's new fruit-stand in the body social of the French Market on that memorable morning. The sausage-women tapped each other on the shoulders and whispered. The butchers walked around it, examined, criticised, and laughed, but all acknowledged that it was "Dog-gone poody!" If they were astonished at the sudden erection of the structure, they were utterly confounded the next morning, when its shelves were tastily decorated with evergreens and furnished with fruits, and a pretty girl took her place before it, and began singing in her soft Italian voice, "Cheap-a banana! 'S-a very nize apple!" over and over again.

Buyers were attracted, as well as neighboring competitors; and the little saleswoman, and 'Manuel, who had appeared during the morning, were both kept busy until the bell rang for closing.

Day after day 'Manuel and his pretty clerk came, and the business grew. 'Manuel was polite to Camelia always, but he was too busy now for much neighborly courtesy. He had introduced the "young lady" as "Miss Marie Cantero," his "saleslady," but had vouchsafed to no one, not even to Camelia, any explanation further than this—and she was too proud to ask him. As time went on, the rival beauty continued to attract, and Camelia had to share her patronage with her. If business waned, Marie introduced some new attraction. Now, it was a loud-talking parrot that cried "Cheap-a banana!" while everybody stopped and laughed and bought. Now, Marie herself appeared in a dazzling new costume, while her laughter was loud and contagious, and her use of slang rather remarkable. At the end of three months, the canopied stall did the principal business in the market, and 'Manuel rented neighboring stands and kept them all busy.

When a year had passed 'Manuel was still prospering. During this time Camelia had had many suitors, who loved her for her beauty, but each one had gone away with his head down. François had repeated his offer of himself and his money several times, but at length the strange truth was forced upon him that she would not accept him. He called her a "crezzy lill fool" for thus standing in her own light, but all his arts failed to effect a change in her mind; and he realized at last that he was finally rejected.

Of course, he went and talked with her sometimes still, to keep up appearances; and, when teased about her, he deported himself as became a man of the world.

"Oh-h! Camelia ees one nize lill Dago gal, an'

good-lookin', yas—*bud*," with a shrug of his manly shoulders, "me, I don' wan' *marry* one Dago. I 'ave a lill pleasure talk wid 'er — daz all !"

And then, to emphasize his position, he would add : "'Spose me, I was marry wid 'er, and dad one-eye Dago pass by my 'ouse, sing oud, 'Swee' po-ta-ders, ten-cen'-a-buck-e-e-e-t !' Yi, yi ! You could knock me down with a fedder ! Oh yas, Camelia 's one nize lill gal, an' poody ! poody ligue magnolias ! But no, no ! Me, I don' wan' marry dad *fodder-in-law*."

In this wise François set himself right with the market gossips, saved the imperilled dignity of the Leboeufs, and — handled Camelia's name like a gentleman.

'Manuel in the meantime was making money. He had never visited Camelia in her home. Before the day of his inspiration, he had loved her hopelessly, as one might become enamoured of a particular star, knowing that he might never reach it, and it would not descend to him. Since his awakening he had been absorbed with his one object—making money enough to become eligible to her under the imposed condition.

It had never occurred to him to doubt her, nor yet to nourish her preference with endearing attentions. The charmed words she had spoken had not been all sweet. There was a bitterness not to be ignored in their underlying implication of his unworthiness.

He would not go to her again until every
vestige of sloth should have fallen from him, and
he could approach her clad in the trig, smart
garments of success—until he could offer her as
much money as "thad sassy Gascon" had dared
offer her.

Whatever pleasure Camelia might have felt in
his prosperity was utterly, spoiled by jealousy of
his pretty clerk. It was plain that 'Manuel was
in love with her. Did they not sit together
every day—on the same lemon-box—and count
over the receipts of the morning? He was even
seen once to pin her overskirt for her! Of course,
he was in love with her; else *why should he pin
her overskirt?* And the bold little thing had giggled all the time he was pinning it! What was
'Manuel thinking about, to fancy such a creature?

Such as these were Camelia's unspoken thoughts,
but she never by one word criticised Marie. Not
she. She would not "give herself away" after
that fashion. She would wear a bright face, flirt
with every new-comer, and keep on good terms
with Marie—if it killed her!

Time passed. It was Christmas night. Camelia
sat alone on her father's door-step. The day had
been a long and trying one to her. Marie had
carried everything before her all the morning in
the market. The children at home, sticky with
Christmas sweets and boisterous with holiday
license, had finally succumbed to fretful sleepi-
ness and gone off to bed. And Camelia herself

felt so weary. The city about her, in its unusual quiet—its stillness exaggerated by contrast,
from following upon a hilarious Christmas-eve—
seemed to be sinking into the heavy stupor of
satiety. It was falling into a drunken sleep.
Nobody came to buy. There was no sound save
of the drowsy diminishing motion of the rocker
in which her mother, nodded, and her father's
half-drunken snore. She thought Christmas was
the worst day, the longest day, in the whole
year. Her hands lay idly in her lap, and she fell
into the universal habit of holiday retrospection.

How certain crises in our lives come back to
us at Christmas! And we smile, and shudder ofttimes, too, as we realize how unconsciously we
met them. How the retrospection dignifies the
commonplace things of life! How it makes us
quail in contemplation of the awful possibilities
of each passing hour, every trivial event! We
laugh in our hearts, too, as we remember how
we agonized over this or that trifle—the trifle
perpetuated in memory only by the agony that
impressed it there—the trifle marked now only
by a tear-stain. And how strangely interspersed
are these tear-stains! In the wrong places! "Ah,
me!" we say—do we not, every one of us?—with
the Amens to our Christmas communings with
self? And we mean—? That depends. There is
a terrible vagueness in this voicing of a sigh. If
the sigh go upward, the heart is better for the
aspiration. Between the "ah" and the "me"

there is, mayhap, a prayer—a renewed consecration of self—a reaching after the best, the real things of life.

"Ah, me!" said little Camelia, sitting in the dimly-lighted doorway to-night. There was a pathos in the very mildness of the ejaculation, for Camelia did not hesitate at profanity, on occasion. Not that she swore. "Cuss'n' an' swearin'" she regarded as a strictly masculine prerogative; but she ran the gamut of mild irreverence twenty times a day, introducing the devil into the society of the saints and the Deity on the faintest provocation—the disputed price of an orange, or a torn armhole—the result of a tip-toed reach for a preferred pineapple.

There was no passion in the laconic "Ah, me!"—her only words to-night. It was but a pathetic confession of weariness, of helpless regret. She simply knew that she was miserable and lonely, and that the light had gone out of her life. She longed for bed-time and sleep and forgetfulness—for escape from intrusive memories of recent humiliations. The review of the year had been a sad picture of her defeat—and Marie was the victor.

The little clock in the back room struck eight—only eight, and the evening had been so long! At eight o'clock last Christmas, where had she been? This and that had happened—and so the year began again to pass before her.

A firm step on the *banquette* startled her. It was 'Manuel. He had stopped, spoken, and seated

19

himself at her side ere she could recover herself enough to speak.

How slender and handsome he looked in his closely-fitting store-clothes! Camelia had never seen him before in other than his market dress. He was actually resplendent to-night. And when he bent his head close to her, and told her in serious way that, having fulfilled the conditions, he had come to claim the promised hand, she could not find voice to answer him. All things were changed. The wretchedness of the last hour receded suddenly into the dim past. It might have been a year ago.

While she only looked into his face and said nothing, 'Manuel went on talking. He spoke in Italian; told her the story of his struggle, his waiting, his success, and how, through it all, he had thought only of her.

And now, he had come to claim her. He looked into her eyes and awaited her answer. She had had time to compose herself a little, and Marie's face had risen up before her. Her heart seemed turned to ice. Instead of replying to his question, she asked frigidly—as always, speaking English.

"For-a w'ad ees Marie sen' you off?"

"Oh-h-h! W'ad you talk ligue thad, Camelia? Marie—tut, tut, tut!" And he burst out laughing. He seemed more amused than disturbed by this unforeseen difficulty.

"Marie ees-a *hi'* to me. Get fif-a-teen dollar de mont," he continued. "Never seen Marie 'n

my life-a, on'y in-a market," and now he drifted
seriously into Italian again.

He talked for an hour, and when he rose to go
he held her hand and something glistened on her
finger.

It was a gold ring, and its pattern was of two
hands clasped. He had said a sweet, pretty thing
about the appropriateness of the design, when he
placed the ring on her finger, and Camelia thought
it the most beautiful speech she had ever heard.
If she had known the word, she would have called
'Manuel a *poet.*

She sat and watched his slender receding figure
until it disappeared in the shadows. And then
she looked down at her hand; 'Manuel had kissed
it when he put the ring upon it. Raising it now
to her face, she laid the spot, still conscious of the
touch of his lips, against her cheek, and blushed
by herself on the doorstep.

And this was Christmas ! Surely Christmas
was the happiest day in all the year !

In a month they were married. The engagement was made no secret from the first, and
everybody seemed pleased. Marie, indeed, appeared quite delighted; but Camelia, remember-
ing her own sorrow, felt sure she laughed to
hide a heavy heart. François was most gushing
and profuse in congratulations, and sent, with his
card attached by a broad white satin ribbon, the
handsomest of all the bridal presents — a deco-

rated liqueur set, mounted in silver plate, with a bottle of anisette to drink the bride's health.

François, by the way, was married, three days before Camelia's wedding, to his second cousin, living "down in the Third." They were married in the Cathedral before the high altar, and had six bridesmaids, "every wan pritty ligue wan pink, and every wan my corzen!" François remarked afterwards.

Camelia's wedding, on the contrary, was conducted according to her own ideas, on economical principles. But 'Manuel spent money in presents without stint. In addition to the wedding outfit, which was his gift, he presented his bride with a "full set of jewelry," even including watch and chain—a gorgeous opera-chain with golden tassels —and every piece was set with an amethyst.

Old Nick, Camelia's father, shed real tears from his good eye when she left home, but he congratulated himself on gaining so progressive a son-in-law. 'Manuel took Camelia to a little home of her own, not a shop, but a neat little cottage, one side of which was rented, and brought in money every month.

Was she happy? Look into her face on this first day, when, having strolled several times through the four rooms of her new home, she at last seats herself in a little rocking-chair and tries to realize things. She has drawn her rocker into the small chamber next her own—this is to be Raphael's room—and her seat here between the doors commands a view both ways, back and front. She sees the kitchen shelves behind the shining new stove, and thinks how ornamental they will be, with coverings of embroidered paper and new tin furnishings. She is so glad that they will show all the way from the parlor. The gorgeousness of her own bedchamber quite intoxicates her with delight. She has turned her chair so that, whenever in repose, her eyes fall upon the Victoria bed. It is this imposing structure, with upholstered scarlet canopy, red-tasselled mosquito-bar, and lace-covered pillows, that dignifies the whole house. And the fringed, red-bordered towels on the towel-rack look so assertively aristocratic. How superior to the roller-towel and tin basin of her father's house! And it is all hers, and 'Manuel is hers, and she is 'Manuel's!

Presently, her attention, satisfied with contemplation of the other apartments, fell upon the little room in which she sat. The arrangement of the furniture here did not suit her. As she regarded it, she hummed a tune and rocked herself briskly back and forth, keeping time to the merry air with the rocking of her chair. Here was a bureau in a dark recess, with no light on its mirror, and a bed in a close corner opposite a window, so that its occupant would get plenty of light full in his face. How little men knew about arranging a house! The plan for a better distribution of the furniture came to her. It came first as a suggestion to her mind, and then seemed to pass quickly down through her arms into her hands. Her fingers fairly tingled to effect the improved arrangement. She quickened her tune and the motion of her chair. Finally, the woman's instinct conquered. Rising hastily from her chair, she peeped out to see where 'Manuel and Raphael were. They sat with her father, who had escorted them home, on the front steps, talking (for this January had borrowed a day from June for Camelia's wedding), and she saw that their cigars were just lighted. She would have plenty of time to make the desired change before the smoking should be over. It would not do for 'Manuel to discover her moving furniture on this first day. She would be ashamed—she had felt strangely shy even when she had walked through the house with him—but after it should be done she would not care, the improvement would be so apparent.

Taking the little bureau by its high shoulders, she moved it easily on its porcelain rollers. She laughed to herself as she pushed it up beside the window, and the little mirror, reflecting her own face, laughed back at her — even threw up its head and laughed as it tilted backward. She gave the bed a gentle pull now. It protested with a noisy creak, and Camelia went and closed the door. Returning now, she pulled and tugged at the cumbersome four-poster until, having gotten it out of its corner, she could step behind it. She would push it out ; it would be easier.

Just as she was throwing her weight against the bed, she happened to look up and saw that the mosquito-netting had caught against the wall. On disentangling it, she bared, not a nail, as she had suspected, but a porcelain knob. Here was a door. It must lead to a closet—a shelved closet, no doubt—the joy of every housewife's heart—and 'Manuel had not shown it to her! It was to be a surprise! She would look in! She did look in. Horrors! What was this? Hanging all around, on pegs against the wall, were Marie Cantero's clothes! She knew them all. Here were dresses, aprons, slippers—even that hateful overskirt! She grew dizzy. What did it all mean? 'Manuel had told her that he had never seen Marie excepting in the market. Had 'Manuel lied to her? Poor little Camelia! She had found a skeleton in her closet on her wedding-day! Pressing her hands to her head, she leaned heavily against the side of the door. A sound startled her. She thought it was a footstep. What if 'Manuel should come now? It would never do. Hurrying on tiptoe to the door, she turned the key, and, returning, closed the closet door, and with nervous strength pushed the bed back where she had found it.

The face in the little mirror looked at her sorrowfully as she moved the bureau into its old place, and, rocking forward, it fell, like a bowed head, crestfallen. Cautiously unlocking the door, and glancing backward to assure herself that everything was just as she had found it, she left the room with a shudder, as if it held a corpse, and went back into the kitchen.

'Manuel's parrot, perched on top of the safe, flapped her wings as Camelia entered, and cried, keeping her whole vocabulary thus in practice, "Cheap-a banana!" It seemed an insult, so closely was the bird associated with Marie.

"Shut yo' mouth-a, you fool!" she exclaimed resentfully, as she hurriedly left the kitchen and sought her own room. Drawing her chair to the side window here, she sat down to collect her scattered senses. How her temples throbbed! If she could only have escaped to weep, it would have been a relief; but this was impossible. She would keep a cheerful face, for her own dignity's sake, but how long the day seemed!

In the weeks that followed, a vague, restless doubting seemed ever present with her. She almost doubted the sincerity of 'Manuel's devotion and its permanence. The secret of the closet, like a Jack-in-the-box, seemed ever threatening to spring out at her, and she found herself growing nervous when she passed the door, or the place where she knew it was, for the bed concealed it. This had, no doubt, been the object of the arrangement. She saw little of Raphael. 'Manuel had put him into the market and kept him busy all day, and so he went early and came late. She had tried once to ask him something about Marie, but he evaded an answer, she thought, with some embarrassment, and then she went into her own room and wept. Why were Raphael and 'Manuel conspiring to deceive her about this girl—this brazen girl whose odious finery was concealed in *her* house?

One day, when Raphael and 'Manuel were both away, she locked both doors of Raphael's room and peeped again into the little closet. The clothing hung as on the first day.

In a few days she went again. *One suit was gone!* She grew faint, and grasped the side of the door for support. Marie had been there! She must have come during the night and taken it. Here was further mystery. She had been troubled before; now she was injured, indignant, outraged! She had come to feel almost comfortable about the affair, and had persuaded herself that there was some simple explanation of the presence of the dresses. She would even have asked about it, had not pride sealed her lips.

Such as these were her thoughts now. In truth, she had never for one moment been satisfied. The closet and its secret had always been a horror to her. But the uncertainty of the past was as joy to the wretchedness of the present moment, for now she was desperate. Slamming the door so that the house shook, she went into her own room. She was too angry to weep, too nervous to work.

After moving about the house abstractedly for an hour, now mechanically arranging the articles on her toilet, now standing at the open window, gazing vacantly into space, she suddenly started, as by a fresh impulse, back into the closeted chamber. The slammed door swung open, revealing the hanging garments. She had resolved to take the matter into her own hands, which she did literally now, gathering the dresses into a bundle and carrying them into the kitchen. She glanced at the clock. It was not yet noon by an hour, and Raphael and 'Manuel would not be home for dinner before nearly one o'clock. She would end this wretched business now—forever! When Miss Marie Cantero should sneak into her house again, she could whistle for her finery! Opening the stove-door, she started the fire with a handful of shavings, and first into the flame put a muslin overskirt. She laughed aloud as the flame burst into fresh life over the combustible fabric ; and she laughed again as she thought of Marie's consternation when she should come for her things and find them all gone.

What would she do ? Would she have the face to inquire about them ? If Marie should, what would she herself do ? She would shrug her shoulders and say she knew nothing about it. Why should she know ? Nobody had told her. But Marie wouldn't ask her—she wouldn't dare ! This would end the whole hateful affair—forever ! It would be neatly and quietly settled !

She laughed a laugh of self-gratulation as, opening the stove-door again, she thrust upon the waning flame a gaudy, lace-covered skirt. The

eagerness with which the blaze seized upon the
flimsy finery seemed in sympathy with her own
passion. Its fiery espousal of her cause soothed
her. The stove was her friend. The voice which
roared through its narrow pipe was the voice of
triumph, of exultation. It was the counterpart
of her own laughter, and when it would have
subsided, the gray ashes in the grate should not be
more tenacious of their secret than she. She had
found companionship in the little stove before,
during the long days when 'Manuel was away.
The secrets involved in the preparation of sundry
new dishes—dishes which 'Manuel had praised—
were they not all between her and her little
friend of the plastic temper?

Camelia was not capable of analysis, but she
was conscious of the charm of companionship
which came from the personality with which she
had unconsciously invested the little stove. And
now, as she fed it with the only available and
tangible elements of her distress, it seemed, in its
greedy consumption of the novel fuel, in its hilarious demonstration of delight, to have followed
her into the realm of passion. The consciousness
of sympathy soothed her spirit, as the genial
warmth did her body.

Presently the fire subsided. Camelia glanced
at the chair on which she had thrown the clothing. A single dress remained. She held this
garment up before her. She would prolong the
joy of its destruction by a last lingering inspec-

tion. How it recalled special days of Marie's
triumph! How vulgarly she had flaunted the
gaudy flouncings of the skirt! And 'Manuel had
tolerated her—liked her—even now held a secret
about her!

There were bright-red spots on Camelia's cheeks
as she opened the stove-door, and as she looked
in, she saw that there were bright-red coals within its grate. She would lay this last garment,
which seemed an embodied indignity, upon the
ardent bosom of her friend, who would quickly
avenge it, and then they would laugh together,
she and the little stove.

Catching the edge of a flounce with a toasting-
fork, she had leaned forward to thrust it into the
fire, when a step startled her. The door had
opened before she turned, and 'Manuel and Raphael walked in.

'Manuel regarded her in questioning astonish-
ment, but she met his glance defiantly. He was
frightened. He had never seen such a look in
his wife's face before, and he did not in the least
understand it. He was first to speak. He approached her gently. "W'a's the mather weeth-a
my lill-a wife?"

His tenderness was more than she could stand.
She resented it as an insult in the face of her
wrongs. The fountains of her wrath, long pent
up, now burst forth in a deluge of violent abuse.
She had endured much, and was proceeding
decently and quietly to dispose of the whole

affair, but—she was caught, and she didn't care.
She charged both 'Manuel and Raphael with de-
ception, conspiracy, insult ; told them that she
had known it from the first, and had put up with
everything until the girl had had the impudence
to sneak into her own house, and now she had
sworn she wouldn't stand it a day longer—no, she
wouldn't ! Finally, however, her anger spent
itself, and she fell to weeping.

The truth of the situation slowly revealed
itself to 'Manuel. He had been strangely obtuse,
but he saw it all now, and he was greatly troubled.
Beckoning to the boy to follow, he left the room.
There were but a few words of conversation
between the two, and 'Manuel's attitude was that
of entreaty. In a moment both returned to the
kitchen, and Raphael, taking up the dress from
the floor where Camelia had dropped it, and
gathering slippers, stockings, and ribbons that
lay strewn around, disappeared with them through
his room into the little closet. Camelia, with her
head buried in her arms over the table, saw nothing of this.

'Manuel approached his wife now, and, taking
her arm, gently, but firmly, raised her up.

"Come, Camelia," said he. "Been-a mague
wan beeg *miz*tague ! 'S all righd now." Camelia
resisted moodily, and he added, " Can'd you truz-a
yo' 'Manu*el* ?"

His voice was so troubled, so tender, that it
moved her, and she suffered him to lead her, sob-

bing afresh, into Raphael's room.   He led her to
a chair, and, stepping to the closet door, rapped
impatiently.

"Say ! Hoary up in-a tha !" said he.

In a moment the door opened. Camelia looked
up. A quick scream escaped her, as Miss Marie
Cantero, in all her glory, emerged from the closet.

"'Ave-a cha'," said 'Manuel, indicating a seat
opposite Camelia.

Turning to her now, he said, "Tague wan-a
good loog, Camelia. Never 's goin'-a see Miss
Marie no mo'."

That young lady now rose, took from her head
hat, ribbon, net, and one by one the feminine
garments fell to the floor, and Raphael, in long
breeches and flannel shirt, stood before her. The
boy laughed nervously, but Camelia was too much
wrought up for laughter—yet. She was humiliated beyond expression. She looked reproach-
fully at her husband.

"For-a w'ad ees-a you neva was-a tell me *biffo'*,
'Man*uel ?*" said she.

"'Ad 'o *prormize Raphael neva was a goin'-a
tell-a nobody !* Neva thoughd-a my lill-a wife
was afrai' trus'-a me !"

He spoke sorrowfully. There was a pathos in
his gentleness. Camelia felt it. She might even
apologize for her mistrust some time, but she had
not the grace to do it now. She preferred a
lateral retreat through a change of subject.
With childish diplomacy, she asked,

"For-a w'ad ees you an' Raphael come-a so soon to-day, 'Manuel? 'S nod leb'n o'clog yed!"

'Manuel held his open watch to her. It was nearly one, though the little clock on the shelf said "five minutes before eleven." It had stopped there when Camelia shook the house, slamming the closet door.

Marie had never appeared in the market after 'Manuel's wedding-day, for Raphael's contract ended then.

When 'Manuel had resolved to bestir himself, the main difficulty in the competition with Camelia in making money seemed to lie in her superior attractiveness over himself. He would not have had this otherwise, but just now—in a business sense —it was in his way. While at home, working on his stall, he had expressed his difficulty to Raphael in this wise: "Nobody's a goin'-a stop-a buy some-a-theen from wan-a orgly man, when wan-a pritty lill-a gal ligue Camelia's a sell-a close by eem."

This led to the wish for a pretty clerk—some shrewd, bright girl who might beat Camelia at her own game. It was then that 'Manuel conceived the idea of Raphael's assuming the disguise. It would be just the thing. Raphael had beauty, wit, and experience, and the plan would steer clear of the embarrassment of dealing with a strange girl. 'Manuel offered good pay and swore secrecy, but he had to beg and bribe a long time before the boy would consent.

The market people never knew what became

of Marie.　Some said that she had committed suicide in a fit of jealousy on 'Manuel's weddingday, and Raphael was so pleased with this solution that he carried a suit of his discarded clothing and left it one night under the wharf at the river's edge.　This was the dress Camelia had missed from the closet.　Some one must have stolen it, for Raphael never heard of it, and when he went to look for it, it was gone.

THE WOMAN'S EXCHANGE OF
SIMPKINSVILLE

"I'VE been kissed once-t—with a reg'lar beau kiss—by Teddy Brooks."

The puffs of smoke from old lady Sarey Mirandy Simpkins's pipe came faster after she had spoken.

"But I never kissed back. Hev you ever been kissed that-a-way, 'th a reg'lar beau kiss, Sis Sophia Falena?" she continued, turning toward her sister, who sat, also smoking, beside her.

"Twice-t."

"Who by?"

"Once-t by Jim Halloway, time he spoken the word fo' me to marry 'im, an'—an' by another person for a far'well."

"An' you kep' two all these years an' never told 'em out, an' here I felt guilty a-hidin' one. Who was that various secon' smarty what done it to you, Sis?"

"He weren't no smarty, Sarey Mirandy. He were Jim Dooley, an' it were time he 'listed in the army."

"Did you kiss back, Sophia Falena?"

"*Yas—I—did!*"

"I 'lowed as much. You was jest the samplin' sort o' young one to tas'e any new-fangled eatin's that was passed 'round. Ricollec' time you tas'e the bull-frog Tom Andrews kilt an' cooked, an' I gagged jest a-lookin'at you?"

The old lady, Sarey Mirandy, chuckled at the memory.

"Yas, I ricollec'. An' I ricollec' how I allus eaten some o' po' ol' Mammy Hester's possum shtew — which you wouldn't so much as tas'e. But that weren't how I kissed Jim Dooley back."

"What put kissin' into yo' head to-night, Sis? It's mighty funny, 'cause I was a-settin' here thinkin' 'bout kissin' too—an' I can't tell when I've studied about sech a thing befo'."

"I don' know. I was jest a-thinkin'. Sometimes it do me good to set an' think 'way back."

"Well, I tell you how I reckon kissin' come into *my* head. I was jest a-thinkin' *s'posin'*."

"S'posin' what, Sis?"

"Well, s'posin' all round. S'posin' Jim Dooley had of came back from the wah, fo' one thing."

A faint blush suffused the thin face of the speaker at the very audacity of that which her supposition implied.

"An' s'posin' Sonny hadn't of taken to birds— an' died. An' s'posin' the bank hadn't o' failed. Why, Sis, I could set here an' s'pose things in five minutes thet 'd make everything different. S'posin' time Teddy Brooks give you that special an' pertic'lar kiss, *you* had jest—ef not to say

kissed back, not *drawed away* neither. S'posin'
that !"

"Well, Sis, since we got on the subjec', I've
s'posened it more 'n once-t—pertic'lar sence I see
how ol' an' run - down the pore feller is. Sally
Ann Jones 'ain't been even to say a half-way wife
to 'im. Seem like ev'ry time she lays a new baby
in the cradle fo' him to rock she gets fatter an'
purtier, an' mo' no 'count ; an' pore Teddy, he sets
an' rocks the flesh clean off'n his bones. Yas, Sis,
I've thought o' *that* s'posin' many a time, but it's
a vain an' foolish thought—if not a ongodly one.
But the one I've s'posened about most is Sonny."

Both women sighed.

"Somehow, I can't get used to thinkin' 'bout
Sonny dyin', no way. No two girls ever had a
better brother 'n Sonny. Sonny was a born genius
if th' ever was one. Perfesser Sloane down to
Spring Hill say hisself they warn't a young man
in the county thet helt a candle to Sonny fo' head-
learnin'—not to speak o' Sonny's manners. An'
when I set an' look at this houseful o' stuffed
birds in glass cases an' think o' what Sonny might
o' been— Well, maybe it was God's will for Sonny
to take to birds, 'stid o' drink or card-shufflin' like
some brothers."

"It's mighty funny, Sis, for you an' me to be
sett'n up here s'posin' an' lookin' back at this pertic'lar time when it so p'intedly behooves us to be
lookin' ahead. Lemme see that paper ag'in. Yas,
here it is in plain 'Merican : 'Failure of the Cot-

ton King's Bank of Little Rock'—a whole col-ume. Nobody to read that would think of its sett'n' two ol' women to studyin' 'bout kissin', now, would they? What you reck'n we better do, Sis?"

"God on'y knows—an' He 'ain't tol' me—yet. 'Twouldn't be no use to try takin' boa'ders, would it?"

"'Twouldn't be right, Sis. They 'ain't nobody in town *to* boa'd out but them as are boa'din' a'ready, an' 'twould be jest the same as askin' 'em to leave an' come to us—'special as we got the fines' house."

"'Twould look that-a-way, wouldn't it? I thought about takin' in quiltin', but there ag'in, you know th' ain't mo' quiltin' give out to be did than Mis' Gibbs can do—an' she half crippled too. No, no. 'Fore I'd give out thet you an' me'd take in quiltin', I'd starve—*that* I would."

"I taken notice to a pertic'lar word you spoke jest now, Sis, 'bout 'God knows.' You ricollec' what the hymn say?

> "'Hev we trial or temptation,
>   Take it to the Lord in prayer.'

Seem to me like our trial been followed by two temptations a'ready. It's mos' nine o'clock, an' I'm goin' to read my chapter an' then lay this case o' you an' me out clear, on my knees, befo' the Lord—an' do you do the same, Sis, an I b'lieve we'll be d'rected."

Lighting her candle, old lady Sophia passed noiselessly into her own room.

Her sister sat for some time longer in thought; then she, too, after shovelling some ashes over the coals upon the hearth, took her candle and went to bed.

The Misses Simpkins were twins, and at the time of the civil war they had been fair, blooming country maidens both, and they were now, since the death, a year ago, of "Sonny," their bachelor brother, the sole representatives of a family that had stood with the best in the Arkansas community in which they lived—a family whose standards and traditions had been religiously observed in all things by the twin daughters upon whose frail maiden shoulders had devolved responsibilities hitherto unknown to the women of the name of Simpkins. Their mother and grandmother had had slaves at their call, and by frugal care had accumulated what there, in those days, was counted as wealth. Such, indeed, is affluence yet in this inland country of simple living.

It had been the fate of the twins to see this fortune slowly dissipated.

They had worn their inherited frugality itself threadbare in the determination to "live like paw an' maw would like to have us live"—and thus far they had succeeded.

Sonny, whose life, viewed retrospectively, seemed even to their loving eyes a failure, had been, when living, their pride and joy.

Sonny was in truth a gentleman. His one year at college, which he left for the army in '61, had sufficed to introduce him into new realms of thought and, it may be, had diverted activity from his hands to his brain. Certain it is that he never grasped the changed situation after the war, and the sisters and he had finally sold all the farm-lands, reserving only the few acres surrounding the homestead. The proceeds, deposited in the failing bank, had yielded an income quite adequate to their modest needs.

Sonny had called himself a naturalist; and so he was—in a sweeter, broader sense than he knew. He was as nature had made him, a true-hearted, unsophisticated gentleman.

He had, despite his country rearing, a certain courtliness of manner, and the sparse oasis of gray that surmounted his else bald pate gave him, at least to his fond sisters' eyes, somewhat the air of a college professor.

Sonny had never done an ungentle thing in his life, nor apparently questioned the wisdom of his own mode of living. For more than twenty years he had been satisfied to pursue his chosen study and take no note of time.

On Sunday mornings he always donned his old broadcloth suit and beaver, harnessed the old horses, which he still called "the ponies," and drove "the girls" to church.

If they had all grown old, Sonny did not know it. He visited the nicest girls in the village with the same gallant dignity with which he had visited their mothers; and had he lived, he would have been ready to recite to their daughters all his selected verses about women and love—when the time should come.

But Sonny was found one day, with a live bird still grasped in his hand, lying dead beneath a tree. Presumably he had climbed and fallen.

And now to the lonely sisters had come a second trial. Into their shadowed door had stalked, unbidden and unexpected, the informal guest called Poverty, with her startling command of " Work !"

It was dinner-time on the day following the conversation recorded before they reverted to the theme again.

" Well," said Miss Sarey Mirandy, " hev anything come to you, sis, thet we can do ?"

" Hev anything come to you, Sis Sarey dear ?"

" Yas, it has. An' I'm 'fraid it's small comfort. Th' ain't but two things I *can* do, an' them's sewin' an' cookin'. Th' ain't any sewin' needin' to be did in Simpkinsville more 'n them as are a'ready doin' it can do, an' as fo' cookin', you know how much chance they is in that—less 'n a person 'd hire out, which I *can't* do, not while ma an' pa's 'ile-painted po'trait looks down from that chimbly at you an' me. Tell the truth, Sis, what *to* do, *I don't* know. Hev you thought 'bout it consider'-ble ?"

" Yas, I have, Sis. You can cook an' sew, an' I can ca'culate figgurs, an' we got a-plenty o' house-room, an' we're right on the public road, an'—"

"In the name o' goodness, Sis, hun, 're you wanderin', or what 're you drivin' at?"

"Well, they's jest this much to it, Sis Sarey Mirandy, I've got a idee, an' *my* idee is thet it's *the* idee—an' that's all they is *to* it."

Miss Sarey Mirandy readjusted her spectacles and scrutinized her sister's face.

"Well, go on, honey. You've done got me wrought up!"

"Why, it's this—an' I'd never o' thought o' sech a thing if it hadn't o' been for my trip to the city, along with me subscribin' to that magazine, both of which you know, hun, you pretty solemn discountenanced. I seen it tried in the city, an' the magazine is continual tellin' how it works everywhere—"

"But for gracious sakes alive, Sis, what is the thing?"

"*It's a Woman's Exchange*—that's what it is!"

"But, Sis, hun, we 'ain't got nothin' to start it with."

"That's jest the beauty of it. They get started on nothin'. We jest give out thet the Exchange *is started,* an' everybody who does any sort o' work to sell sends it in, an' we sell it for her an' *deduc'* ten pre cent. You see?"

"Well, I don't know as I do."

"Well, here: S'posin' ol' Mis' Gibbs, 'stid o' totin' her heavy comforters all 'round the country an' losin' maybe two whole days' time a-sellin' one for two dollars, jest sends 'em in here, an' we sell 'em for her. She gets—ten from one dollar leaves ninety cents, an' nine an' nine's eighteen, eight an' carry one— She gets—"

"You don't mean she gets eight dollars? 'Twouldn't never do in the world. People wouldn't pay it. An' besides, I thought you said she wouldn't have to carry none?"

"Don't put me out, Sis; I'm all frustrated—'f I jest had a slate! Now I got it. You don't carry at all. Ought's a ought, an' nine an' nine's eighteen. She'd get a dollar 'n' eighty cents, an' we'd get the two dimes. Then you could put any kind o' cooked things in an' sell em., Them lemon pies o' yours 'd sell like hot cakes."

"An' who'd get the pre cent on them, Sis?"

"Well, reely, hun, I—I hardly know. We got to deal fair. We might give it to charity. How'd it do to give it to Mis' Gibbs to make up the *deduct* on the comforters?"

"That might do if it's got to be give; but look's if it would naturally *b'long* somewheres, don't it?"

"It do seem so. Maybe we might keep that fo' rent o' the room."

"Well, I don' know. If we do, we had ought to give it out, so's every person 'd understand."

"Then, maybe nex' thing some smarty 'd be offerin' to give a room an' sell *rent free*."

"Even so, Sis, if it's principle, it's got to go so, but—"

She closed her eyes in thought.

"Seem to me—if—we—make—an'—sell—both —we got a free right to *collec'* for both."

"Why, yas. That's so—that's so. An' yet— if we sell our pies for a quarter, an' Mis' Stith send in some thet gets *de*ducted—seem like we're gett'n' a advantage over her."

"We get that by *sellin'* 'em, Sis. If she want the whole quarter, let 'er sell 'em herself."

"That's so, of co'se. Well, how'll we start, hun?"

"Why not have it called out in church? It's a good, helpful work."

And so it was done.

When, on Sunday following, the minister stepped aside to read the notice, Miss Sophia Falena grew so flurried that she untied her bonnet-strings. Her sister, however, though sniffling vociferously herself, nudged her, and she tied them again, and only cleared her throat at short intervals.

The notice simply called a meeting of all interested in the project, which was duly set forth on the next day at the Simpkins residence.

The response was most encouraging, all the chairs in the house and one from the kitchen being called into requisition to seat the attendants.

Miss Sophia's voice trembled distinctly, as did the hand that held the paper from which she read, standing in the midst of the assembly, her "Idees on the Subjec'," which she had thought best to commit to paper.

It was a trying ordeal, but her sister had seen to it that a glass of water stood at her elbow, and at the first quaver of her voice Miss Sarey thought best to step behind her and fan her solicitously.

The meeting was in all respects a success. Besides the assorted bits of advice, which all gave freely on the spot, each promised to "enter" something.

While Miss Sophia Falena, an atlas balanced upon her knee, made a note of articles promised, Miss Sarey Miranda passed around raspberry vinegar and crullers on an old silver tray.

The two were similarly attired in gowns of shiny black silk, whose swishing sound at every movement seemed, with the clink of the high goblets against the silver waiter, reminiscent of a bygone and more prosperous period.

The change wrought in the Simpkins household by the new enterprise was marvellous.

It was as if time had turned backward and they were young again, so quickly did they move about, so animatedly discuss the numerous details of preparation.

After considerable parley they decided to use the mahogany centre-table for cakes and articles of special showiness, while fancy-work could be advantageously displayed on the piano. If the time should come again when they cared to hear music in the house, they could move the things. Miss Sophia, who had been from home more than her sister, hated to open the old piano anyway.

Indeed, she was once heard to say, " When that *piano* is shut an' kivered up, a person can look at it an' think music, because the shape seems to favor it ; but jest open it, an' I declare Methusalum ain't nowhere. It makes a person ponder on death an' *eternity*."

The twins were much interrupted by company during the first days after the announcement ; such as had not been able to attend the meeting dropping in as occasion allowed.

Some even came after tea to talk it over, as did their next neighbor and his old wife, when he facetiously announced, " I heerd th' was a woman's *ex*change over here, an' I come to see if I couldn't change off my ol' 'oman for one o' you twinses—air one thet 'll come."

This joke travelled and was perpetrated by all the good-humored happy husbands in the county, to the unfailing delight of every one present.

The Exchange opened briskly. The centre-table fairly groaned beneath its burden of cakes — " White - Mountain," " Lady Washington," " Confederate layer," " Marble," " Dolly Varden," " General Lee," and a score of others, iced and decorated with reckless elaboration; while in the centre, completing the effect of a spread feast, stood—under glass, it is true--a glowing pyramid of wax fruits.

The piano was a bazaar of many-hued zephyrs, from the miniature sacques and stockings of shrimp-pink and kindred raw tints, relegated by provincial taste to the adorning of babes, to the chinchilla and purple capes, suggestive of grand-mothers' rheumatic shoulders.

On a side table, wrapped in snowy linen, were heaped loaves of home-made bread, buns, rolls, lemon-pies—the home contribution.

A stream of people were coming all day, examining things, pricing, but rarely buying. Indeed, nearly all had something in stock *to sell.*

The two old ladies flitted briskly about, ever and anon putting their heads together, only to dart off in other directions, as busy and buzzy as two happy house-flies on a sunny day—only the bright red spots on their cheeks testifying to the unusual agitation of their minds.

That they had need of tact, discretion, and judgment, not to mention patience, a bit of conversation, caught up at random, will perhaps best illustrate.

"An' who sent in this curious cake, Miss Simpkins?"

The querist was a patroness of influence.

"Kate Clark sent in that'n, Mis' Blanks. It's a 'will-o'-the-wisp,' made out'n five times sifted flour 'n' whites of eggs. She says she *made it up,* name an' all."

"Seem to me, she'd have 'bout all she could do makin' up rhymin' po'try. What price does she put on it?"

"She wouldn't name no sum. She says she never prices the work of her mind in money, an' that cake is jest the same to her as a po'try-verse. She'll be grateful for whatever it 'll fetch."

"Well, I vow! Time a person taken to writin' po'try seem like they all but lose what little sense they got. How you goin' to sell it 'thout no price?"

"Well, we 'lowed that anybody thet 'd want it 'd deal *fair*. I s'pose bein' as they's nothin' but eggs, an' only the half o' them, in it, they mus' be consider'ble flour. An' *siftin'* it five times—you know that's worrisome work. An' the eggs is well beat, you can see that. Don't you reck'n it's wuth two bits?"

"Maybe it is for them as are willin' to buy a quarter's wuth o' wind. When I want air, I'll go out-do's an' sniff it! That's all I'm askin' fo' mine, an' it iced all over, an' eight whole eggs in it, an' them beat sep'rate, an' a cup o' butter, not mentionin' the other things, nur the *extrac'*. They's a spoonful o' v'nilla extrac' in my cake if they's a drop, for I dashed it in by my eye—an' I've got what you call big eyes, come to measurin' food-stuffs."

The speaker's little blue eyes snapped sharply, and she sniffed twice in hesitation ere she proceeded, with some embarrassment:

"If you goin' to charge twenty-five cents fo' Kate Clark's pile o' baked bubbles—you can lift it an' see it's nothin' else—you better rub that twenty-five off o' my iced cake an' put a forty on it. That's it, a four an' a ought; an' whoever buys *mine* gets four dimes' wuth o' good nourishment, if I do say it."

She moved on apace.

"I see Kitty Baker's sent in a lot o' things. Well, them as want to eat after Kitty *can*—that's all *I* got to say."

"Kitty's a well-meanin' girl, Mis' Blanks, an' needy too. S'posin' you don't say nothin' like that to nobody. I see the flour is caked some roun' the edges of her cakes, but that ain't sayin' they's anything wrong with her cookin'."

"Why, Miss Sarey *Mi*-randy Simpkins! I'm a perfessin' Christian, as you know—an' tryin' to live up to my lights. I wouldn't say nothin' to injure Kitty *fo' nothin'*. Them remarks I make to you is jes' to say 'twix' you an' me an' the bed-pos'. One o' my motters is, 'Live an' let live,' an' another one"—she added with a laugh—"'What don't pizen, fattens.' What you askin' fo' yo' lemon-pies, Miss Simpkins?"

"Twenty-five cents, Mis' Blanks."

"Mh—hm! I s'pose they're made by yo' ma's ol' recipe—three eggs to the pie, savin' out the whites to whip up fo' the top?"

"'Deed, Mis' Blanks, Sis made 'em, an' I couldn't tell you jest how she po'tioned 'em; but I know she ca'culated that they come to eighteen cents apiece, not countin' firewood, which, sence pore Sonny's gone, we have to hire to have cut."

"Cert'n'y—an' yet, I'd think a little thing like

21

a pie you could slip in whils' the other things are bakin'."

"That's so, we do; an' yet—? Do you think two bits is too much for 'em, Mis' Blanks?"

"Law, child, the idee! I was jest a-thinkin' *this.* You know, business is business, Miss Simpkins, an' I was jest a-thinkin'—they *can't, noways,* be more 'n *five* eggs in a pie—even if they was guinea eggs — an' they's eight in my cake — *an' it iced — an'* flavored. Jest rub out that *four,* please 'm, an' put a *five* on my cake, will you? 'Cordin' to the gen'ral valliation it's wuth a half-a-dollar if it's wuth a cent. Well, I mus' be goin'. What you chargin' fo' yo' bread, Miss Simpkins?"

The old lady addressed scarcely found voice to answer,

" Ten cents a loaf, Mis' Blanks."

" Well, you better gimme a loaf, please 'm. You see, makin' cake an' bringin' it to the Exchange, I didn't bake to-day. I s'pose you make with salt-risin', don't you?"

"No, Mis' Blanks, we raise with 'eas'-cakes."

" Jest so it don't tas'e hoppy I ain't pertic'la_r, but from hoppy bread *deliver* me. Well, good-by, Miss Sarey Mirandy, honey, *good-*by, an' I'm goin' to pray for you to succeed. Lemme know who buys my cake. I do wish I could be there to see it cut. Well, good-by again. Law, here comes Mis' Brooks with a bundle big as a Chris'mas-tree. I *must* stop an' see what she's fetchin'. I do declare this here Woman's *Exchange* does tickle me all but *to* death. Simpkinsville 'ain't been so stirred up sence the fire. Howdy, Mis' Brooks? I see you keepin' the ball a-movin'!"

"You better b'lieve I wasn't goin' to be outdid by all you smart seamsters an' fancy cooks."

And Teddy Brooks's wife, drawing off its loose wrapping of paper, set upon the table a gorgeous pair of old brass candelabra.

"How's them for antics?" she exclaimed, resting her hands upon her fat hips and stepping backward.

These candelabra had been the proudest possession of Teddy's mother to the day of her death. To sell them seemed sacrilege to the loyal mind of Miss Sarey Mirandy.

"Are they—for sale?" she asked, with an effort at composure.

"Why, yes indeedy. Of course they're for sale, Miss Simpkins. 'Ain't nobody else brought in no antics? They're the special special*i*ties they sell *in* Exchanges, antics are. I wanted to fetch over Teddy's ma's gran'ma's bellowses. The wind's all out of 'em, an' they're no good 'cept'n *as* antics, which I naturally *d*espise. But Teddy taken it so hard I had to leave 'em, to keep the peace. You ask if they're fo' sale. Ain't ev'rything here fo' sale, Miss Simpkins?"

"Ev'rything thet *is* is, of course, but they's some things that *ain't*. Sonny's birds ain't, nor pa's an' ma's 'ile-painted po'traits, nor none o'

them things which them as are gone seem to stan'
guard over."

"Well, the way I look at that is, if the spirits
that stan' guard over things, as you say, would
jest keep 'em dusted an' cobwebbed off, so's we
could be sure they *was* keepin' up with 'em, they'd
be some sense in it. Teddy took on some over
sellin' the ol' things, but I tol' him he hisself was
the only Brooks antic I cared to keep. How much
you reck'n I ought to get for 'em, Miss Simpkins ?"

"I'm 'feerd I was too ol' a frien' to ol' Mis'
Brooks, Sally Ann, to put a price on them candelabras; but you're at liberty to put whatever
tag you like on 'em—an' Sis an' me 'll do our
part, fair an' square. I see they's one dangle
missin' on this one."

"Yes, I give it to the baby to cut 'is eye-teeth
on, an' he dropped it an' it snapped. The things
're no manner of account. They cost a hundred
dollars, an' I doubt if I'll get ten for 'em, but
I'm goin' to start 'em at that anyway. I'm dyin'
for a swingin' silver-plated ice-pitcher, an' have it
I will. I've *got* the price all to seven dollars.
Teddy laid it by to have the children's pictures
took, but I told him the young ones could see
their pictures in the side o' the ice-pitcher." And
Mrs. Brooks laughed heartily at her own wit.
"When I can swing back in my red-plush rockin'-
chair an' tilt ice-water out of a silver-plated pitcher, I'll feel like some. I see you've got lots o'

goodies for sale. I'm bound to have *somethin'* from th' Exchange for supper. What kinds have you got?" She slipped a piece of liquorice-root from her pocket to her mouth as she began a circuit of the room, chewing vigorously the while. "Better do up that choc'late layer for me, Miss Simpkins," she said finally. "Teddy don't eat choc'late, but I don' know but he's better off 'thout cake, anyway. Jes' charge it, please, to Teddy—Mr. Theodore Brooks—that's it. Might's well open a 'count here first as last, 'f you're goin' to have choc'late fixin's—that's the one thing I c'd get up in my sleep to eat—an' I don' know's I'll bother bakin', if you're goin' to have bread. Jest lay by a couple o' loaves every day, please 'm."

When Mrs. Brooks passed out, the sisters, from their opposite corners of the room, managed to exchange glances, and both sighed.

When the first day was over, all the bread and rolls were sold; indeed, nearly all the housewives who had taken this first step in bread-winning went home with bought loaves under their arms.

It was only after some days, when the gorgeous array of sweets was growing stale, that the sisters and their patronesses began to realize that there were few buyers of luxuries in their frugal little village.

Besides several purchases of Mrs. Brooks, there had been but one cake sold. The "will-o'-the-wisp" had passed on the second day into the possession of a certain pale young telegraph operator, the same who was "keeping company" with its poetic fabricator.

Perhaps the materialistic circle of housewives whose substantial contributions were further solidifying before their eyes should be pardoned the numerous pleasantries expended on this purchase.

That the objects of their mirth, two ethereal young persons, dealing professionally in commodities so unsubstantial as poetry and electricity, should choose "wind cake" for nourishment, was a combination too prolific of humor to be passed by. The portly contributor of the still unsold eight-egg cake waxed especially facetious over it; and on the occasion of the unanimous vote of "stockholders," to send the entire stale lot as a donation to the inmates of the poorhouse, she even went so far as to withdraw hers from them, and to bear it in her own hands, as a gift, to her friend the poetess, who, she declared, should have "one good bite o' solid substance, if she never had another."

Thus she did, after all, enjoy the delight of "seeing it cut," while she sampled its flavor. Then, between slices, it was such a joy to drop delicate insinuations about the telegraph operator, and to glean points as to the expected wedding; while she saw to it that a few good seed, in the shape of admonitions as to the nutritive properties of certain foods, were let fall during the visit. For she was a motherly soul and a Christian.

The exclusion of confections, excepting those supplied to order, practically converted the Exchange into a bakery; for the fancy department, after passing through a fading process, had shrunken, through many withdrawals, until a single glass case—an unused one among Sonny's possessions—held the entire stock.

Screened from the odium of professional bread-making by the prestige of the "Exchange," the Misses Simpkins were thus enabled to earn in this simple manner a modest living. True, the vocation had its trials, but there were compensations.

If their delicate wrists and arms were decorated with a succession of bracelets in the shape of burns from the oven doors; if they agonized many nights over the intricacies of numerous recipes sent in by kind advisers, and were oft disquieted in spirit by the vicissitudes of salt-rising, compressed yeast, or potato-leaven; it was yet a new, youth-restoring life to be always professedly and really busy with work that left no time for repinings. It was a sweet, secret pleasure to Miss Sarey Mirandy to make the loaves Teddy Brooks paid for as large as she dared without attracting notice. And sometimes, on anniversaries—which, perhaps, she alone cherished—of their young days, it pleased her tender maiden heart to slip a few raisins into his loaf, with a suspicion of cinnamon, in loving memory of his boyish fancies.

For some time she was tortured with a dread

that some one should offer to buy the candelabra. Should such a time come, she would calmly reply that they were already sold, when from an old stocking she would produce one of the ten-dollar coins that represented her own funeral expenses. It should buy Teddy's wife a swinging pitcher, and the candelabra would descend by will at her death to Teddy's daughter—his mother's name-sake.

For a long time she scarcely left the house, fearing her sister should sell them during her absence. Indeed, at times she was in such a state of suppressed panic over the matter that she would gladly have bought them outright, were it not for gossip.

People would talk. In her calm moments, she knew that no one in Simpkinsville would pay half the amount asked for useless, old-fashioned bric-a-brac that they had seen all their lives. In fact, she had often heard the women jokingly wonder who would buy "Mis' Brooks's antics," and "if, because she'd visited in Washington"—a distant town in the State, noted for its social distinc-tion—"she was the only person in Simpkinsville who knowed about swingin' ice-pitchers." When they "had change to fling away, they'd buy ice-pitchers for themselves, an' not swap it off for glass Noah's-ark dingle-dangles."

So in time Miss Sarey grew to feel pretty secure about the candelabra, and at night, when her sister knitted or nodded beside her, she would often half-close her eyes, and, looking at the glass pendants, seem to see, as the fire sparkled from the prisms, bright memory pictures of her youthful days. A rosy-faced girl with curls, her young self, often smiled at the retrospective old woman from the familiar scenes, and Teddy was there and Sonny, and another—a boy who had not come home from the war—and every one was young, and the trees were green, producing nuts, berries, persimmons, or sustaining grape-vine swings, as reminiscence required. Only the missing dangle, on which Sally Ann's baby had cut his teeth, made a painful gap in the panorama.

In this vacant place Teddy, grown pale-faced and weary, seemed somehow always to stand, and while she looked at it all the other pictures went out. So she would turn the defective side to the wall.

When the winter had passed, the Exchange had gone through some changes, shaping itself to the needs of the community by contraction or extension, according to indication. A few, who seemed especially fitted to become at once its patrons and beneficiaries, had resented its overtures as an insult, as did Mrs. Gibbs, the respected quilter of comfortables. From every point of view the Exchange was an offence unto her sensitive nostrils. To its bid for her patronage she had protested with a sniff that " she hed never ast no mo' 'n they was wuth fo' her quilts, an' the day she took off two dimes on one she'd

own that she owed jest that much to every person as ever bought one. As fo' totin' 'em 'round
the country, she didn't know as 'twas anybody's
business in special. The roads was free, and
she reckoned her rheumatism was her own—not
but what she'd be glad to give it to anybody
that was honin' to take keer of it. As to her
time, she hadn't bound herself out to nobody
but the good Lord, an' she 'lowed to claim the
time he gave her till he changed it for eternity,
when she guessed she'd take that too, ef the
Simpkinsville folks didn't have no objections.
The only visitin' she ever done was takin' orders
in the spring o' the year and deliverin' her money's
wuth *to a cent* in the fall. Them that thought
she gadded too much was welcome to do 'thout
comforts an' freeze, jest to give her the hint."

The truth was that the social side of Mrs.
Gibbs's profession was her very life. A habit of
spending a day with her patrons at both ends of
each transaction kept her in touch with the home
lives of the people. If she had conducted her
business through an agent, she would long ago
have shrivelled out of existence. There was much
in her work to develop an interest in what to
outsiders might seem trifles—such, for instance,
as which among her patrons' families kicked in
their sleep—and in her social rounds it became
her pleasure to discover whether the solution lay
in the eating of hot suppers or in guilty consciences.

She would hold up before her a quilt that was "clean kicked to strips before the battin' was matted," and exclaim with a grunt that was half a chuckle, "Hot suppers! Like as not fried chicken at eight o'clock all winter long!" And then she would unwittingly smack her lips.

Though theoretically respecting the quiet sleepers, whose quilts, although often "made out'n the back brea'ths of ol' skirts, lasted their time out," it was nevertheless true that their greater patronage fostered nearer friendships with such as were able to bid her remain to steaming waffles and to send her home in a wagon.

If the Exchange failed to fulfil all its possibilities in some directions, it did unforeseen duty in others, especially supplying an oft-felt want in the open door which it soon offered to the passing stranger.

Simpkinsville had never boasted a hotel, and so it naturally came about that, in the common parlance of the village, travellers understood that "at the *Exchange* they could get comfortably et an' slep'" for a reasonable consideration.

This was robbing no one, as previously it had been an unwritten law of hospitality of the town that strangers be entertained gratis. It seemed odd that its leading family—that which not only lent the dignity of its solitary gabled front to its highest eminence, but had bequeathed to Simpkinsville its name and traditions—should have been first to put a price on the bread broken with a stranger; but such is the irony of fact, for, with a sensitiveness revealed to the close observer by the slight pursing of their lips, which perhaps the wayfarer interpreted as having a mercenary meaning, these two old ladies did actually charge him twenty-five cents who consumed a hearty meal, reducing the bill with minute scrupulousness to fifteen and even to ten cents to such as failed in appetite. Further than this their most rigorous consciences did not lead them, as they agreed that it was "wuth a dime to cook things an' then not see 'em et."

That they were sensitive to their changed social relations through the ever-present atmosphere of trade was evinced by a conversation one night, when Miss Sophia Falena broke a long silence by saying,

"Sis, hun, I been figgurin' to see how we can contrive to move the Exchange out'n the parlor. When we *do* have outside comp'ny, I declare I hate to set 'em 'round that centre-table piled up with sech as we been raised to offer our comp'ny free—an' it fo' sale. Time the Jenkses come in last week, an' we sat 'round so solemcholy, every now 'n' ag'in glancin' at the table, which was covered up with mosquito-nett'n', I vow if the thing didn't seem to me like some sort o' dead corpse, an' 's if we were some way holdin' a wake over it—an' oughtn't to laugh out loud."

Her sister chuckled nervously.

"It's funny, Sis, but d' you know, I thought

about that too, an'—maybe I oughtn't to say it, but it 'minded me o' pore Sonny's buryin', an' ma's an' pa's. But I don't see how we can help it. We might clear off the table entire, an' put the bread an' rolls on shelves. I never knew of no dead person bein' laid on a shelf—not literal, though the way they're forgot they might 's well be."

"Let's do it, Sis, an' get shet o' that ghostly covered table. Maybe you didn't take notice to it, but last Sadday, when ol' Mis' Perkins sidled up to the table so stately an' raised up the nettin', she said the identical pertic'lar word thet she said time she taken a last look at Sonny; 'Jes' as natural as life,' says she, jes' so. Of course, she was referrin' to Inez Bowman's case o' wax fruits, but it gimme the cold shivers to see her standin' there again, a-sayin' them same words. An' they's another thing strikes me, Sis. When a day or a night boa'der *do* drop in, it seems to me the house mus' seem sort o' gloomy with nobody in it but a lot o' dead glass-eyed stuffed birds an' two ol' ladies—which you know to outsiders we are, Sis— an' them dressed in black, solid as Egyp'. Seem to me it's enough to sort o' take away a travellin' man's appetite. How'd it do fo' you an' me to bas'e a little white ruchin' in the neck an' sleeves o' our black comp'ny dresses—not meanin' no disrespec's to the dead, but in compliment to the livin' ?"

"Well, ef you say so, Sis, hun. Seem like our first duty *is* to the livin'. Maybe if we *do* lighten our mo'nin' a little, these worldly drummers an' sech won't feel called to talk religion to us like they do. I can see it comes pretty hard on 'em."

"An' I declare, maybe it's foolish, but I *do* wish Tom wasn't a black cat. He looks mighty doleful, layin' asleep on the hearth of evenin's. A pink ribbon 'roun' his neck wouldn't look too worldly, would it—not for the pore soulless beast, hun, of course, but for us?"

"Why, no, I reck'n not—or a blue one. The blue bow on my valedict'ry is purty faded, but if you think it 'd do, why, th' ain't no use in keepin' it no longer. If Sonny had o' lived an' married— which, for a man, as long as they's life they's hope—they might in time o' been sech as would care fo' they ol' auntie's valedict'ry. That ribbon cost five dollars a yard in Confed'rit money, an' 'tain't all silk, neither—but for a cat—"

"'Tain't any too good fo' Tom, Sis—he been a faithful ol' cat. But they's another p'int on my mind. Don't you think maybe we better open up Sonny's room an' sun it good an' reg'late it, so's if we're pushed fo' room we could let comp'ny go up there to sleep? As 'tis, we can't sleep mo' 'n three strangers *no* way, an' if a crowd *was* to come—not thet they're likely— But I b'lieve if we'd do it, we'd be relieved ourselves. As long as we keep it shet tight, jest the way Sonny left it, we'll feel like death is locked in—an' I don't know as it's Christian. What you say, Sis?"

" Well, maybe you're right, dearie. S'pose we

go up in the mornin' together. I've done started
up there three times a'ready, an' my knees trembled so they give way under me—but if you was
with me, maybe— You don't s'pose strangers
would mind sleepin' with so many birds, do you?"

"Cert'n'y not. Why should they, les'n maybe they was high-strung, an' their mind got excited? Ef so, they *might* imagine they was all
singin' at once-t, quick as the light was out. If
sech a person was to try to sleep there—well, I
dunno. They's thirty-one hundred an' sixty-three
stuffed birds in that garret room, an' all in sight
o' the bed."

"Shucks, Sis! you're talkin' *redic'lous*—I vow if
you ain't! D' you s'pose any right-minded man
would think o' sech as that? Of course we ain't
goin' to put no skittish person to sleep in Sonny's
room, no way—jest reel gentlemen, an' only them
if we're pushed."

"It cert'n'y do behoove us to take in all we
can hones', Sis, for seem like the Exchange money
don't mo' 'n to say hardly pay our boa'd, somehow."

The truth was, the profits of bread-making were
steadily shrinking. Not only did Teddy Brooks's
loaves grow larger and larger as he waxed paler
and more careworn, but among the "customers"
of the Exchange there was scarce one whose circumstances did not seem to the old ladies an appeal for generosity—hardly one who was not, as
they said, "mo' in need 'n we are."

It would have been a hopelessly weary business but for its rich perquisites in opportunities of sympathy and helpfulness.

The spacious garret chamber was thrown open none too soon, as only a week later it was called into unexpected requisition through the arrival, late one evening, of a party of five dust-begrimed travellers, whom the ladies would have feared to receive had they not been accompanied by a neighbor who had taken charge of their horses, and who, in a whisper aside, announced them as "Uncle Sam's men, with a-plenty o' greenbacks."

While the strangers sat at supper that night, it was pathetic to see the solicitous scrutiny with which their hostesses scanned their faces in turn, eager for some sign by which to decide whom of them all should be counted worthy to sleep in Sonny's bed.

A chance remark settled the question.

"Well," said one, "I believe we are in the land of the myrtle and orange."

"Hardly," rejoined another ; "but better yet, we are in the country of the night-singing mocking-bird. Do you ladies ever hear them at night?" he added.

"From the up-stairs bedroom," replied both sisters at once, while Miss Sophia continued,

"The winders open right out into the maginolia-trees, where they set an' sing all night long, some nights."

The stranger's eyes beamed.

"How delightful! If one might be so fortunate?" he replied with a rising inflection, smiling.

"It's yore room, sir, for the night," both said together, again exchanging glances, "with whichever one o' the other gentlemen you choose. They's a wide, easy-sleepin' bed in it, a-plenty broad fo' two. An' if you want to hear the birds sing, jest open any winder you like. They's four, not countin' the dormers, an' they all open into trees, an' every tree's full o' birds' nests."

"Isn't that remarkable? Are all the trees here full of nests?" the stranger asked.

"No, sir. Sonny—Mr. Stephen Decatur Simpkins, our brother thet's passed away—he had a gift. He got 'em to nestin' there."

"He was a lover of birds, do I understand?"

The sisters exchanged glances again, and Miss Sarey answered simply,

"Yas, sir. He was a naturalist."

"Ah, indeed."

Around the speaker's mouth played that ghost of a smile which, being interpreted, means amused incredulity, while the conversation, becoming general, passed to other things.

With such an introduction, an hour later, Mr. John Saunders, of the Smithsonian Institution of Washington City, accompanied by his associate, Ezra Cox, proceeded, candle in hand, to the modest roof-chamber that held the life-work of Stephen Decatur Simpkins, naturalist.

The next morning, though the twins appeared

22

at breakfast in their fresh white-ruched dresses, and Tom sauntered around the table resplendent in a blue neck-ribbon, the ends of which hung to his knees, a distinct depression marked the spirit of the household.

Despite their best efforts in the direction of cheerfulness, the twins were haggard and wan.

The eyes of their guests, on the contrary, beamed with pleasure, especially those of the occupants of the upper chamber.

In the first interval of silence after serving the dishes, Miss Sarey Mirandy, turning to the strangers, asked timidly,

"May I ask, sir, what perfession you gentlemen perfess?"

"Certainly, madam," replied John Saunders, his eye twinkling; "the three at your left, Messrs. Green, Brown, and Black—men of color, you perceive—are members of the National Geological Survey, whom Congress has sent out here to hunt up some mineral specimens. My friend here, Mr. Cox, and I—my name is Saunders—are from the Smithsonian Institution at Washington City, at present loafers, as we are off on a vacation. We are called scientists, I believe. Naturalists is a name we like better; but really "—he hesitated for a moment as if to gain entire seriousness—"but really, here, in the presence of your brother's beautiful work, we should appropriate the name timidly—with heads uncovered. Is this collection of birds known in the State, may I ask?"

"Well, yas, sir. I reckin 'tis. 'Tain't never been to say *hid*. It's been right here. Th' ain't nobody, black nor white, in the county but *knows* they're here."

"It is not registered. I know of all the important recorded collections in America. I wonder if you ladies realize what a treasure you possess. My friend and I studied it until our candle burned out. Then we crept down and begged those of our friends and burned them up—besides one we found in the dining-room. I hope we didn't disturb you, ladies?"

The sisters exchanged glances and colored.

"Th' wasn't to say 'xactly noise enough to disturb nobody, sir, if we'd knew what it was; but th' ain't nobody slep' up in Sonny's room sence he passed away tell now, an' the sound o' every foot-fall seemed like him back ag'in—so we naturally kep' list'nin' for 'em to stop; an', to tell the whole truth, sir, when we heard 'em so late, not knowin' nothin' 'bout you gentlemen, we got nervous an' scared like, 'n' we got up an' dressed an' set up the livelong night, 'th our valu'bles all in reach—not thet you gentlemen look like peddlers, which even ef you was, you might be hones'—"

The professional gentlemen present thought it unsafe to look at one another, while they expressed the sincere sorrow they felt at so unfortunate a *contretemps*.

The occasion of their late hours, however, soon

became the absorbing theme, resulting in a full restoration of confidence.

John Saunders's enthusiasm was genuine.

"I actually counted sixty-one beautiful specimens not existing in any registered collection," he said, addressing his companions.

"An' they wasn't all easy got, neither," replied Miss Sophia. "Why, Sonny slep' in a crêpe-myrtle-tree ev'ry night for a week once-t, jest to find out how a little he-bird conduct hisself—if he changed places with his settin' wife, or jest entertained 'er settin' on a limb beside her."

Her interlocutor smiled. "And how was it, do you remember?"

"Well, reely—how was it, Sis?"

"'Deed, sir, I disremember. Either he did 'r he didn't—one. I clean forget, but—but it's put down in the book."

"So there is a book?"

"They's five leather-backed books, sir, with nothin' but sech as that *in* 'em. Sis an' me 've read in 'em some, an' for anybody that *keered* for sech, I s'pose it's good readin'. They's *one* thing, it's *true*, an' thet's more 'n you can say fo' the triflin' novels thet folks pizins their minds *an'* principles with."

"You have, indeed, a valuable possession here, ladies. Have you ever thought of selling it?"

"Sellin' Sonny's birds? No, sir. No mo' 'n we'd sell pa an' ma's 'ile-painted po'trits or Sonny's Confed'rit clo'es, *ragged* as they be. No, sir. They's some things thet money don't tech. We wouldn't sell them birds, not ef we got ten cents a head for 'em—an' that's mo' 'n most of 'em 'd be wuth, even if they was baked in a pie 'n' the crust an' gravy throwed in."

"But, my dear ladies," said Mr. Cox, "they are worth far more than that. As a collection they are worth considerably more than a dollar apiece—"

"Sis," said Miss Sarey Mirandy, "the gentleman don't understand. Them birds, sir, ain't nothin' but feathers an' skin, an' it full o' rank pizen arsenic. Th' ain't a blessed thing in 'em but raw cotton, an' it physicked, an' nine out'n every ten of 'em never was no count fo' neither cookin' *nur* singin'. We wouldn't deceive you *'bout* 'em. But if they was birds o' paradise caught before the fall o' Adam, jest swooned away, an' li'ble to come back to life any minute, 'n' you offered us the United States Mint for 'em, even so, th' ain't fo' sale—*no ways*."

This was somewhat a rebuff to the first overture of the Washington scientist, who, indeed, seriously meant that the Institution should become possessed of the new-found treasure, if possible.

He had inserted the edge of a wedge, however, and was satisfied to wait before pressing it.

Breakfast over, it was but natural that Miss Sophia should follow the visitors into the parlor, while she, with evident and pathetic pride, exhib-ited the additional species there.

When a half-hour later she rejoined her sister in the kitchen, she was so full to overflowing of this tender theme that some time elapsed before she remarked, in a tone betraying a secondary interest,

"Well, I reckin Sally Ann 'll have her swingin' pitcher after all, 'cause I've done sol' the candelabras—"

Miss Sarey stood kneading dough, with her back to her sister. She came near falling for a moment.

" Wh—what you say, honey? H—who bought —*what?*"

She kept on kneading and did not turn.

"That slim, light - complected one, I say, has done bought ol' Mis' Brooks's candelabras, 'n' I mus' say, I never sol' a thing with a worse grace. I'm a - puttin' the ten dollars which he give for 'em here in this pink vase on the dinin' - room mantel - shelf, an' do you give it to Sally Ann, honey. I don't want nothin' to do *with* it, nor with her neither. She gets me riled enough to all but back-slide 'th her 'xtravagance 'n' super-*fluo*usniss."

Miss Sarey had not realized until now how attached she had herself become to the old candelabra. Their shimmering prisms were crystallized memories. Themselves, their long-familiar fantastic shapes, were friends, antedating in association any surviving friendship.

When she had completed her task, great beads of perspiration stood upon her pale brow.

Passing out, she nervously seized the ten dollars and hastened to the parlor. The purchaser stood admiring his new possession.

Laying the money before him, she said, with a masterful effort at composure,

"They's been a mistake made, sir. Them candelabras is already sold."

"Indeed? I'm sorry," he said, bowing; and as she moved away, he added, "I should be glad to give five times the price—if they could be secured!"

Miss Sarcy Mirandy hesitated.

"Sir?"

There was something almost tragic in the apprehension expressed in this one word.

The offer was repeated.

Fifty dollars! Half her secret hoard! In a twinkling the sum resolved itself into a difference in the quality of a shroud and coffin. Without apparent hesitation she replied firmly,

"The lady thet's bought 'em don't ca'culate to sell 'em, thank you, sir." And, her old heart thumping absurdly, she went out.

Declining the fifty dollars had seemed a simple matter of decision and principle at the moment, and the offer a bribe to her loyalty; but all day as she moved about the house her secret kept growing, first naturally, from the germ, as the extravagance seemed to grow in enormity, and then by accretion, as one by one the sundry deceptions it would involve gathered about it.

Of course she would "deal fair." Sally Ann should have the fifty dollars. But this soon became the slightest consideration.

She must not be known as the purchaser—not even to her sister. If she hadn't told her of that long-ago kiss, it would be different. Sally Ann would naturally tell every one the price she got—and she would ask questions.

Excepting for the *amount*, she might arrange it so that Miss Sophia Falena would have to pay Sally Ann, when she could honestly say that she had herself sold them to the stranger. But the price!

Should she pay Sally Ann herself, and even say that the purchaser wished to remain incog.? Miss Sophia would tell the whole story—price and all.

Even fancying all these difficulties passed, where should she hide the things? Her sister, "the greatest rummager thet ever drawed breath," would be sure to come across them. How would she ever convey them from the parlor for temporary concealment in the top of her mahogany wardrobe? The pendants tinkled like bells if they were moved.

At what critical moment on the departure of the guests would she dare to have them disappear?

Miss Sophia would be sure to ask searching questions. She had already "wondered how the gentleman was goin' to tote 'em."

Again—and this aggravated her mental panic

—Sally Ann might come in at any moment. Miss Sophia would refer to the sale, and all would be lost. This was verily the·most trying ordeal in all her experience.

For the first time in her life she was shame-faced and afraid, responding even to her sister's enthusiastic remarks about Sonny in an incoherent manner.

In the midst of her greatest apprehension the front gate was heard to slam, and Sally Ann Brooks did actually appear, coming up the path.

Seeing her enter, however, Miss Sophia said, "Sis, you set Sally Ann down in the parlor an' talk to her, honey. I'm 'feer'd if I'd see her tickled over that ten dollars I might not be polite. Maybe if a more Christian spirit comes to me, I'll come in after whiles ; but it's mos' supper-time, any-how."

As she passed through the parlor to receive Mrs. Brooks, Miss Sarey was astounded to per-ceive the " red - complected " coveter of the an-tiques still standing before them.

If the devious ways of deceit had been an old-travelled road to her, her dilemma would have been less trying.

Not to introduce those who chanced to meet in her parlor would be a social dereliction of which she was incapable. To do so in the present in-stance would invite disaster. She did not hesitate. Come what would, she would be a lady worthy the name of Simpkins.

What she said at the door was,

"Walk right in the parlor, Sally Ann, an' I'll make you 'quainted with a gentleman thet's here from the North."

"Law, Miss Simpkins!" exclaimed Teddy's wife, shrinking back, "I 'ain't got on no corset nor nothin'. I jest run over in my Mother-Hubbard as I was. I wouldn't go before a strange gentleman the way I am, nohow, for nothin'."

One crisis was safely passed. Trembling within, and with two solferino spots upon her thin cheeks, Miss Sarey Mirandy invited Mrs. Brooks into her own room.

"We hear you've got a houseful o' Yankees," said the guest, taking a rocking-chair; "but Mr. Jakes says they're reel nice, an' he says the way they're a-praisin' up Mr. Sonny Simpkins roun' town you'd think he might o' been George Washin'ton, or maybe Jeff Davis hisself."

"Yas, Sally Ann. It's been mighty gratifyin' to Sis an' me to hear them as knows a-praisin' of Sonny. One of 'em's been a-studyin' over Sonny's books the livelong day."

"Is that so? If they read them books they *mus'* shorely be educated. Kitty Clark's beau says they been a-telegraphtin' all day to Washin'ton—an' he says the name o' Simpkins has gone over the wire more 'n once-t, though neither he nor she nor I got any right to tell it. Three of 'em, you know, 's been out to Mr. Jakes's farm all day, a-spyin' out dug-up things with a spy-glass.

Mr. Jakes is diggin' a new cow-pond, an' they do say he's dug up enough to undo the whole Bible. That's the way the talk's a-goin', but I'm thankful to say I was raised a good 'Piscopal church-woman—not sayin' nothin' 'gainst the Baptists, Miss Simpkins—an' the prayer-book don't, in no place *I* ever opened it, make no mention o' Mr. Jakes's cow-pond, nor the ins an' outs of it. An' talkin' 'bout the Church, Miss Simpkins, fetches me to what brought me here, not that I needed any excuse; but this is Lent, you know, in our church, an' we're 'xpected to make some sort o' sacrerfice—if not fastin', some other—an' I thought 'stid o' denyin' myself spring onions or maybe choc'let, since Teddy's mind seems to run on 'em consider'ble, I'd come over an' get them candelabras o' his ma's, an' set 'em back on the mantel where she left 'em. Don't you think the Lord might take that the way it's meant, for a Lenten off'rin'?"

"I do, indeed, Sally Ann, an' a good one." And she added in a moment, "'Cause you know, honey, they *might* o' sold for what 'd fetch consider'ble worldly vanities."

"Yes 'm, so they might, tho' I doubt if th' ever would."

A moment's silence followed, broken finally by Miss Sarey.

"But I'd advise you, Sally Ann, child, to examine yore deed pretty close-t, before you offer it to the dear Lord, 'cause you know, honey, He sees the inside *inness* o' all our purposes. Suppose somebody now was to offer to buy them candelabras 'n' pay a big price, cash down. How 'bout Lent, honey?"

The old lady's heart was thumping furiously.

"Well, Miss Simpkins, tell the truth, *they couldn't get 'em*—not if they offered me the first price of 'em."

Teddy Brooks's wife's eyes filled with tears as she continued,

"Teddy seems right porely these days, Miss Simpkins; an' another thing I come to ask you was, if you had any more o' that blackberry wine o' yores left. It helped him a heap las' spring. Some days I get so worreted the way he seems a-failin', seem like if he'd get good 'n' strong, I wouldn't care fo' nothin' else."

When Miss Sarey went for the wine, she moved with the alacrity of a happier and younger woman than she who had entered the room ten minutes before. While she had the opportunity, she thought it but safe to look into the kitchen in passing, and to say,

"Sis, I don't know 's you'd better bother comin' in. I'll make yore excuses to Sally Ann."

"Well, maybe it's jest as well, though I was jest untyin' my apron *to* go in—guess I'll tighten 't up ag'in an' pick these berries."

For the first time in years Miss Sarey Mirandy kissed Teddy's wife at parting, and bade her "keep good heart an' not forgit thet the good

Lord loved her an' hers." And as she turned to go in, she drew a long, free breath, as she said to herself, "An' yet some folks 'll set up an' say th' ain't no sech a thing as special providence."

It was quite tea-time now, and in the rush of last preparations she had no opportunity for confidential talk with her sister until supper was ready.

She stood at one end of the table, bell in hand, while her sister moved about, touching here and there, preparatory to taking her station at the other end.

"Well, what do you think, Sis? Sally Ann has done took the candelabras home," she said, plunging into the subject.

Miss Sophia stared. "But they're bought an' paid for, Sis—hun—an' I tol' you so—'n' the price's in the vase."

"I've done give the money back, dearie, an' it's all fixed. D' you reckin' I'd let a little foolishness like that stan' in the way o' gettin' Teddy's ma's candelabras back to 'im—an' he porely, too?"

"I hope you dealt fair, honey. Did you tell 'er they was sol'?"

"No, but I ast 'er if she'd take a offer, 'n' she said she wouldn't take a hundred dollars for 'em. I reckin' she's consider'ble worreted about Teddy. I got a bottle o' wine out to send 'im, but she was so loaded up with the candle-sticks, she said she'd sen' back for it. I reckin' Sally Ann means better 'n we give 'er credit for. She looked purty 'nough to eat to-night. No wonder she taken pore Teddy's eye."

"Well, I'm glad they're back. What did you tell the gentleman thet bought 'em?"

"I tol' 'im they was a'ready disposed of, an thet you didn't know it—which was true."

"Mh—hm. I s'pose it was, though I'm not right shore. I trus' neither of us 'll ever be pushed to say nothin' thet won't stand in the Jedgment fo' the truth, Sis. Ring the bell, honey. An' don't ferget to offer secon' cups o' tea. Wait—yore placket-hole's a-gappin'; lemme pin it. That's it. Kitty, Kitty! Come here, Tom! I declare, Tom gets his neck-ribbon awful twisted. Ring now, Sis!"

The entertaining of five strange, college-bred men, who talked familiarly of things beyond their ken, albeit the bird-theme was a bond of sympathy between them—was a somewhat formidable undertaking to these old, timid women of narrow and hitherto protected lives, though they had congratulated themselves many times to-day that "the household was perpared for 'em, even down to Tom."

When supper was over to-night and Mr. Saunders, with a formality that was significant, begged an interview with the ladies in the parlor, they were seized anew with a vague mistrust.

These Yankee men, who wore the United States initials "promiscuous" about their persons, and

"THE HOUSEHOLD WAS PERPARED FOR 'EM, EVEN DOWN TO TOM."

made so free with the telegraph, might be—
What? Spies? Detectives?

Neither confided to the other what, in truth,
was but a suspicion of a suspicion, as they repaired
together to their chambers to secure their turkey-
tailed fans and fresh hemstitched handkerchiefs,
and slip bits of orris-root into their mouths.

The gentlemen were already assembled, and the
meeting lost nothing, but rather gained in formality, on the entrance of the twins, who, bowing
slightly, proceeded to seat themselves side by side
upon the sofa.

"Ladies," said Mr. Saunders, rising, "yesterday
a party of tired men came to your door, asking
for supper and a night's lodging. They had come
from a distant brilliant city, with its art-galleries,
its institutions of learning, its glare, its music.
Coming into this little inland Arkansas town,
they expected to find rich, deep forests and fertile
fields. tilled by true-hearted children of the soil.
Within your hospitable door they hoped for what
Solomon meant when he said, 'A dry morsel, and
quietness therewith,' as they were both hungry
and tired. Instead of a dry morsel, you have
given us sumptuous fare, ladies. And for the
quietness we sought, we have found—what shall
I say?—the stillness of a temple, where, instead
of sleeping, we have since sat in reverence. Two
of us have spent a day and half a night in studying
the beautiful life-work of Mr. Stephen Decatur
Simpkins. Here we have found science, art, lit-

crature, romance, poetry, music—for the birds at our windows have filled the night with melody.

"There are in the world but two larger personal collections of birds than that we find here. There is none so exquisitely perfect in every detail. I have not found a gun-shot in a single specimen, gentlemen, nor a ruffled feather—"

"Th' ain't but thirteen shot birds there," interrupted Miss Sarey Mirandy, "an' them was give to Sonny. He spent five years livin' 'mongst 'em so 's they'd know 'im, before he ever ketched one. An' *then*, he never took 'em in nestin' time, less 'n he got both the he and the she. He never left a mo'nin' bird in his life, or a new-hatched nest, Sonny didn't."

There was something very like a quaver in John Saunders's voice when he resumed his speech.

" All the valuable known collections, ladies, are on exhibition in public institutions. As its representative, I am authorized to say to you that the United States Government wishes to place the work of Mr. Simpkins in the Smithsonian Institution at Washington—"

Simultaneously, as if electrified, the twins rose to their feet. Miss Sophia first found voice. What she said, in a quavering tremor, was this:

" If I may please speak, sir, Sonny lived a peaceful an' law-abidin' citizen clean since the wah, an' he hedn't no more hard feelin's to them he fit ag'in' 'n we've got—not a bit. If, after all these years, the North see fit to converscate his pore voiceless birds thet show *theyselves* how harmless Sonny spent his time—not havin' even to say a shot *in* 'em—why, all we got to ask is, jest wait a few more years till two ol' women pass away, an' then, why, if the North cares for 'em, they'll be nobody lef' to claim 'em."

As she sat down, her sister spoke.

"Them words we let fall to you Northerners 'bout Sonny's Confedrit uniform wasn't intended fo' no insult to you gentlemen. We jest prize it, bein' his sisters, 'cause seem like it's got all his young shape in it yet—thet's all. Th' ain't a livin' bit o' strife mixed in our feelin's 'bout it—not a bit. Thet's all we got to say, I reckin'—ain't it, Sis?"

John Saunders was not the only man present who found it necessary to use his handkerchief before he could trust his voice again. There was a very tender note in it when he said,

"I have blundered shamefully, my dear ladies, and I beg you to forgive me. Your brother's property is yours. No power on earth can take it from you. The war and confiscation are no more. Were Mr. Simpkins living, he could desire no greater honor than national recognition as one of America's first naturalists. This is what we would accord him now. His work lies buried in this little town. In the National Museum thousands will visit it daily. His portrait will hang beside it, and his poetic and exhaustive treatises adorn the public libraries. These books alone,

23

describing numerous hitherto unclassified species, and giving original methods of capture and preservation, are worth several thousand dollars. I am not yet authorized to offer a specified sum. We cannot always pay as we should like to, but I can guarantee that to the estate of Mr. Stephen Decatur Simpkins the United States will pay certainly not less than ten thousand dollars for the collection entire — it ought to be double that. We feel quite sure that when you ladies fully understand, you will not let any feeling stand in the way of his getting his full honors."

For answer, the sisters turned to each other, opened their arms, and fell sobbing each upon the other's shoulder. Thus they sat for some moments, and when they raised their heads they were alone.

"I hope," said Miss Sophia, wiping her eyes, "I hope pa an' ma 's been a-lookin' on an' a list'nin', Sis. 'Twould make 'em happier, even in Heaven."

"Yas—an' Sonny too, dearie. I hope he's been present—though I doubt if he'd keer so much. I b'lieve he'd enjoyed more bein' up-stairs las' night, a-studyin' the birds with them gentlemen."

"I reckin you're right, Sis, an' maybe he was. I don't b'lieve the good Lord 'd hinder 'im if he wanted to come."

———

If some supposed the fortune coming to the Misses Simpkins would prove a death-blow to the

Exchange, they were mistaken. A comfortable income gave its machinery just the lubrication it needed for smooth and happy working according to the pleasure of its proprietors.

Three years have passed since Sonny's collection of birds went to Washington, and every spring the sisters plan to go north to visit it at the Institution; but each season finds Teddy Brooks "lookin' so porely," that Miss Sarey Mirandy finds an excuse to put it off. When pressed, she did even say once to her sister,

"Though Sally Ann is growin' in grace ev'ry day, an' 'll make a fine woman in time if she lives, you can't put a ol' head on young shoulders—an' like as not before we'd be half way to Washin'-ton, she'd run out o' light-bread an' feed Teddy on hoe-cake, which always was same as pizen to 'im, even in his young days."

"OH, SHOUTIN'S MIGHTY SWEET"

"OH, SHOUTIN'S MIGHTY SWEET"

"OH, SHOUTIN'S MIGHTY SWEET"

PLANTATION PARTING HYMN

OH, shoutin's mighty sweet
    When yer shout when yer meet,
An' shek han's roun', an' say :
    " Bless Gord fur de meetin' !
    Bless Gord fur de greetin' !"
Shoutin' comes mighty easy dat a-way.

    But ter shout when yer part,
    An' ter shout f'om yo' heart,
When yer gwine far away, far away,
    Wid-a lettin' go han's,
    An' a-facin' strange lan's—
Shoutin' comes mighty hard sech a day.

    " Glory" sticks in yo' th'oat
    At de whistle o' de boat,
Dat cuts lak a knife thoo yo' heart ;
    An' " Hallelujah" breaks
    At de raisin' o' de stakes
Dat loosens up de ropes ter let 'er start.

But ef yer fix yo' eye
On de writin' in de sky,
Whar de " good-byes " is all strucken out,
An' read de prormus clair
Of another geth'rin' there,
You kin say far'well, my brothers, with a shout.

Den shout, brothers, shout !
Oh, tell yo' vict'ry out,
How neither death nur partin' kin undo yer.
Look fust at yo' loss,
But last at de cross,
Singin' glory, glory, glory hallelujah !

LUCINDY

LUCINDY

WHEN Lucindy's eye do shine
Lak a ripe, ripe muscadine,
An' 'er lips sticks out
In a tantalizin' pout,
I counts Lucindy mine.

When she droop 'er eyes so shy,
Lak she gwine ter pass me by,
An' des afore she pass
Drap 'er hankcher on de grass,
My courage rise up high.

When she sets up in de choir,
An' 'er voice mounts higher an' higher,
  In unisom wid Jim's,
  A-singin' o' de hymns,
I sets back an' puspire.

When she lean down on 'er hoe,
'N' dig de san' up wid 'er toe,
  An' look todes me an' sigh,
  Des lak she 'mos' could cry,
I don't know whar ter go.

When she walk right down de aisle
At de cake-walk wid a smile,
  An' she an' yaller Jake
  Ketch han's an' win de cake,
I steam an' sizz an' bile.

When she claim me fur her beau,
An' den dance de reel wid Joe;
  An' when she swing me by,
  Squeeze *my* han' on de sly—
I don' know whe'r or no.

Tell de trufe, Lucindy's ways
Gits me so upsot some days
　　Dat, 'cep'n dat I knew
　　Dat's *des de way she do,*
I'd do some *damage,* 'caze

Some days when she do de wus',
Ef 'twarn't dat I hates a fuss,
　　An' loves 'er thoo an' thoo
　　Wid all de ways she do,
De *least* I'd do'd be *cuss.*

THE END

By MARY E. WILKINS

SILENCE, and Other Stories.   Illustrated.   16mo, Cloth, Ornamental, $1 25.

JEROME, A POOR MAN.   A Novel.   Illustrated.   16mo, Cloth, Ornamental, $1 50.

MADELON.   A Novel.   16mo, Cloth, Ornamental, $1 25.

PEMBROKE.   A Novel.   Illustrated.   16mo, Cloth, Ornamental, $1 50.

JANE FIELD.   A Novel.   Illustrated.   16mo, Cloth, Ornamental, $1 25.

A NEW ENGLAND NUN, and Other Stories.   16mo, Cloth, Ornamental. $1 25.

A HUMBLE ROMANCE, and Other Stories.   16mo, Cloth, Ornamental, $1 25.

YOUNG LUCRETIA, and Other Stories.   Illustrated.   Post 8vo, Cloth, Ornamental, $1 25.

GILES COREY, YEOMAN.   A Play.   Illustrated.   32mo, Cloth, Ornamental, 50 cents.

Mary E. Wilkins writes of New England country life, analyzes New England country character, with the skill and deftness of one who knows it through and through, and yet never forgets that, while realistic, she is first and last an artist.—*Boston Advertiser.*

Miss Wilkins has attained an eminent position among her literary contemporaries as one of the most careful, natural, and effective writers of brief dramatic incident.   Few surpass her in expressing the homely pathos of the poor and ignorant, while the humor of her stories is quiet, pervasive, and suggestive.—*Philadelphia Press.*

It takes just such distinguished literary art as Mary E. Wilkins possesses to give an episode of New England its soul, pathos, and poetry.—*N. Y. Times.*

The pathos of New England life, its intensities of repressed feeling, its homely tragedies, and its tender humor, have never been better told than by Mary E. Wilkins.—*Boston Courier.*

The simplicity, purity, and quaintness of these stories set them apart in a niche of distinction where they have no rivals.—*Literary World,* Boston.

The charm of Miss Wilkins's stories is in her intimate acquaintance and comprehension of humble life, and the sweet human interest she feels and makes her readers partake of, in the simple, common, homely people she draws.—*Springfield Republican.*